CHILDREN of the VOICE · the TRILOGY

Special love and thanks to: Irene, Joss, Dans and Suzy.
Steve Legg, Trevor Perkins and all my family and friends.
Also, Revelation Church, Pioneer, Kingsway Publications,
and of course Silver Fish Publishing.

Children
of the
Voice

the trilogy

ISHMAEL

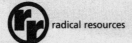 radical resources

Silver Fish
publishing

Omnibus edition published in Great Britain 1998 by
Silver Fish Publishing in association with Radical Resources.

Children of the Voice 1 first published 1990 by
Kingsway Publications Ltd
Children of the Voice 2 first published 1991 by
Kingsway Publications Ltd
Children of the Voice 3 first published 1993 by
Kingsway Publications Ltd

British Library Cataloguing in Publication Data
A record for this book is available from the British Library

ISBN 1 902134 03 6

Printed and bound in Great Britain by
Cox & Wyman, Reading, Berks.

Silver Fish Publishing is a division of
Silver Fish Creative Marketing Ltd
44c Fermoy Road, Maida Vale
London W9 3NH

contents

CHILDREN of the VOICE - BOOK 1

CHILDREN of the VOICE - BOOK 2

children of the voice - book 3

Children of the Voice

Book 1

a story for those who are kids at heart

1. OLDCHURCH

'Dear Voice, please perform a miracle and make Sunday disappear this week,' prayed Little Trouble with all the concentration he could manage. 'And Voice, while I'm talking to you, do you think you could explain to me why such a great day as Saturday seems so short, and why such a boring day as Sunday never seems to end?' No voice answered him, and he assumed that no one was listening.

Little Trouble walked with his parents downstairs and out of the front door towards the church bus. As he looked up he saw the enormous cloud that always hung over the

City of Oldchurch. He wondered why the weather never changed; it was always so dreary and miserable.

No one spoke as they boarded the vehicle. Everyone just sat facing the front, looking as depressed as the weather. 'Obviously deep in prayer,' thought Little Trouble. He glanced round and saw two of his friends, Little Pest and Little Nuisance, but even they didn't give him a wave; in fact, they didn't even seem to notice he was there.

Although the distance to the church building was short, the silence made it drag out. 'Sunday has begun,' thought Little Trouble.

The engine of the old bus droned on, sounding like a swarm of frustrated bees that were pushing their noses against a glass pane perceiving beautiful sweet smelling flowers, but unable to get to them. He yawned, then started to beat out a rhythm with his fists on the hard, scarcely-padded plastic seat that he was perched on, until a lady whom he vaguely recognised leaned over and condescendingly wagged a finger at him. He obediently stopped beating with his hands and began to tap his feet annoyingly on the back of the seat in front of him, which made two miserable male occupants turn around and glare at him until again he stopped. Through Little Trouble's eyes, every Sunday was like an action replay from a very old movie; week in, week out everything looked the same, sounded the same and even smelt the same. A touch of the déjà vu. The word 'boring' would have been too complimentary.

It was just at that moment he felt like doing something really outrageous; something that would show people that he could live up to the name his parents had landed him with. So he leaped up onto the bus seat and yelled, 'I'm going to take all my clothes off.' With that, his hat went flying up in the air and his T-shirt followed. Seeing that there was still no reaction, off came his trousers, pants, socks and shoes, then he proceeded to make up a little song and dance which went something like, 'If it was good enough for Adam, then it's good enough for me.'

But even a twelve-year-old performing a naked song and dance routine was not enough to get Little Trouble noticed, so he put his clothes back on again.

The bus ground to a halt and all the adult travellers alighted and walked slowly towards the enormous doors at the Old Saints Church. When they had disappeared from view, two large Kiddiecontrollers, armed with sticks in one hand and large boards in the other, the sort that were used to herd pigs (the word 'Fison's' could still be seen faintly on one), told all the Littlekids to leave the bus slowly and quietly. They herded them towards another door in Old Saints Church and one or two of the tinies managed to push past the Kiddiecontrollers, and ran off somewhere, but in a reasonably short time all the Littlekids were installed in the Junior Church Hall.

Every Littlekid from one day old to twelve-years-old was expected to be there, and as everyone sat down on the rough wooden floor Auntie Mona stood up and welcomed one and all to the next three hours of mindless entertainment in the Littlehorrors Junior Church, and all the other Aunties around the room said a solemn Amen. The next ten minutes were taken up with announcing the rules, which went as follows:

Number 1. No talking.
Number 2. No shouting.
Number 3. Only sweet singing allowed.
Number 4. No sliding about on the floor because last week Little Monkey spent most of the three hours having splinters removed from his backside.
Number 5. No trying to escape.

At this point, the Kiddiecontrollers gave a sort of salute to show that they were on guard at each door, so the Littlekids had better beware. And so the rules continued.

Little Trouble was getting bored and quite angry. All the other Littlekids seemed to be docile and willing to suffer in silence; but he was not. His mind was full of burning questions and he wanted some answers.

As Auntie Mona was approaching rule number 53, he leaped up and shouted, 'Excuse me, I have a question.'

She glared at him, hating to be interrupted. 'What is your name?' she demanded.

'Can't you read?' he cheekily replied, pointing to his T-shirt which had the words 'Watch out, here comes Little Trouble' written in large letters on it.

'Well, Little Trouble,' she snapped, 'what is your question?'

Little Trouble stood silently for a moment and then suddenly shouted, 'Why can't we be with our parents in the Real Church on Sundays? Where do all the thirteen-year-olds disappear to when they leave the Littlehorrors Junior Church, and who is the Voice, what is the Voice, and why doesn't he speak to anyone so they can hear him?'

'Silence! That's enough!' shouted all the Aunties together. It was then that Auntie Mona looked very seriously at him, with eyes that were as cold as ice. 'Who do you think you are to ask such questions?' she growled. 'You are a born rebel. I've met your sort before. You want answers, do you?' she continued. 'Well, you can go and see the Elder. He knows how to put Littlekids like you in their place. Kiddiecontroller, take this troublemaker away,' she yelled looking at one of the guards on the doors.

The Kiddiecontroller obediently came over and told Little Trouble to follow him, and together they left the Junior Church Hall and made their way towards the Real Church.

'You will have to wait in the Church Office,' said the Kiddiecontroller. 'There is another two-and-a-half hours of the meeting to run, and then the Elder will see you and sort you out.'

Little Trouble had other ideas. He had no intention of waiting in some stuffy office for all that time, and as the Kiddiecontroller was unlocking the office door he made a run for it.

The controller followed him in hot pursuit, but was no match for the young and healthy Little Trouble. He ran down an endless series of corridors, not having a clue where he was heading, because he had never been allowed in this part of the building before. Then he stopped in front of three doors. The shouts of the Kiddiecontroller had faded away. 'Oh Voice,' thought Little Trouble, more in panic than in prayer, 'where do I go now?'

It was at that very second he heard a voice in his mind that he had never heard before. It was gentle and warm, and as it spoke a wonderful feeling of peace came into Little Trouble. 'Go through the door on the right,' the Voice said, 'then the second door on the left and the third door on the right.'

'I'm sorry, could you repeat that?' said Little Trouble who had a terrible memory. And the Voice did so.

Little Trouble did not dare argue with the Voice and began to perspire as he realised that he wasn't actually running away from someone, but it was like he was being led by someone. As he walked through that third door on the right, his heart leaped with fear as he realised that he was standing in the huge Real Church building, but not at the back. Unfortunately, the door he had come through had brought him right into the preacher's pulpit and there, staring straight at him, were hundreds of adults.

He felt like running back through the door, but it was as though his feet were cemented to the floor.

Everyone was deadly silent, and as he gazed around everyone looked so old and so sad. Then a voice called up to him, 'Little Trouble, what are you doing here? You know this building is for adults only.'

Little Trouble guessed that this must be the Elder because his hair was pure white and he looked as though he was at least ninety-years-old. Courage was rising from somewhere inside Little Trouble and he shouted to the Elder, 'Why do you ban us Littlekids from this building?'

The Elder smiled, 'Well surely even you can understand that you are not old enough to be part of the Real Church. That is why you are in the Junior Church Hall, and anyway you would be bored being in here with the older ones.' At that point, the majority of the adults accidentally yawned.

'Now will someone call a Kiddiecontroller and inform him a Littlekid has escaped, then he can take this Little Trouble away and we can continue our meeting,' said the Elder.

'No, I'm not leaving till you answer my question,' screamed Little Trouble. The adults gasped. They had never had rebellion in the Real Church before.

The Elder, seeing that this was all getting very embarrassing, said that he would agree to answer his question as long as he promised to leave quietly afterwards.

Little Trouble agreed and climbed down out of the pulpit and stood beside the Elder. Little Trouble began, 'All I want to know is, why can't we be with our parents in the Real Church on Sundays, and where do all the thirteen-year-olds disappear to after they leave the Littlehorrors' Junior Church, and who is the Voice, what is the Voice and why doesn't he speak to anyone so that they can hear what he is saying?' He just about managed to finish his paragraph without swallowing or pausing for breath.

The Elder thought for a moment then said, 'I think that was more than just one question, but here are the answers. The first I have already explained: this building is not for you, and your parents need to be away from you so they can spend time talking to the Voice without you disturbing them. Secondly, the teenagers leave the Littlehorrors' Junior Church and go to a place called the Bigwideworld. We don't know where it is, we don't know what they do when they get there. All we know is that once they leave us they never come back to us.'

It was at this stage that Little Trouble noticed that this question was having an emotional effect on some of the adults. Handkerchiefs were appearing as tears began to flow.

'Finally,' said the Elder, his voice now beginning to tremble, 'many years ago we all knew the Voice like a real friend. He would talk to us every day and tell us of his plans for our lives. But that was long ago. Nowadays we don't know how or even if we want to move on to new things, so although we spend all our time in sadness and prayer, we are not convinced that the Voice hears us. To tell you the truth, we have forgotten what the Voice sounds like.'

Suddenly an old lady jumped up and wailed, 'If only my son and daughter were still around. They were young enough to lead us back to the Voice.'

'Quite,' said the Elder, 'but we cannot live on "ifs".' This faces us with a major problem, Little Trouble. Our Littlekids are all Littlehorrors, we lose our teenagers, and our adults are all getting older. I, the Elder, have only a short time left on this earth and there is no one wanting or able to take my place. In a few years' time Oldchurch will cease to exist because we have no up-and-coming generation.'

By now even Little Trouble was sad. 'But we can't just give up,' he shouted. 'Why don't you make me an Elder? I don't mind being one.' At this point the adults' tears stopped flowing, smiles spread across their faces turning into huge grins then tears of laughter. One shouted out, 'Will you lead us with your clothes on or off?' remembering the incident on the bus journey. 'Yes, and will you make a grand entrance out of the door in the preacher's pulpit every Sunday?' joked another.

'Quiet!' shouted the Elder. 'This has gone far enough. You could never be an Elder, Little Trouble. You don't even seem to respect and hear the voice of those adults present here. What hope have you of hearing the one true Voice? Kiddiecontroller, come and take him away now and I don't want him put back with the other Littlekids. He is a bad and rebellious influence.'

'Wait,' cried Little Trouble. 'Give me a chance. Allow me to go to the Bigwideworld and let me find the Voice and new Elders and bring them back to you.'

All went deathly quiet. 'You are unique, Little Trouble,' said the Elder, 'and although I don't believe for one minute that you will succeed, we cannot stop you. You have now reached the age of twelve. Follow me.'

That very moment the Real Church emptied as they all escorted Little Trouble to the perimeter wall and the huge gates of Oldchurch. This was no new experience for some adults. They had waved goodbye to hundreds of twelve-year-olds before, but even they were murmuring that Little Trouble seemed different from the rest.

Standing with Little Trouble's parents, the Elder looked at Little Trouble and said, 'Beyond those gates lies the

Bigwideworld. It is full of Enemy Superpowers and danger. That is why no adults will leave the safety of these walls. This is your last chance to change your mind, Little Trouble,' he warned.

Little Trouble didn't answer. He kissed his tearful parents. Everyone knew he had to go. As he walked out through the gates, he shouted, 'I will be back... one day.'

'No one has ever walked through those gates and returned,' said the Elder. 'May the Voice have mercy on his soul.'

As he walked out, Little Trouble heard the gates of Oldchurch slam shut behind him. He was on his own.

2. smoke mountain

Little Trouble walked a long way before he turned around and saw the fading shape of Oldchurch which had almost disappeared from view, and strangely enough it was only when he turned around and saw the past disappearing that he suddenly felt a little afraid and not half as confident as he had felt when he first strutted out through those big gates. Where would he find the Voice? Was he going in the right direction? Never mind, the day was sunny and warm, and the trees and flowers surrounding him were very beautiful, so he tried not to think about the important issues too much and concentrated on the surroundings.

After a while, he came to a fork in the road. 'What a strange place for someone to leave a fork,' he thought, but then as he looked closely at the handle he read the words inscribed, 'Pull me out of the ground.' With a lot of effort and huffing and puffing Little Trouble obligingly did as the message said and saw on the end of one of the prongs a piece of paper wrapped in polythene. Quickly, he unwrapped the polythene and the paper inside had these words written on it:

Are you in a little trouble?
Then you must act at the double,
This path leads in the wrong direction.
If you want the Voice's protection,
Ascend the steep track on your right.
Then at the top, I think I'm right,
You'll see Smoke Mountain, it's not that far.
I've news for you... love Angela.

'Wow,' thought Little Trouble, 'I wonder if it's for me? After all, it *has* got my name on it.' He sat down by the roadside and looked up once at the steep track on the right, then down at the lovely smooth road. He looked up for the second time to the right and saw it looked cold and shady. Then he looked down for the second time at the smooth road which was hot and sunny. 'No, it can't be for me,' he thought. 'I'm sure the Voice will be down this nice easy road.' And up he jumped and off he set again.

As he walked he started whistling and the sun was getting hotter and hotter. The sun had never been able to break through the clouds in Oldchurch so he was thoroughly enjoying this new experience. What he had failed to notice, however, was that it was melting the tar on the road and the surface was getting softer and softer. And when he did eventually realise it he thought it great fun, and decided to play a game of jumping up and down as heavily as he could to see how big an impression he could make with his boots.

Then suddenly, to his horror, his boots stuck fast and he couldn't lift them out. Worse still, the more he tried, the further into the tarmac he started to sink. Within ten minutes he was up to his waist and being pulled down fast. The hot, thick, gungy, black mess was horrible and as it sucked him down as far as his shoulders, he realised that he was about to die.

As he struggled, Angela's words haunted him: 'This path leads in the wrong direction, if you want the Voice's protection.' He felt like kicking himself, but that was an impossibility due to the sticky mess that was trapping his legs.

The black mass came up to his chin then started to creep into the corners of his mouth. All he could move was his eyes and as he took what he thought would be his last look at the world around him he suddenly heard a voice say, 'What's up, kid? In a spot of trouble?' Then the voice changed and sounded like thunder as it said, 'Enemy Superpowers, I demand you release that kid now in the name of the Voice.' Little Trouble was convinced that he heard a screaming sound as the tarmac obediently pushed him back up to the surface and went back to its solid state.

'Hi, Little Trouble. I'm Miraclekid and I've been sent by the Voice to walk all over the Bigwideworld and rescue kids like you from the Enemy Superpowers.'

'But you could never tackle the Enemy Superpowers,' gasped Little Trouble. 'After all, you're not much older than I am.'

Miraclekid smiled, 'Where on earth did you learn that age has anything to do with working for the Voice? Oh, don't tell me, you must have come from Oldchurch.'

Before Little Trouble could bombard Miraclekid with questions, Miraclekid explained that he must dash off to give the Enemy Superpowers some more grief, and told Little Trouble to get moving because he'd heard that the Voice was waiting to meet him. 'But where do I go from here?' exclaimed a poor, filthy, sticky, black Little Trouble.

'Your next stop must be to see Angela. Didn't you get her message?' Even though his face was black, Little Trouble felt it blushing a brilliant red. 'Oh, I didn't think her message was for me. After all, to find her was a lot harder climb.' Miraclekid smiled as he walked off. 'Take my advice, Little Trouble. Following the Voice may be the harder way, but at least you won't end up being suffocated by a road surface. See you around.' And off he went.

Little Trouble quickly made his way back to the fork in the road and began his climb up the steep path. Although it was shady and the slope hurt the backs of his ankles, it was a funny thing but he still felt a lot better than when he was walking along the flat, sunny road earlier. He was fascinated by the number of little animals and reptiles that kept running across the track. He counted one hedgehog, three little lizards, four frogs or toads (he never could tell which was which), and dozens of playful rabbits leaping all over the place. These creatures took his mind off the steep climb and made time pass very quickly.

As he reached the end of the long track, his heart jumped. There facing him was the Smoke Mountain that Angela had said he would see, and boy, was it enormous. As he sat down on the grass at the foot of the mountain to get his breath back before starting the big climb, he heard the sound of music in the distance. The more he listened, the more he realised that the music was travelling around the side of the mountain and towards him. Little Trouble squinted his eyes to try and focus them, and he could just make out the outline of a person in the distance. The person was not walking normally. This strange character seemed to be leaping all over the path.

As the music grew louder, so the person grew larger and Little Trouble's eyes nearly popped out of his head when he noticed that the person vaguely approaching him not only had a great big ghettoblaster on his shoulder, but also wore a funny hat and dark glasses. 'Perhaps he is blind,' thought Little Trouble as he watched this gyrating oddball dance straight past him without even noticing him.

'Hello,' shouted Little Trouble at the stranger, but as he got no response he grabbed hold of the stranger's arm and stopped him. 'Hello,' shouted Little Trouble, again trying to make his voice louder than the earpiercing din. 'Who are you?'

The dark glasses turned and faced towards him and then started to half sing, half talk the following words:

Hey listen, do ya know what you just did?
You touched the arm of the Coolkid.
My clothes are smart, my hair is neat,
I was always the best-looking kid in our street.
I do not panic, I have no fear,
I'm off to find the Voice you hear.
But climb Smoke Mountain I will not,
No sweat for the Coolkid, I won't get hot.
But I've an idea I think is ace:
If I keep walking around the base,
Angela will soon come down to me.

She'll say this Coolkid I must see,
So I'll boogie on with my music loud,
But I ain't going up, I'm much too proud.
I said she'll come down, you wait and see.
No chick can fail to notice me.
Excuse me now as I split this scene,
Angela may be asking where I've been.
But don't forget when you next pray
Give thanks that Coolkid made your day.
I said, don't forget when you next pray
Give thanks, give thanks
That Coolkid... made your day.

And with that he continued down the path. 'Wow,' thought Little Trouble, 'what a cool kid! I wish I could be like him, but I'm scruffy and not as good looking, so I think I'd better start climbing this mountain as there is no way Angela would ever come down for me.' So off he set.

Smoke Mountain was rough and steep. Little Trouble's tar-stained clothes tore as they caught on sharp rocks. At other times he lost concentration and found himself climbing up three metres then sliding down four. His legs were covered in cuts and scratches, and parts of his body were aching and bruised. It was only now that he realised he was starving hungry and very thirsty. He had left Oldchurch in such a rush that he had not thought about such essentials as food and drink.

The darkness of night descended quickly on Smoke Mountain and now with cold and lack of visibility to add to his other problems, Little Trouble felt like giving up. 'I can't go on any further,' he whimpered. 'I just can't take any more punishment.'

All was now pitch dark and he could not even see his

hand in front of his face. He dragged his battered, dirty, bleeding body up just a fraction more then quietly breathed out the words, 'This is the end,' allowed his eyelids to close and slumped into a heap, unconscious.

3. ANGELA

The sun had just begun to rise on Smoke Mountain as
Little Trouble opened his eyes, and although he was still
filthy dirty and covered in wounds, he did feel a lot better
after his long sleep. As he slowly lifted up his head he saw
that he was facing some little pink trainers. Looking up
further he saw that the trainers were attached to a pair of
long, skinny white legs, a thin body in a pair of jogging
shorts and T-shirt and eventually the pretty face of a
young girl who, he was astonished to see, was about the
same age as he was.

'Wakey wakey, Little Trouble,' said the female standing in front of him, in a very unrefined voice. 'I woz expectin' ya yesterday afternoon. Wot kept yer?'

Little Trouble grew angry at the lack of sensitivity of this person talking to him. What a cheek she had to talk to him like that after what he had been through. To make it worse, she wasn't even a boy, she was only a girl.

Trying to keep his temper and sound mature he stood up on his feet and, feeling rather pleased that he was a little taller than she was, said in a very stern voice, 'I don't know who you are, and what is more I don't particularly care. I had a terrible day yesterday and I haven't climbed all the way up this mountain to spend my time talking to the likes of you. I am here to talk to a lady called Angela, not a silly little girl. Now perhaps you would be so kind as to tell me where I can find her before I waste any more of this precious time that you are wittering on about.'

The girl collapsed on the floor in a fit of laughter. 'I'm sorry,' she said. 'I know I shouldn't be laughin', but ya look so funny tryin' to be all serious with yer clothes and body covered in some dried-up black mess, and with that little bit of white clean skin from yer top lip to yer hair line ya remind me of a majorette's baton.' She burst into another fit of laughter.

Little Trouble felt totally humiliated and knew he must get back some respect from this stupid girl. 'Do you realise I am like this because I saw a baby stuck and about to drown in a tar swamp?' he lied. 'As I dived in, without any thought of the dangerous mission I was embarking upon, I suddenly realised that underneath the surface of the swamp lived the tar monster which is fifty metres long, has three heads, razor-sharp teeth, poison fangs and breathes fire out of his ears.'

Little Trouble's imagination was running wild. 'Anyway,' he continued, 'after fighting this monster and tearing it to pieces with my bare hands, I dragged the child to safety. Only then did I discover that the child was an heir to the throne. So, yes I am a little late getting here, but that is only because I had to deliver the prince back to the palace, and the King and Queen invited me to stay to a banquet and be knighted.'

The young girl stopped laughing, but still kept smiling. 'Let me introduce meself,' she said. 'I'm Angela.'

Little Trouble nearly fell back down the mountain in amazement. 'No... you can't be,' he gasped. 'You don't talk properly, and you are much too young to be employed by the Voice,' he stammered. 'And you are certainly not serious enough for such a responsible position.'

'So ya want some proof doz ya?' said Angela.

'I certainly do,' replied Little Trouble.

'OK, owz this then? The reason yer so late in arrivin' is because ya chose to ignore me note on the fork in the road and chose to take wot ya thought would be the easy way. 'Ere ya got into deep water, or more to the point deep tar, and if it 'adn't been for me mate Miraclekid ya would now be 'istory. Am I right or am I right?'

Little Trouble thought it was time to interrupt and to put his side of the story, but then decided to keep quiet as he realised he didn't have a side of the story. 'How does she know all this?' he thought.

'So you have found out all this from Miraclekid, have you?' said Little Trouble, saying the next best thing that came into his mind.

'Nah,' said Angela, her voice becoming quieter. 'Truth to tell is that I got worried about ya and the Voice spoke to me and told me not to fret as 'ee was takin' care of ya, but ya would be arrivin' a few hours late.'

'Oh,' said Little Trouble taken aback a bit. 'But who are you really, and why don't you talk properly?'

'It's obvious yer 'aven't met the Voice yet, have ya?' said Angela. 'Ya see, the Voice 'as chosen me to be one of 'is Directors. In other words, me job is to 'elp, encourage, guide, an' as 'ee says, direct people like you. The Voice don't just choose all the clever posh kids. 'Ee gives everyone that 'ears, obeys and loves 'im a special job to do, and this is mine.'

'But where I come from we were taught that Littlekids were of no use to the Voice.'

'Don't tell me, yer from Oldchurch, ain't ya?' said Angela. 'We've 'ad loadsa trouble with yer lot, but 'opefully in time you'll realise that yer've been told a pack of lies. Anyway, follow me, Little Trouble and let's 'ave some breakfast.'

Little Trouble wasn't about to argue with that idea, and as the two of them sat down, he ate some of the freshest fruit and the most delicious home-baked bread that he had ever tasted. Then he asked if it was possible to have a wash as he was very embarrassed by his appearance. Angela pointed to a small hut which was a bathroom and Little Trouble was soon sitting in a lovely hot bath, scrubbing away with soap and a brush to try and remove the tar.

After thirty minutes he hadn't returned and Angela was a bit worried that he may have fallen asleep again or worse still passed out, so she gave him a shout, 'Hurry up, Little Trouble. Time's goin' on and I've things I gotta tell ya.'

At that moment Little Trouble reappeared and Angela could not believe her eyes. After all that time bathing and scrubbing, he looked in exactly the same state as he did before he went in.

'Ah, that's better,' said Little Trouble, trying to reassure himself. 'I know I couldn't quite get it all off but after all this time I think I must be a bit cleaner.'

Sadly, he failed to convince himself and though he was usually so brave and fearless and would never show any sort of emotion (he had been taught that this was a sign of weakness, especially in front of girls), he still could not hold back the tears from rolling down his cheeks.

'I'm going to be filthy dirty for the rest of my life,' he sobbed, 'and I really want to be clean.' Angela came up and put a comforting arm around him. 'I'm sorry, Little Trouble, us Directors tend not to be very good at the gentle stuff, and me words of condolence don't come natural, but I promise yer this: yer'll change once ya meet the Voice.'

Little Trouble wiped his eyes with a corner of his T-shirt, then quickly pulled away from Angela, realising that she had put her arm around him and the last thing that he needed was any of that cissy stuff.

'OK,' he said, 'if you really are a Director, are you going to show me how I can find the Voice?'

'Well, if yer sure yer ready, follow me,' said Angela.

She led him to a massive rock which happened to be the side of the mountain. 'We're goin' in,' she said, and after mumbling a few words (the only one Little Trouble recognised was 'Voice'), the rock parted as if by a miracle and revealed a crack which was just about large enough for them both to walk inside. As they entered, it was very bright, not dark as Little Trouble had imagined it would be, and there was a warm refreshing smoke which filled the enormous cavern. It was a strange sort of smoke—not like a thick fog, but more like a gentle mist which gave the whole cave an air of secrecy.

'Wait 'ere,' instructed Angela, 'while I go and 'ave a quick word with the Voice,' and then she slipped off her shoes.

'What are you taking your shoes off for?' enquired Little Trouble. Angela explained that although the Voice was her best friend, he also was the one she worshipped, and this was Smoke Mountain and holy ground. 'No one says I 'ave to do it,' she continued, 'but it's one way that I like to show me respect.'

As she moved out into the middle of the cave, he saw her kneel down. At first she just knelt with her hands in the air, and although he could see her lips moving he could not understand the language she was speaking. Then she said some words that he could understand, but which still didn't make any sense to him. She bowed her head and went silent as though she were listening to someone, but Little Trouble could hear nothing.

After a few minutes she returned, put her little pink training shoes back on again and told Little Trouble to follow her. She walked over to where two rope ladders were hanging and immediately started climbing one of them. Little Trouble didn't fancy the climb, although he would never admit it. He was quite scared of heights, but he thought he'd better follow. Up they both went. The higher they climbed the more Little Trouble fearfully looked down and realised how the floor of the cave seemed to be disappearing from view. 'C'mon, scaredy cat,' shouted Angela, sensing her obedient follower had misgivings about this venture, 'we're nearly at the top.'

By "the top" she meant the roof, and the ropes actually finished on a narrow ledge. Angela leaped off the ladder onto the ledge with all the agility of a professional trapeze artist while it took another ten minutes before poor Little Trouble even reached the ledge, and a further ten minutes to get onto it from the ladder. 'Well done, Little Trouble,' she said. 'Now then, lie down on yer tummy and look over the edge at the floor of the cave.'

Poor Little Trouble was by now feeling quite ill but still

thought it was best to do as he was told. He was not really in any position to argue.

As they looked down, they could see very little except the swirling mist. 'I can't see anything worth looking at,' grumbled Little Trouble, who was looking at the rope ladder dangling below him and was still wondering how on earth he had managed to climb up it.

'OK, watch this then. Ready when you are, Voice,' she shouted. First there was a noise like an earthquake, then the cave shook and the flat floor that just a short while earlier they had been standing on began to be pulled and pushed, twisted and contorted into every imaginable direction and position. Large lumps became even larger mounds and these started shooting up towards them like enormous rockets. Other pieces were dropping down, way down, and these formed large canyons which filled up with a swirling blue liquid. 'I've heard of floor shows before,' screamed Little Trouble, 'but this one's come alive!' Angela just continued to smile.

After a few minutes all movement stopped and everything went silent. The mist again started creeping in from the edges and left just a large clear circle in the middle. Little Trouble's eyes nearly popped out of his head. 'It's... it's... it's a real life size map right in front of us,' he shrieked excitedly.

'Nah, it's much more'n that,' explained Angela. 'Little Trouble... this could be yer life. Down below yer lookin' at the route that the Voice 'as planned for ya to follow.'

'Can I ask you some questions?' he enquired.

'Fire away. That's what a Director's for,' she replied.

'Why can I only see what's inside that circle? Why can't I see the rest—you know, the whole of the rest of my life?' he asked.

'Easy,' said Angela. 'The Voice only allows us to know one step at a time. Our minds wouldn't be able to cope with any more.'

Little Trouble again glanced down at the circle that he was allowed to see. 'Surely,' he said, 'everyone who comes up Smoke Mountain sees the same map and route?'

'Wrong again,' said Angela. 'There's not two people in the whole wide world who are the same, and the Voice treats everyone individually and each will 'ave their own special route planned.'

'Am I being forced to follow this route?' asked Little Trouble.

'Nah,' said Angela. 'You can choose whether ya follow it or go yer own way. Like yer did when yer 'ad yer tar experience.'

Little Trouble still shuddered at the memory. 'One last question,' he said. 'How will I remember which way to go, even with just the little bit that I have been allowed to see? My memory is not brilliant, you know.'

'Don't ya think that the Voice don't know that?' said Angela. 'Watch this.' Immediately, there was the brightest flash of light that he had ever seen.

'What's that?' he shouted.

'Calm down,' said Angela. 'Yer've gotta learn that even though there's a lot of excitement, there's never nothin' to be afraid of when the Voice is in charge.'

As they looked down they saw that all the floor had returned back to normal.

'Let's go,' said Angela and got up and walked along the ledge to the side of the cave where a door suddenly opened, revealing warm sunshine and a nice green grassy bank which led down to the cave entrance. 'Hey, we could have come in this way instead of that horrible climb up the rope ladders,' said Little Trouble.

'We could 'ave.' said Angela, 'but that wouldn't 'ave been 'alf as much fun, would it?'

At the cave entrance Angela explained that the large flash was in fact a very ingenious camera which took a picture of where Little Trouble was to go next, and then after waiting three minutes for it to develop, it came shooting out of the side of the mountain and landed straight in Little Trouble's hands.

He looked at the photo and saw that not only was it a map of the area, but there was a clear red line with arrows on it so it was almost impossible to get lost.

As they both walked to the edge of Smoke Mountain, Angela was sad at having to part ways and, amazing as it may sound, so was Little Trouble. 'Thank you for your direction and help, Angela,' said Little Trouble. 'Will I ever see you again? I would really like to, you know.'

He noticed a little blush appear on Angela's face that he had never noticed before. 'Once yer've met the Voice, I'm sure we'll see each other again.'

Next Little Trouble did something which required more courage than anything he had done so far: he gave her a little kiss on the cheek. Angela giggled and waved goodbye as he hastily made his way down the steep side of Smoke Mountain. As Angela became a dot on the horizon, he realised that maybe girls were not so bad after all. Well, this one certainly wasn't. To take his mind off her he pulled out the photograph and looked carefully at it. 'Right then,' he said. 'Next stop... Crosscountry.'

4. fruit farm

Little Trouble was quite surprised while staring at the map to find that it seemed to be such a short distance between Smoke Mountain and the borders of Crosscountry, but knowing the hardships he had faced en -route so far, he guessed that this short stroll could still be a dangerous one.

Once at the foot of Smoke Mountain he set off walking along a nice grassy path which had high hedgerows each side. These were packed with every conceivable coloured flower and were quite the most beautiful sight he had ever seen. He even noticed some luscious fruit just hand -picked and eaten. Always willing to oblige, he did just that.

As he became more interested in what was at the side of the path than where the actual path was going, he noticed a small opening in the hedge and a little sign which read: 'For the best possible fruit that you have ever tasted, you must visit Greedy Gutrot's Pick Your Own Farm. Only 100 metres down the path on your left.'

Little Trouble hesitated for a moment, remembering that last time he strayed off in the wrong direction it ended with him up to his ears in tar. But the wonderful taste of the fruit he had been eating seemed to come back into his mouth and tickle his tastebuds as he tried to imagine eating fruit that was even tastier. It did not take him a lot of time or a lot of thinking to realise that this was very different from the tarmac experience. After all, he was not going to go in the wrong direction deliberately. No, he was simply going on a 100-metre detour to see what Greedy Gutrot had to offer, and then he would rejoin the path again. There seemed no harm in that.

As he wandered down the little path he felt quite excited, but was not sure why. His excitement was interrupted by the loudest snore that he had ever heard, and as he followed the noise he saw its owner lying flat on the floor fast asleep.

Little Trouble could not believe his eyes. This guy was enormous. In fact, he had never seen nor even imagined it possible that anyone could reach these mammoth proportions without bursting and making a horrible mess over a five-mile radius.

'Still,' he thought, 'I'd better not be rude,' so he walked up to the sleeping blubberball and tapped him on the shoulder.

'Eh, what's that?' came a sound from underneath a multiplicity of chins.

'Excuse me,' said Little Trouble. 'I read your signs and have come down to see what you have to offer.'

A smile stretched across the fat man's face. 'Oh have you, young sir?' he said very politely. 'And you are very welcome to do so. Let me introduce myself. My name is Greedy Gutrot. I am the owner of all the beauty you see around you.' Little Trouble glanced around and saw that he was surrounded by the most delicious-looking fruit he had ever seen.

'Now give me a hand up, young man, and don't touch any fruit till I tell you, because all that you see now is the worst of what I have grown. I will take you to a secret place where I keep my very best.'

Little Trouble again felt a shiver of excitement inside of him, but then looking down at the huge bulk of Greedy Gutrot he wondered how on earth he was going to be able to help him onto his feet.

Greedy Gutrot could see what was going through Little Trouble's mind and again gave an enormous grin which showed a set of the blackest most decayed teeth that he had ever seen. 'Look above me,' he said, 'and you'll see a chain attached to a winch and pulley in the tree. Just pass the chain to me, will you?' Little Trouble did as instructed, then Greedy Gutrot fastened the chain to his belt, took some sort of remote control gadget out of his pocket, pressed two buttons and simultaneously the chain tightened up and started pulling him off the ground. A little truck with very wide wheels and an even wider seat appeared from nowhere and parked right beneath him so he was able to lower himself carefully onto it. The tree seemed to sigh with relief and the truck seemed to groan as Greedy Gutrot transferred himself from one to the other and unhooked the chain.

'Brilliant, don't you think?' he chuckled. 'I had it specially made for me as I don't like walking much. I find it so tiring and unnecessary. Now come on, follow me and see the most wonderful sights that a hungry man has ever laid eyes on,' and with this he steered his little truck off in the opposite direction from the Crosscountry path that Little Trouble had left. They wove in and out of the apple trees, the pear trees, the raspberry and loganberry bushes until eventually they reached a large wire cage.

'It's to keep the birds and thieves out,' said Greedy Gutrot, before Little Trouble had time to ask what the cage was for. 'Look inside, my little friend, and what do you see?' Little Trouble gasped as he faced the largest apple tree that he had ever seen. Greedy Gutrot smiled as he saw his new-found friend walking closer to the cage, with his eyes almost popping out as they stared at this unbelievable apparition.

'Wow!' blurted out Little Trouble uncontrollably as his vision was locked into this mind-blowing sight. The leaves of this magnificent specimen were bright green and looked so shiney that one could have been forgiven for thinking that someone had gone round and polished each one by hand. The strong branches were creaking and bending low under the enormous weight of the fruit they were having to bear. And the apples proudly hung there, portraying the most succulent, juicy irresistible temptation since Adam and Eve in the Garden of Eden. Little Trouble's mouth was watering so much at the sight that he couldn't speak a word without dribbling.

'Well, this is what you came for, isn't it?' said Greedy Gutrot. 'The first perfect apple tree. Why not go and give your stomach the treat of its life?'

Little Trouble did not need to be asked twice. He rushed into the cage, grabbed the largest fruit that he could see and took an enormous bite. Crunching it between his teeth it tasted... awful. It was sour, bitter. It looked like an apple, but tasted like a lemon. Then he started to feel a strange sensation in his mouth. He looked up to shout to the fat man, but he was locking the cage door, and still smiling.

'What are you doing?' asked Little Trouble.

'Now, how shall I put it?' said Greedy Gutrot, whose smile had turned into a leer. 'Yes, how about, "You are about to die"? Fool! Did you really think I caged those apples in because they are the best? If you did, then you are more stupid than you look. This fruit is lethal. I experimented with it and sprayed it with certain untried chemicals and yes the apples grew freakishly large, but they are also deadly poisonous.'

As Little Trouble fell to the ground, unsure whether to hold his fiery throat or his aching stomach, the fat man drove away shouting, 'An apple a day keeps Littlekids away!'

'Help me,' whispered Little Trouble. 'Please someone, help me. Miraclekid, Angela, are you around? Can you save me?' But no one leaped out to rescue him.

'Dear Voice, wherever you are and whoever you are, can you hear me? I'm so sorry I left your path. Please don't let me die here. I've seen the map of my life. This can't be my next step. I must meet you and take you back to Oldchurch.'

As he rapidly sunk into a state of semi-consciousness he heard someone speaking to his mind and he recognised it as the same voice that had instructed him on where to go when he had been lost in the maze of corridors back in the Old Saints Church building. 'I am going to clean out your insides,' said the Voice, 'and all you need to do is cough when I tell you.'

Little Trouble didn't really understand what was happening, but gradually he felt the pain at the pit of his stomach change into a hot sensation. This heat slowly spread throughout his stomach and right up his body until it reached his throat. Then he heard the Voice say, 'Cough!' He obeyed, and immediately he vomited up the poison. He was very sick. It was a horrible experience, but Little Trouble realised that it had saved his life. More to the point, the Voice had saved his life. He felt no weakness or aftereffects. In fact, he leaped straight onto his feet feeling even stronger than before, but he was also very angry that he had allowed himself to be tricked.

Grabbing one of the poisoned apples and sliding it into his trouser pocket, he rushed at the cage door and kicked it down as if it were made of paper. Then he hurried off in the direction he had seen Greedy Gutrot disappear. 'Where is that fat freak?' he thought, as he followed the tyre tracks.

He didn't have to follow them very far because soon the familiar sound of snoring could be heard and Little Trouble knew that the great deceiver was lying in wait for the next Littlekid to come along.

Quietly, Little Trouble crept up on the incredible hulk, who was dreaming merrily under the same tree where he had first met him, and with the utmost care he gently put his hand into Greedy Gutrot's pocket and very carefully pulled out the remote control gadget. Then, with the same stealth and precision, he hitched the chain onto his over-sized belt and stood back.

Now Little Trouble felt a smile creeping over his face as he pressed both buttons. The chain quickly tightened and Greedy Gutrot instantly woke up as he started to be hoisted up into the tree. 'What the...' he yelled. 'What the—are you doing alive, you little...'

Little Trouble was by now sitting in Greedy Gutrot's truck with the big seat and thought that he may as well make use of it as there was no way the dangling Greedy Gutrot was ever going to need it again. It seemed that as long as he possessed the remote control, then the tree, the chain and Fatso had a permanent future together.

It was then that Greedy Gutrot's face turned red with uncontrollable fury and he started spitting every filthy word he knew towards Little Trouble. Amid this onslaught he screamed out that he worked for the Enemy Superpowers and no one, not even the Voice, was as powerful as they were.

'Liar!' shouted Little Trouble, his anger rising again. Greedy Gutrot was beginning to struggle, using all his weight to break free. And he was going to do it! Quickly Little Trouble dismounted from the truck. He had to do something. Suddenly he felt the poisoned apple in his pocket. He took it out and, holding it as he would a cricket ball, he-threw it with all his might towards the face of Greedy Gutrot. As his great mouth was still open, cursing and swearing, the apple easily found this large opening and went straight in.

Greedy Gutrot went silent. Then, after turning various shades of green, he started to deflate and shrink. Little Trouble watched in amazement. Within seconds, the oversized glutton became not just thin but flat, as though he had been run over by a steamroller. Then, when he was wafer thin, he shrivelled into what looked like a tiny piece of paper and fluttered down to where Little Trouble was standing. Little Trouble picked up the piece of paper and read the words, 'I will be back to get you.' He felt no fear.

In fact, his smile reappeared as he tore up the paper, threw it over his shoulder and jumped back onto his newly-inherited vehicle.

'Now to get back to the path. I've wasted enough time,' he thought. 'I just hope that I have learned something from this experience, and not just been put off fruit for life.'

Little Trouble drove the little truck back through the hole in the hedge, carefully making sure that he ran over and smashed the Fruit Farm sign to pieces, and then continued towards Crosscountry.

5. CROSSCOUNTRY

Little Trouble felt good. He felt that he was really getting somewhere. He'd learned how to contact the Voice, he'd defeated one of the Enemy Superpowers, and now he was making good time, thanks to this wonderful little truck. He hadn't dared to look too much at the hedges, but the only thing that he had found a bit depressing was that all the beautiful colourful flowers and fruit had gone and the further he drove down this path the more bleak the surroundings were becoming.

'I wonder why the green grass is now scorched and black

and all the bushes and trees look burned and dead?' Then he noticed a large sign at the side of the path in the shape of a cross, saying: WELCOME TO CROSSCOUNTRY.

'I'm here,' thought Little Trouble, 'but it's not quite like I expected.' He got out his photomap just to check that he was at the right place, and discovered he was right on course.

After a few more kilometres, he had lost that good feeling and was now feeling quite scared. Everything was silent, deathly silent. No birds sang, no animals could be seen and there was no sign of any green vegetation. The clouds cast a huge grey shadow over the whole of the land. It was a country with no life.

He stopped his truck as the path had ended. The skeletons of giant old oaks made the way impassable for any vehicle. He placed his feet upon the ground which crunched as he stood on it. It was like treading on a substance similar to coal; like walking on a deserted slag heap. It was eerie, and what made it worse was that a wind had started to blow and made frightening noises as it whistled through the charred outstretched remains of old branches circling above his head.

He started to shiver, but was unsure whether it was because the clouds had made him feel much colder or whether he was shaking through fear. He looked at his photomap and he saw that he had to keep going straight ahead in between the trees, and although that was the last thing he wanted to do, he knew that there was no other way. He walked very quickly, then even started to run until he went flying over a tree stump which was very hard to see in the gloomy light. Picking himself up, he looked even blacker than he had before, but that was the least of his worries.

The further he walked, the more the trees thinned out and

eventually they stopped altogether. Then he saw the most frightening sight he had ever seen, and his heart leaped inside of him and started beating so fast he thought it would burst.

There in front of him was a high, jet black hill and at the top of it stood an enormous gravestone. Someone was standing as still as a statue on top of it.

Little Trouble slowly made his way up the steep black incline and even though he was freezing, he was perspiring like mad. Whose grave was it, and who was that standing on top of it? The closer he got, the darker the sky became and it was only the moon above that was offering any light at all.

'I can't read it,' he thought. 'There's a name on it, but every time I go to read it it gets darker.' He started to run towards it in panic. What was it that was making him act like this? When he was a few metres away from it, a star flashed like a celestial spotlight onto the stone and Little Trouble shrieked in horror. It had these words on it: 'LITTLE TROUBLE (DECEASED).'

He fell to the ground sobbing, 'So this was where the map ended. I'm to die on this slagheap.' Crushed by disappointment, he had forgotten all about the figure who was standing on his tomb—until he heard a loud voice shout out, 'Oi!'

He looked up, and not really knowing what he was saying, said, 'What do you want with a dead kid, whoever you are?'

'I can't hear you. Hold on, I'm coming down,' replied the loud voice.

Little Trouble stood up and saw a figure abseil down the slope and land just in front of him. It was another Littlekid, but as the moonlight shone down upon him Little Trouble could see that he was dressed from top to toe in bright red.

'Little Trouble, I am Hearthunter. I am sent by the Voice to ask you a few questions.'

'A sort of last request?' said Little Trouble, still thinking of his impending death.

'Question one,' said Hearthunter, having whipped out a clipboard and questionnaire from seemingly nowhere, and fumbled around the top of his ear trying to find a pencil. 'Do you think that you have ever done anything or thought anything which you consider the Voice would not be happy about?'

Little Trouble thought for a moment and then said, 'That is a hard question. Do you have any easier ones?'

'Hard?' shouted Hearthunter in surprise. 'This should be the easiest one.'

'Can I pass on it?' asked Little Trouble. 'I know I may not be perfect, but I don't think I'm that bad, so I can't find an answer to it.'

'Right, follow me,' said Hearthunter, and at the bottom right hand corner of the stone appeared some steps going downwards. Down they both climbed until they reached a very large circular auditorium with an enormous screen going around the wall.

'Brilliant, a cinema!' exclaimed Little Trouble, already forgetting about his impending death. 'I love the movies. But hold on, there's only one seat in the middle of the hall. Where am I going to sit?'

'That is your seat,' explained Hearthunter patiently. 'You don't think that I want to stay around and see this sort of rubbish, do you? Now you have a choice of films: either, *What the Littlekid did* or *What the Littlekid thought*. I must warn you, however, that there is no censorship. Both of these movies are horrific, but the latter is even more explicit than the first.'

'Superb, I'll see them both,' smiled Little Trouble. 'Maybe the tame one first.'

'OK,' said Hearthunter. 'Now go and sit in the chair. Your films have true-to-life 3D sound and picture so you will feel like you are really part of the movie. Should you not be able to cope with what you are seeing, press the red button on your chair and the film will instantly cut and I will return.'

'Not much chance of that,' boasted Little Trouble. 'I have managed to sneak hold of some of the worst videos available at home while my parents were at meetings, and I've never had to switch one off yet.'

The lights went out and Little Trouble settled into the chair, although he wasn't sitting that comfortably because of the tar that was still stuck to him. The first frames of *What the Littlekid did* began running through the projector. 'Wasn't I a cute little baby,' he chuckled, as a tiny Littlekid appeared on the screen. He assumed it must be him as he was in the arms of his very much younger mother and father. Then, as he saw himself growing older, his smile disappeared. For the first time he started seeing himself as he really was, and it was worse than a horror movie. He saw how when still very young he started to lose his temper, very regularly. He saw himself being greedy, selfish, bullying, lying, cheating, criticising, bragging, hating, and destroying things and people around him, to name but a few character defects. While all this was going on, flashbacks kept appearing on the screen of his parents praying and weeping over their uncontrollable, rebellious Littlekid. Within a very short time, Little Trouble had rammed his finger on the button, stopped the film and was weeping in a heap on the floor. 'That was me in the film. I remember those things I did as if it were yesterday. I don't want to see any more. I'm evil,' he cried. 'I've nothing good in me. I deserve to die.'

'Yes you are right. You do,' agreed Hearthunter. 'But just sit back in the chair once more. I've got one more movie to show you.'

Little Trouble agreed, as long as Hearthunter stayed by his side. 'The film is about the Voice. You will see the pictures of his life, but you will hear no sound through your ears, because the Voice is going to speak directly into your heart.'

The film ran and Little Trouble saw all the wonderful things that the Voice had done. How the Voice became a human being; how he healed those who were ill, loved those who nobody else loved, and enjoyed spending time with Littlekids. As he watched he could see there was a direct link between what Miraclekid and Angela were doing, and what the Voice was doing. The film was action packed with a love portrayed by the Voice that he had never encountered before. Throughout the film he had noticed that the Voice had his enemies, but even though they wanted to kill him there was no way that they could. After all, he was the Voice, the good guy. It was then that the screen grew darker. He saw the Voice being beaten up. He then saw some adults hammering big long metal spikes into the Voice's hands and feet and nailing him to a wooden cross shaped thing.

Little Trouble jumped up out of his chair: 'Fight back, Voice,' he screamed, with tears welling up in his eyes again. 'Kill them before they kill you.' But as he stopped shouting, Little Trouble heard the Voice whisper something about forgiving them. Then massive red letters blazened across the screen in front of him displaying the words: 'It is finished!' The projector stopped and the lights came on.

'No wonder people have a hard time hearing the Voice,' sobbed Little Trouble. 'It must be very hard to understand what a dead Voice is saying. Those adults who killed him must have been working for the Enemy Superpowers. If only I could get my hands on them.'

'Hold on a minute,' interrupted Hearthunter. 'Just a short while ago you discovered that your life is being run by Enemy Superpowers, the same as those adults. We have all done things that have hurt the Voice, but just as you heard the Voice forgive his murderers, so he will also forgive you.'

'But what must I do to be forgiven?' asked Little Trouble.

'Try watching the next reel,' replied Hearthunter as the lights went off and the projector started again.

As Little Trouble watched the final reel, he couldn't contain himself and started cheering, shouting and dancing around the chair. 'Yippee! The Voice is not dead after all,' he hooted. 'He came back to life again. Wow, that really must have been a kick in the teeth for the Enemy Superpowers.'

'Wait,' said Hearthunter. 'Read those words written on the screen. This is the best news of all.'

Little Trouble read the words, 'If you are really sorry for the way you have hurt the Voice, and if you believe what you have seen, you will be forgiven. This includes you, Little Trouble.'

Little Trouble sat silently as the lights came back on. 'Let me complete my questions now,' said Hearthunter. 'First, I repeat: Do you think that you have ever done anything or thought anything which you consider the Voice would not be happy about?'

'Yes I do, but please don't show me my film again,' pleaded Little Trouble.

'Secondly, do you believe what you have just seen about the Voice and what you have heard from him?'

'Without doubt,' said Little Trouble. 'There's something inside of me which is telling me that it's all true.'

'Finally, are you willing to let the Voice be in charge of your life and to live your life for him?'

'You bet,' shouted Little Trouble, too excited to notice his poor choice of words.

Then Hearthunter stood back and shouted, 'Be clean!'

With this, water gushed out of the ceiling of the auditorium, crashing down on Little Trouble. It wasn't a clear water. It was bright white, and as it covered him it cleaned every bit of tar from his body. But better even than that, Littlekid felt clean inside.

'Look to your left,' shouted Hearthunter, and as Little Trouble peered through the water he could see both of the films of his past life being burned in mid air. He knew that he would never have to see or even hear about them ever again.

Once the water stopped, Hearthunter gave a second command: 'Be filled!' And a gale like a whirlwind wrapped around Little Trouble and all the gaps in his life where all the bad old ways had been washed out were now filled by the whirlwind of the Voice. Little Trouble fell to his knees, giving thanks in words that he didn't understand. For the first time in his life he felt really clean and full of power to serve the Voice.

Hearthunter went over and put his hand on Little Trouble's shoulder. He then gave out his third command: 'Little Trouble is dead. You have seen his grave and tombstone above us. Arise; Little Christian.'

As they both walked through the doors of the auditorium, they stepped into brilliant sunshine. All the blackness had gone and they were treading on bright green springy grass. The birds were singing, little animals were prancing excitedly all around them, and even the oak trees had come back to life and were producing acorns.

Little Christian looked down at his brilliant white clothes and then turned round and looked up at the massive towering gravestone behind him. It came as no surprise when he saw there were two words added to 'LITTLE TROUBLE (DECEASED)'. They were in bright red and scribbled right over the top of the other words. They simply read: 'THE VOICE.'

'He really did die for me,' said Little Christian, not realising he was standing alone and talking to himself.

Suddenly another flash penetrated his eyes, but this was one that he had seen before. Yes, Hearthunter had one of those Polaroid cameras and couldn't resist taking a picture of the new Little Christian standing in front of the old Little Trouble's grave.

'Souvenir for you,' said Hearthunter, 'so you'll never forget what happened today.' He handed him the print.

'I'm sure I'll never forget what happened today,' said Little Christian, putting the print carefully alongside his map. 'That reminds me,' he said, taking out his photomap. His new route had been clearly marked out.

'What did you expect?' said Hearthunter, smiling. 'Not everything that the Voice tells you to do is easy, but as to where you should go, only a fool could go wrong.'

Little Christian smiled back at him, and took Hearthunter's words both as advice and as a warning.

'One last gift,' said Hearthunter, taking a small book out of his pocket. 'Little Christian, may I proudly present you with your very own copy of The Voice's Manual. Inside this very special book you will find the answers to some of your questions, and you will also discover that the more you read it, the more you will get to know the Voice personally.'

'Wow,' said Little Christian, grabbing it very excitedly. 'Thank you. I promise I'll read it regularly and guard it with my life.'

Having put it safely in his pocket next to his photomap, he said goodbye to Hearthunter and thanked him for everything.

"Think nothing of it,' shouted back Hearthunter. 'It really was my pleasure,' and Little Christian could see that he really meant it.

6. wastetime UNIVERSITY

Little Christian was very proud of his brand new transformation. He looked good and, by golly, he felt good. He sat down on a large rock by a crystal clear cool stream to have a study of his new Manual and started to read the first chapter which was simply entitled 'The Book of Beginnings'. He was amazed to discover how the world, animals and people came into being, and also how quickly the Enemy Superpowers made their presence known. After a good long read he put his Manual away and opened up his map.

'So now I'm heading for the Voice's Training Module. Well, that doesn't seem too far away.' But as he looked even more closely, he noticed that the only way to the Training Module was across the Distraction Desert, which was part of the Temptation Terrain .

There were three oases also marked out along the route on his map, but as these were very small they didn't have any names marked down. 'Still, at least they are spread out nice and evenly, so I should be all right for a bit of hospitality and maybe make a few friends,' he mused.

It was not long after leaving the stream that he came to the desert. He hadn't seen such a large mass of golden sand since a few years ago when he had a holiday with his parents at Clackpool-on-Sea, but even there he couldn't remember seeing this much sand.

He took his socks and shoes off and ventured out into the desert. It was a wonderful sensation as the warm sand pushed up between his toes, and as he came to the first dune he forgot all about his lovely clean clothes and rolled down it, laughing his head off.

After a few hours, both the sand and the air had become much hotter. In fact, he had to put his shoes back on again as the sand was starting to burn his feet, so it was a welcome treat when he saw a sign which read: 'Wastetime University Oasis 2 Kilometres.'

'This must be the first oasis,' he thought, and even though he was hot, sticky and quite tired, he still had a bit of bounce left in his step as he headed towards his first resting point.

As he drew closer and was expecting to see a few scattered palm trees he had quite a shock when he noticed in the distance a large fortress which was reminiscent of the sandcastles he had once built in Clackpool. The nearer he got to it, the larger it seemed to be, and when he eventually stood next to the enormous wooden doors he felt a bit like an ant standing next to a dustbin.

He walked over to the doorbell which had the words: 'PRESS... (ON AND SUCCEED).' This he did.

He waited for about five minutes until somebody came and the large gate opened.

'Welcome,' said a stern and very posh voice. 'You must be... ahem, a Littlekid.'

'Yes, that is correct,' said Little Christian. 'But I'm not just a Littlekid, I'm also Little Christian,' he said proudly.

'Oh,' said the posh voice, showing absolutely no emotion whatsoever. 'Well do come in and follow me. Professor Bulgebrain is ready to give you an audience.'

As they walked, they passed tall buildings which were all grey, and most of them had steeples and bells on the top, very similar to Old Saints Church back in Oldchurch. They also passed a lot of people, but none of them said hello because they were all walking around with various books in their hands, obviously deep in study. 'I wonder why none of them is reading the Voice's Manual,' he thought. The other strange thing that Little Christian noticed was that although the age range was from Littlekids to oldies, everyone including the Littlekids wore long black robes, spectacles and had bald heads (except the girls).

While he was thinking about all this, he arrived at what he assumed was the Professor's study and was shown in and told to stand in front of a large wooden desk. 'The Professor will be with you directly,' said the person with the stern voice, and with that he picked up a book from the Professor's desk and walked off reading it.

Little Christian glanced around the room. He had never seen so many books. Every wall was covered in shelves which were filled with books. Any bit of spare floorspace had been taken over by a pile of books, and even an empty fishtank was now overflowing with yet more books.

At this point another door opened and in walked a tall, robed, totally bald gentleman, who had a pair of half spectacles perched on the end of his nose. Little Christian put his hand out to shake hands, but the Professor looked at him in horror. 'Young man, we do not allow any sort of familiarity, friendship or physical contact in this institution. We are way above those vulgarities, but you may salute me if you so desire.'

'Why? Who are you?' said Little Christian, getting rather annoyed by this man's snobbery.

'I, my illiterate little friend, am the world famous Professor Bulgebrain, the Principal of Wastetime University, which happens to be the foremost Further Educational Establishment worldwide.'

'Never heard of it,' said Little Christian.

'Well, your sort wouldn't have, would they? I can see that you have no breeding and come from a working-class background,' snapped the Professor.

Little Christian ignored that statement and asked the Professor to give him the lowdown on the University.

'Well, my simple little fellow, here we train up all ages of students in how to succeed in the Bigwideworld that the Voice has made for us. When our ambitious graduates leave here, after many many years of hard study I might add, they become the pinnacles of society. They have all the top jobs, you know, and they are guaranteed enormous salaries, detached houses, high pension schemes, easy living, a wife or husband, two children, a dog and a cat.'

'But what about the Voice's map for their lives?' asked Little Christian.

'I haven't got a clue what you are talking about,' said the Professor. 'The Voice has given us brains, abilities and talents, has he not, and we are here to develop them so that we can be huge successes. I'm sure the Voice is very proud of us.'

'Does the Voice ever visit the University?' asked Little Christian in despair.

'Visit *us!*' exclaimed the Professor. 'What a silly idea! But he hasn't stopped young ambitious students arriving here, so I am totally convinced that he has the greatest respect for us.'

'Anyway,' said the Professor, 'enough of this. After all, I am interviewing *you*. I am sorry to have to inform you that you do not have the right qualifications, or the right attitude, even to sit the entrance exam. We have taken one or two of your type before, but I'm afraid they were disastrous failures and dropped out within a very short time.'

'Forgive me, Professor, but I wouldn't want to stay here even if you wanted me. I am on my way to the Voice's Training Module, and I only dropped in for some food and drink, and maybe a bed for the night if possible.'

'Tut tut,' said the Professor. 'The Voice's Training Module, such a low-grade establishment. Many Littlekids call in here on their way to that place, but after they see what we have to offer, they choose to stay with us. But they are only the bright ones, I hasten to add. Do you realise, I have yet to hear about anyone leaving that place with any real qualifications. Still, having been in conversation with you, I would imagine that you and it are ideally suited.'

Although the Professor would have loved to boot Little Christian right out of Wastetime University immediately, he felt word of his lack of hospitality may leak out to other future applicants. Also, thinking in his own mind that those outside of his gates thought of him as being highly educated and respected, he didn't want any bad press which may make people think to the contrary. He considered the wisest course of action was to allow this Little Christian to stay for just one night.

He rang a bell and the same person who had met Little Christian at the gate returned. 'You rang, Professor?' he asked.

'Yes. Please take our guest to room 3002 where he can stay the night and have a tray of sandwiches and a drink delivered to his room. I don't want him mixing with the students. He is the sort that could be a major distraction to their studies.'

Little Christian was led along a stone corridor, up three flights of stairs and shown into a very sparse room which had only a bed, a chair, a table with a reading light aimed at a copy of the University Prospectus. But there was also something that thrilled his heart: an en suite bathroom. He was told he would be awoken at 5:30 am sharp so that he could continue his travels, and his supper tray would be brought to his room shortly.

Little Christian lay in the hot soapy water of the bath and thought of his adventures so far. What was most in his mind was the Voice and how he had met him, but he also couldn't help thinking about his parents back in Oldchurch and of course Angela. He wondered if he would ever see them again.

As he climbed into bed, having had his fill of the food and drink that had obediently been delivered, he read another portion of his Manual, then he thanked the Voice for his protection and decided to make a resolution that he would do this each night. He never wanted to take the Voice for granted, as the Professor and all the people in this University seemed to be doing.

The minute his head hit the pillow he sunk into a deep sleep and although he dreamed a lot, all his dreams were pleasant ones.

It was three o'clock in the morning when he was awoken from these lovely dreams by a gentle knocking on his door. Then he saw the door slowly opening.

Little Christian leaped from his bed and ran towards the table light, but in his panic he tripped over the chair and landed with a thump on the floor. 'Who is that? Who's there?' he whispered from his embarrassing prostrate position.

The door quietly closed and he heard the patter of little footsteps coming towards him and a voice say, 'Ssshhhhh...'

He stood up, not so scared now that he realised his intruder was much smaller than he was, and managed at last to switch the light on. There in front of him was a tiny female Littlekid, about eight years old he guessed.

'Please help me,' she whispered.

'Come and sit down and tell me all about it,' said a surprised and still very sleepy Little Christian.

The little girl's name was Wanda and she explained how bored she was, because she couldn't manage the work. She didn't like the people either, and she had no desire to grow up to be intelligent. She then went on to ask Little Christian if she could leave with him in the morning.

'But I am going to the Voice's Training Module to be trained up,' said Little Christian.

'You know,' said little Wanda in a very matter of fact voice, 'that's where I believe I should be going as well.'

Little Christian had grave doubts, but then it was three o'clock in the morning, and anywhere must be better for her than this place, so he agreed to let her tag along with him. 'It will be no problem for you to leave here,' he continued. 'They all walk around with their noses in their books and they won't even notice that you are missing. Go back to bed now and meet me at the gates soon after 5:30 in the morning.'

Little Wanda went back to bed very excited, but Little Christian didn't sleep too well for the rest of the night as he was wondering if he was doing the right thing.

Five-thirty came and as he was escorted to and through the main gates, nobody noticed, except him, a little girl slip through the gates and join him. Together the two of them took off their shoes and socks and started to walk across the now cool sand.

A short while on they faced a sign which pointed to: 'LEISURE BEACH OASIS' which was about a day's walk away. 'That's our next port of call,' said Little Christian, checking his photomap.

'That place sounds great fun,' said Little Wanda.

'Yes it does, doesn't it,' replied Little Christian cagily, and wondering what on earth he had let himself in for as a full-time baby sitter.

7. Leisure beach

Little Christian didn't find it so easy walking with his tiny companion. She kept wanting either to stop and have a rest or else to keep talking the whole time. 'Oh for a bit of peace and quiet,' he mumbled to himself.

She told him all about herself, but was strangely vague when she mentioned her father. She went into detail explaining about how her mother had died many years ago, but all she would say about her father was that he was very intelligent and had no time for her.

Leisure Beach Oasis was one of those places that could be

heard before it could actually be seen. With the screams and shouts of laughter, and music blasting away, it certainly seemed a fun place and the opposite of Wastetime University that he had just left.

As it came into view, it was an assortment of bright colours. Everything had been painted almost as loudly as the music which could be heard from miles away. The apartments and hotel roofs, the restaurants and bars, plus the numerous sun umbrellas all added to this eye-catching decor.

Little Christian and Wanda made their way down the main street which was packed with very friendly people dressed in bikinis and bathing trunks, sun hats and sunglasses. All the residences and shops were on their left-hand side. On the right-hand side was an enormous man-made beach and lake with a built-in wave machine.

While Wanda was babbling on about how great everything was, Little Christian was getting rather steamed up, wondering what all these people were doing lazing around here instead of following the Voice's map.

Outside one of the buildings, Little Christian noticed the words: 'RECEPTION FOR NEW ARRIVALS.' He thought this might be a good place to go and see if Wanda and he could get booked into a couple of rooms for the night.

As he entered the door, a very attractive lady with a big smile shouted, 'Yes sir, can I help you?'

Little Christian explained where he had come from and as the lady seemed to be interested in his travels he went over them again in even greater detail.

'Oh dear, you poor young thing,' she exclaimed as he eventually wound down. 'You take a seat over there and I'll go and get the boss. I know that he would love to meet you.'

A few minutes later a tubby little man came rushing

towards them. He had a heavy tan, brightly patterned Bermuda shorts, a T-shirt with 'Hug Me, I'm Free' written on it, and a large cigar sticking out of his mouth.

'Wow,' he said, 'you must be Little Christian. My secretary has told me all about you and it's my pleasure to meet one of the Voice's heroes. Let me introduce myself. My name is Idol. Boney Idol. Boney, by the way, is just a nickname that my friends affectionately use due to my shape being the opposite of boney. Get it? Ha Ha Ha! And who's this Littlekid?'

'I'm Wanda,' said Wanda.

'Well aren't you a little cutie,' he giggled. 'Now, Little Christian,' he said, putting on a more serious voice, 'bearing in mind all that you have been through in the service of the Voice, it is my pleasure to offer you the keys of Leisure Beach. In other words, you can stay as long as you want. I have a penthouse apartment all ready for you, and everything you want is yours for free, and the same goes for little cutie here.'

Little Christian didn't know what to say. Nobody had ever offered him anything like this before. He now found that two voices were speaking into his mind. A clear voice was telling him to stay a night and then to move on towards the Voice's Training Module. Another voice, however, which was not as clear, was reminding him that he deserved a break after all he had come through. This voice continued to ram home its point by saying that everyone needs a holiday retreat and there's nothing wrong with that, is there? Even the Elder in Oldchurch went on a sabbatical holiday every seven months.

Little Christian hesitated, as the latter voice got louder and clearer. He preferred what that voice was saying, so he thanked Boney Idol for his very kind offer and said he would accept it, but only for a short period of maybe a couple of days.

'Excellent. You know it makes sense. Very wise,' said Boney.

'Wowie, great!' said Wanda.

Boney then gave them both keys and a special Cashquik Card which Little Christian would find was accepted anywhere in the oasis, or he could even draw what cash he required out of the local Lendezee Bank, any time, day or night.

Both Little Christian and Wanda settled into the lap of luxury very quickly. Neither of them had ever experienced this sort of good life before. They lazed by the lake throughout the daytime, swimming and getting beautifully tanned. Then in the evenings over food and drinks they would meet up with other Littlekids who, although they had been there for a few years, were convinced that one day they would continue their journey to the Voice's Training Module. But there was no rush, they would say, and Little Christian tended to agree.

Each Sunday everyone on Leisure Beach would meet up for a service which Boney led, and although the Voice was never allowed to speak there, they had some wonderful times singing and telling the Voice about the fun they were having. Then they'd conclude by hearing Boney read a bit from the Manual and he'd have everyone in fits of laughter with a few hilarious jokes.

After a few weeks had passed, Little Christian found himself getting very friendly with a pretty Littlekid called Sandy. He first met her on the beach. This relationship came just at the right time. He now saw very little of Wanda and he assumed that she too must have made friends with Littlekids of her own age.

Little Christian really enjoyed walking about with a girl-friend holding onto his arm all day long. And it was an added bonus that she just happened to be the best looker on Leisure Beach, so it was also fun to watch the other male Littlekids looking enviously at him.

Two months had passed, and now Little Christian himself was saying that he would move on to the Voice's Training Module soon, but there was no rush. In his heart he had no thoughts of moving on. Sandy seemed set here for life and as Little Christian was becoming more serious about her, this was another reason he was not too concerned about moving on.

One morning, as Little Christian was lying dozing on the beach with Sandy cuddling up to him, a cloud suddenly covered him. He thought nothing of it, even though he had not noticed any clouds before on Leisure Beach. But then he heard a voice he recognised.

'So just wot do ya think yer doin' 'ere, Little Trouble?'

Little Christian froze rigid, then he leaped up, pushing Sandy to one side, and there looking straight into his eyes was... Angela.

'Oh, hi there, Angela. What a nice surprise,' he said nervously. 'Let me introduce you to a friend of mine: this is Sandy.'

'She ain't no friend. She's a distraction to the Voice,' said Angela very sternly.

Sandy leaped up, eyes blazing. 'Who do you think you are calling a distraction?' she screamed. 'I happen to be Little Christian's girl and I think that you are just a jealous cow.'

'Hold on,' said Little Christian joining in. 'I don't think you need to use language like that, Sandy. After all, Angela is just an old friend.'

'Oh, I see. So you're sticking up for her now, are you?'

Sandy yelled. 'Well, I won't be treated like this. After all, I am the prettiest girl on Leisure Beach and I have the choice of any bloke around. Little Christian, you and me are history. If I see you in a hundred years' time, it will be too soon for me,' she screamed, stomping off up the beach.

'Well, I admire ya taste. You really know how ta pick 'em,' said Angela turning on Little Christian.

'Women!' shouted Little Christian.

'Women nothing,' said Angela, her eyes now staring straight into Little Christian's. 'Don't kid yerself. I'm not 'ere chasin' after a time waster like you. I've got more important things ta do wiv my time. I'm on a mission for the Voice.'

Little Christian went silent and even redder than his suntan. 'The Voice 'as been tryin' to get through to ya, but yer've bin ignoring 'im. That's why 'ee 'as sent me to find ya and try and talk some sense into ya.'

'But, Angela, you know I had a rough time. Surely there is nothing wrong with taking a holiday?'

'Little Trouble, there is a time for 'olidays and a time for servin'. Per'aps when yer've done a bit of servin' yer'll 'ave earned the need for an 'oliday, but that time is certainly not now.'

Little Christian felt tears welling up in his eyes. It had taken him such a short time to forget what happened in Crosscountry.

'Angela,' he said, changing the subject, 'would you like to see a photo?' and he handed her the picture of him standing in front of his tombstone.

'That's beautiful,' said Angela, trying to hold back her own tears. 'I'm sorry for callin' ya "Little Trouble" when I should 'ave said "Little Christian".'

'No, you were right to call me that,' argued Little

Christian. 'I was acting more like the old me, not the new me,' he continued.

'Nah, don't ever say that. Yer'll never be Little Trouble again. Remember 'ee is dead and buried. Once the Voice renames ya, that is who ya really are, faults 'n' all. I can't force ya to continue with yer journey—it's not me place. Besides,' said Angela, 'no one can, not even the Voice. It is yer own choosin'. You can waste the rest of yer days 'ere with people like Sandy, or ya can continue, to be trained and take the Voice back to yer loved ones in Oldchurch.'

Before he could answer he saw Boney Idol running towards him. 'Little Christian, I've just seen Sandy and she's furious and very upset. I really think that you two lovebirds should kiss and make up.'

'Sorry, Boney, I'm afraid that relationship is over,' said Little Christian. 'Please apologise to her on my behalf as I didn't mean to hurt her. Now, though, I must be leaving Leisure Beach. I've a mission to complete and if I stay here it will never get done. Thanks for everything. Maybe I will return one day when I've spent some time serving and deserve a holiday.' He winked at Angela and she smiled back.

'Well, take care, Little Christian,' said Boney Idol. 'You are a bit of a weirdo. I've never known anybody leave Leisure Beach once they have settled here, but I guess it takes all sorts to make up a world. Oh, and by the way, do give my love to the Voice, won't you,' and with that he disappeared.

As Angela and Little Christian reached the edge of the oasis he suddenly remembered Little Wanda.

'Oh, I wouldn't worry about 'er,' said Angela. 'Er dad came and found 'er and when 'ee saw wot Leisure Beach woz like, an' wot fun it woz, 'ee decided to stay on with 'er.'

'Well, who is her dad?' asked Little Christian in surprise.

'I think ya met 'im,' said Angela. 'A certain Professor Bulgebrain, and the University at this very moment is lookin' for a new Principal. Fancy applying for the job?' she said jokingly.

'I think you'd make a better applicant, especially with the way you talk,' said Little Christian.

Angela gave him a thump and then they both sat down in the hot sand and rolled around in fits of laughter.

As the laughter subsided Angela said that it was time they were moving on as she had more work to do, and Little Christian had a few hours' walk before he would reach Securicity, which was his last stop before the Voice's Training Module.

'Angela, I really do like you,' said Little Christian, trying to be serious.

'Yeah, ya know I think I quite like you too,' she giggled. 'But, Little Christian, 'aven't ya learned from yer experience with Sandy that romance isn't yer immediate priority?' She paused. 'Maybe one day,' she said giving him a wink and a smile, 'but until that day the Voice 'as much more important things for ya to do and ya don't want any more distractions, do ya?'

Little Trouble had to agree, and as they parted yet again he hoped this wouldn't be the last time he saw her. He had learned his lesson though. From now on the Voice was going to remain more important than any girl, however pretty she may happen to be.

8. securicity

Little Christian seemed to have found a new bounce in his
step after his time with Angela, and within what seemed a
very short space of time he reached a signpost which said:
'You are now half way between Leisure Beach and
Securicity.'

As he had made such good time he thought he would
have a rest for five minutes. The desert was hot and the
warm air made him feel quite sleepy. Sitting down under
the shade of the signpost, he heard the sound of an engine
in the distance, and looking very carefully he could also see

a cloud of dust. The dust and noise grew closer and louder as they approached him and then circled the signpost three times before eventually grinding to a halt. It took a few minutes for the dust to settle, but when it did, Little Christian was facing the most modern and powerful motorcycle he had ever seen, with a Littlekid perched on top of it.

The Littlekid jumped off the mighty machine and started to walk over to Little Christian. He had no crash helmet or protective clothing. In fact, all he was wearing was a pair of extra large leather boots, a pair of extra tight leather shorts and a pair of spectacles with extra thick lenses.

'Hey, hiya man,' he said in an unusually deep voice. 'I'm Dangerkid,' he continued, tripping over a rock which he had failed to notice and ending up lying alongside Little Christian.

After hearing Little Christian's story about who he was and how he was heading for Securicity, then on to the Voice's Training Module, Dangerkid shook his head and made a few tutting noises with his mouth.

'Nah, ya'll listen hear, little dude. Where you're goin' there ain't no excitement, and the Voice promised ya'll a life of excitement now, didn't he? I mean, ya'll can't be even sixteen yet, but by the time ya'll complete the route yer on, ya'll be an old timer and too frail to enjoy yourself.'

'Be that as it may,' answered Little Christian. 'This map in my pocket was given to me by the Voice and he must know what is best for me.'

'Nah, come off it,' argued Dangerkid. 'I ain't arguin' that the Voice knows best. Naw, all I'm sayin' is that he also knows ya'll and being a young whippersnapper, Littlekid, he also knows that ya'll need a bit of excitement in yer life. Look ya just told me yer makin' good time. Hows about comin' for a quick spin with me? Surely that can't do no harm?'

Little Christian was very tempted. He had never been on a machine as powerful and fast as the one facing him. 'But I haven't got a crash helmet,' he said.

'Hey, them things is for girls and wimps. Us menfolk don't need them. Anyhow, ya'll believe that the Voice will protect us, don't yer?'

Little Christian was not sure of the answer to this question. He didn't know if the Voice did a motorcycle insurance policy, so he didn't reply.

'C'mon, get along there,' said Dangerkid, standing up and walking straight into the signpost by mistake. 'Now where did I leave ma bike? I can't seem to see it.'

Little Christian led him to his bike, and without meaning to sound too personal asked him if he was sure he was OK to be riding with such poor eyesight. Dangerkid laughed, 'You betcha,' he said. 'That's what makes it even more excitin'. Anyway, I drive by faith not by sight. That's what the Manual teaches, don't it?'

Again, Little Christian had no answer for him. He had not read up to that bit in the Manual, but it did sound right. So he nodded so as not to look too stupid.

'Now jump on,' shouted Dangerkid with the bike already started and the throttle wound up to maximum revs. Little Christian hesitated, then jumped aboard.

Immediately there was a screech of tyres and a smell of burning rubber as the machine went straight into a wheelie and shot off like a rocket. Little Christian flung his arms around Dangerkid's waist and held on for dear life. For the first few minutes he kept his eyes tightly closed, but as he opened them he realised that he could still see nothing due to the dusty sand that the bike was throwing up into the air.

Dangerkid was by now very excited and was making all kinds of whooping noises. Little Christian began to suspect that even he could not see anything.

For ten minutes the bike spun over the flat surface at maximum speed, but neither driver nor pillion could see that they were on a direct course for a large ravine with steep sides, and it was filled with the most vicious, spikey cacti imaginable.

The bike reached the top of the ravine and then left terra firma and entered into space. 'Yippee!' screamed Dangerkid. 'We're flyin'!' Little Christian just closed his eyes and started to pray.

Since motorbikes were made to go on solid surfaces and aeroplanes were made to fly, it is not surprising that in a very short time both riders had left the machine and the bike flew on by itself unaccompanied.

All went quiet. Even the bike had stalled. Little Christian opened his eyes and he was in terrible pain. His body was covered in the cactus spikes which had penetrated deeply into his skin. Although he knew that no bones were broken and he was not very seriously injured, just the sight of himself covered in blood made him feel worse.

He staggered up the steep wall of the ravine, and glancing back saw Dangerkid looking around trying to find where his bike had landed. He was shouting at the top of his voice about how exciting the ride had been, and how this was really living. Little Christian couldn't cope with facing him again, so once at the top of the ravine he painfully followed the tyre marks back towards the road to Securicity.

After a few miles he felt he could walk no further, and knowing that it was his own stupidity listening to that idiot Dangerkid that had got him into this position, he thought that maybe he would lie down by the side of the road and give up. Every now and then he would feel another cactus spike and pull it out of his skin.

It was then that he heard a loud horn noise behind him, and turning around he saw that he was face to face with a brand new Mercedes Benz. What a quiet vehicle—exactly the opposite of the bike. He hadn't even heard it approach him.

The car door opened and out stepped a very posh man dressed in what looked to be a very expensive suit. 'I say, old bean,' said the man, whose voice was as posh and refined as the clothes he was wearing, 'if you don't mind me saying so, you look in an awfully bad way, what? My name is Investments, Andy Investments. Can I be of any assistance?'

Little Christian explained that he had just been in a collision with a cactus without going into any great detail, and that he was heading for Securicity.

'Well, what a stroke of luck, old man,' said Andy. 'That is in fact where I reside and if you would care to hop in, I will see that you get there safely.'

As the two drove along, Little Christian could not help thinking about the two contrasting people and rides that he had experienced all in one day. First, reckless, scruffy Dangerkid riding as fast a his motorbike would go, and now immaculately posh Andy who claimed he drove a Mercedes because it was the safest car on the road. He was also driving at a steady thirteen-and-a-half miles per hour because he considered that anyone who raced along at the excessive fiteen miles per hour was an absolute cad and roadhog and should be banned from driving.

Even though he was still in pain, Little Christian couldn't help but smile.

Even travelling at such a low speed, Securicity was soon reached, and although it was called a city, and was bigger than Wastetime University and Leisure Beach, it didn't have a very large residential area.

As they arrived Little Christian was surprised that it had a very high wall and a very deep moat surrounding it and hence they had to drive over a drawbridge to get inside. Once inside the gate they were surrounded by quaint old buildings. Unlike Leisure Beach this place was spotlessly clean and everyone had very smart clothes on. An extremely wealthy and prosperous place.

'Welcome to Securicity,' said Andy. 'Are you thinking of putting your roots down here?'

'No, I'm just staying the night then moving on to the Voice's Training Module,' replied Little Christian.

'Oh my,' said Andy in horror. 'Are you sure that's wise, old fellow? After all, it's all right you thinking about today and even tomorrow, but you must also consider your long-term future. Look here, pop into the Treasures on Earth Arms, get a room for the night, have a nice hot bath to clean up and I will meet you in an hour and take you on a sightseeing tour.'

Little Christian agreed and did just as Andy suggested. He wondered how he would pay for the room, however, as he had no money, but the landlord told him that no one had any money here and that cash currency was very out of date. Everyone now just owned plastic Loancards which were far more interesting, and he gave Little Christian one for himself.

His bedroom was very luxurious. It was fully equipped with an olde worlde four-poster bed, antique coffee table and chair, a loud ticking grandfather clock, an en suite bathroom where the carpet was so deep that he almost lost sight of his feet when he trod on it, plus every mod con imaginable. On the wall he noticed some words printed inside a picture frame which read: 'A Littlekid's home is his castle, and Securicity is a castle for Littlekids.'

Having soaked in a lovely hot bath and pulled out all the offending bits of cactus, he went back downstairs to meet his new friend Andy. Good to his word, Andy arrived precisely on time and off they both set. Andy seemed to know everyone and they all seemed to know him. They were all so polite and sophisticated.

'This is my building,' said Andy, proudly facing a beautiful large old building with the words: 'Andy Investments... Sow a seed today, and reap a harvest in the future.' 'I have a very important function here and that is to see that all you Littlekids invest all that the Voice has entrusted you with in the best possible way.

'You invest your giftings and talents into this city,' Andy continued, 'and I will see that you are set up for life. Depending upon what the Voice has given you, you could end up with a lovely old cottage, plus a vintage car, and being surrounded by these big walls there is no fear of any danger. I will set you up for life. Do you really think that the Voice who loves you, wants you to go through hard and difficult times? Don't you think that he wants you to have the best of everything? And it's all here.'

It was funny, but Andy's voice sounded very reminiscent of one of the Aunties back in the Littlehorrors Junior Church.

'But wouldn't it be a waste just living in this luxury?' asked Little Christian. 'Wouldn't it be a waste if my gifts and talents never really got to the people who need them, like the people in Oldchurch and the Bigwideworld, for instance?'

Andy smiled a smug smile. 'Do you really consider that those sorts of people are worth throwing your talents away on? I mean, some of them don't even know the Voice and don't even want to. You will be... how shall I say it... casting pearls before swine.'

The tour continued. Andy showed Little Christian around Prosperity Palace, the Stock Market, the Tithes Trust Storehouse, and encouraged testimonies from many happy Littlekids who had decided to settle down in this wonderful Securicity for the rest of their earthly days.

But still Little Christian was not convinced that this was for him. 'This is not where my map ends up,' he argued.

'Don't be naive,' said Andy. 'Nobody's map ends up here, but your common sense will tell you this is the right place to be. After all,' he said, 'does it not say in the Manual that the Voice helps those who help themselves?'

'I'm not sure,' said Little Christian, confused. 'But I do know that my time on earth must be more than just making a cosy life for myself.'

'Well, if you want to be a martyr, so be it,' said Andy sadly. He was convinced that Little Christian was just immature and misguided and was throwing his life away.

With this, Little Christian said goodbye and walked back to the Treasures on Earth Arms. He decided to go straight to bed because he found that the more people he talked to, the more confused he was becoming.

After spending a time reading the Manual, he reassured himself that living by faith and not by sight had nothing to do with blind motorcycle maniacs. And as for 'the Voice helps those who help themselves'—he couldn't find that anywhere. Eventually he fell fast asleep, convinced that both Dangerkid and Andy Investments did not know the Manual and were not hearing the Voice.

Little Christian woke up very early the following morning and quietly left the hotel and Securicity. He did not want to face Andy again because he was one of the most dangerous, deceived people that he had met in the Distraction Desert, and the worst thing about it was that some of what he said made sense. And he was such a nice person.

9. THE VOICE'S TRAINING MODULE

As Securicity vanished out of view, so Distraction Desert and the Temptation Terrain came to an end. The sand made way for some nice lush grass again and the cacti were replaced by beautiful plants and trees.

Little Christian was now determined that whoever he met he would not stop and talk to them since nearly everyone he had encountered so far had brought him to the brink of disaster. He did in fact pass two Littlekids. He simply said hello then hurried on, even though they looked like they would not have minded stopping and having a chat.

Then he saw it. There in the distance was 'THE VOICE'S TRAINING MODULE'. He had to squint as he gazed at it because the ultra-modern domes and buildings reflected the bright rays of the sun. It was like he was standing staring at an enormous glistening crystal. His heart leaped at the very thought that he would soon be entering the most brilliantly futuristic construction ever built. There would be nothing old-fashioned there.

He did still have one problem to face, however, and that was how he would actually get to it, because it was situated on an island in the middle of a big lake. As he walked down the bank to the edge of the water, he noticed a small rowing boat heading towards him with two Littlekids in it. It stopped by the bank and a female voice shouted, 'Hello, I'm Harmony and he's Buddy. Please allow us to row you over to the Voice's Training Module.'

'Not likely,' shouted Little Christian. 'I've met your sort before and I don't trust any of you.' With that he dived into the lake and started swimming towards the island.

'Wait!' shouted Buddy. 'That water is dangerous.'

'Not half as dangerous as you,' called back Little Christian, ignoring the warning.

He was about halfway across, thinking 'so far so good', when he noticed some weed popping up out of the water. He kept swimming, but the weed got thicker, and as he looked more closely at it he saw that each plant had hundreds of little suckers attached to it. He swam a bit further, but it was getting harder and harder to move forwards as the suckers were not only sticking to his clothes, but they were also sticking to his hands, feet and face.

Then he stopped. The weed had covered him, and the

thousands of suckers now began to pull him beneath the surface towards the bottom of the lake. Just as he started to swallow and breathe in the dirty water, the water suddenly became very hot around him and the weed that had a murderous grip on him instantly scorched and shrivelled up. He felt a strong hand grab hold of his hand and the next thing he knew was that somehow he was lying in the boat with Harmony and Buddy staring at him.

'You must learn who your friends are,' said the Littlekids together sternly. 'The Voice has given us this job to help people like you to reach the Voice's Training Module safely. You need us just as much as you have needed Angela, Miraclekid and Hearthunter. That Loneranger Weed would have drowned you had it not been for my Gooddeed Ranger Repellant.'

'I'm sorry,' said Little Christian, 'but you didn't seem as important as Angela, Miraclekid and Hearthunter. Now I see you are, please accept both my thanks and my apologies.'

Harmony smiled warmly. 'Oh, that's all right,' she said. 'A lot of Littlekids think we are inferior to some of the more powerful giftings, but when they, like you, are in a time of need, they soon discover that we're not. One thing you must always remember is that whatever the Voice calls you to do, it is vital. Not one of us is more important than the other, and none of us can survive without each other.'

'I'll remember that,' said Little Christian, feeling well and truly rebuked.

As the little boat drew into the bank, Little Christian thanked Harmony and Buddy once more, then turned and gazed at the glass complex facing him. Feeling very small, he made his way to the large glass doors of the module. As he reached them, the doors automatically opened, making a gentle buzzing sound. He walked straight in and saw someone sitting at a large black desk in the middle of a raised rotating patio area, his head buried in a computer screen. 'Over here, if you please, Little Christian,' called the serious yet friendly voice, still not looking up.

Little Christian walked obediently over to the bowed head which then suddenly looked up at him. The face was kind but a little stern, and without speaking he pressed a button and the computer monitor spun around so that the screen faced Little Christian.

Seeing a list of dates on the monitor, Little Christian assumed that it was some form of calendar.

'Oh, is it your diary?' he asked observantly.

'No...it's your diary,' said the man behind the desk. 'And if you look carefully, the first date written on our memory banks was when we expected you, but that was months ago.'

'Ah,' said Little Christian, blushing. 'I'm afraid I got a bit waylaid.'

'You certainly did,' came the reply. 'Now, what would you like first: the good news or the bad news?'

'Um... the good news, please,' said Little Christian.

'All right, the good news is that the Voice has forgiven you for all your "waylayings" and is very proud of you for reaching here.'

'Brilliant!' shouted Little Christian. 'What about the bad news?'

'Well, due to your late arrival you are going to have to study very hard if you wish to be awarded your gift by graduation day, which happens to be only a few weeks away.'

'I'll do it,' said Little Christian. 'You just watch me.'

With that, the man got up from behind his desk and smiled. 'I'm sure you will,' he said encouragingly. He walked over and gave Little Christian a hug and introduced himself. 'I, Little Christian, am a Truth Extractor. It will be my privilege to go through the Manual with you and help try to explain what it means, so that when you eventually go to the Bigwideworld you will know a lot more about the Voice, and how he can speak to you. Now, follow me and I will show you where you are staying.'

The building was very clean and everything that wasn't glass was either dazzling chrome or painted brilliant white. It was very warm and comfortable, but not as luxurious as Securicity. Little Christian was led into a large light room where the Truth Extractor flicked a few more switches and three beds appeared as if from nowhere through the wall.

'You are to share your room with a couple of other Littlekids. We believe that it is one thing to get on and obey the Voice by yourself, but another thing altogether to learn to work and be friends with others.' Little Christian just smiled as this was going to be a new experience for him.

As the Truth Extractor left, he sat on the bed, feeling rather nervous. He had never found it easy to make new friends and here for the next few weeks he was going to be sharing a room with two strangers. Supposing they didn't like him? Supposing they were a bit weird?

He lay on his bed in trepidation as he heard the sound of voices coming down the corridor. Then suddenly two Littlekids rushed into the room, and before he could get a good look at them they had jumped on him playfully. In no time at all Little Christian was lying on the floor with the two Littlekids sitting on top of him.

'What kept you, Little Trouble?' they shouted laughing. He hadn't heard that name for a long time.

Little Christian gasped in amazement at what he saw, then breathed a sigh of relief. He also burst out laughing, for there, sitting on top of him, were his old friends from Oldchurch: Little Pest and Little Nuisance.

For the rest of the afternoon, and until the early hours of the morning, they talked, laughed and shared adventures. Then eventually, feeling totally exhausted but wonderfully happy, they all fell asleep.

Tomorrow was going to be a big day.

10. THE COMMISSION

It was at six o'clock sharp that Little Christian and his friends were awoken with the words, 'Wake up, Littlekids, your day has begun,' booming over the intercom. They quickly washed and dressed, then walked down to the dining hall to have some breakfast.

There the Truth Extractor joined them. 'Good morning, Littlekids,' he said, smiling. 'Are you ready to begin your first assignment?'

'Yes,' they replied excitedly.

They left the residents' building and came to a small door

in the side of a large tree. 'This is where you begin,' said the Truth Extractor. 'Inside here are hundreds of rooms, and once you get inside you will be so confused that you will be immediately lost. There will be many voices in there giving you all sorts of advice, but only the Voice himself will give you the right advice. The object of the exercise is to learn how to discern, hear and recognise the Voice. Is that clear?'

'Yes,' they all said confidently.

'Now, you have to be outside of the tree within one week, otherwise you will have failed this first section and will have to start all over again. You will find food and drink in various rooms. Now off you go.'

The three Littlekids walked through the small door, and it closed automatically behind them the minute they were inside. Then it immediately vanished, and they were left staring in a room with tunnels going out from it in all directions. They decided to split up, and having wished each other all the best, each departed down a different tunnel.

Little Christian's tunnel led to a room that was full of telephones. He had never imagined that there were so many different types and colours, and they ranged from real museum pieces to the latest in cellular models.

'Yes,' he thought to himself, 'it's obvious that the Voice would speak through one of these. But which one?' He had hundreds to choose from. Right now he was staring at quite an old model similar to one he remembered seeing back in Oldchurch. He picked that one up first, but it was dead. 'That makes sense,' he thought.

He then proceeded to pick up a bright red modern one, and a voice told him that if he wanted to find the door he should pick up the antique brass one at the other end of the room. He ran to the other end and there was the antique brass phone. 'Great,' he thought, 'I'm getting there,' but as he picked up the antique brass phone a voice informed him that if he wanted to find the door he should pick up the black phone in the centre of the room. And so he continued, until he had picked up all the phones at least twice, some even three times.

Little Christian sat down, exhausted. His ear was sore and his mind was spinning with all the different voices he had heard, but he had not once heard the real Voice that was to tell him how to find the door.

After a few minutes he stood up and walked down another tunnel, but just before he entered the next room, he saw a great big wooden chest filled to the brim with identical silver coins. A little note was on the lid which said:

> Take plenty of coins, you have no choice,
> if you really want to hear the Voice.

Little Christian obediently filled his pockets with coins and entered the room. It was crammed with plastic heads which were surrounded by little pulpits like the one the adults had in their building back at Old Saints Church. They all had a coin slot in the side of the head, so Little Christian put his first coin in the first head, which was a model of a trendy young man who looked ultra up to date.

Once the money was in, the little mouth started flapping open and shut, and the head started moving up and down. It even spun right round a couple of times. It was shouting very loudly and passionately and even some beads of sweat appeared on its brow, but although it put on a great performance, it wasn't saying anything of any relevance about the door.

He tried the head of a young lady, but it spoke so quietly that he couldn't hear a word she was saying. Then there was a very old man whom he couldn't get to start talking, followed by a middle aged lady whom he couldn't get to stop talking. Then he tried a man and lady who were doing a double act, but they only sang in different languages. He used up the rest of his coins more out of interest than expectation of actually hearing the real Voice, and then passed down another tunnel to another room.

Little Christian had lost all track of time. He had eaten and he had slept numerous times. He had listened to voices coming from computers, televisions, radios, records, tapes and compact disc players. He'd listened to rock bands, choirs and sacred soloists, and he had even listened to talking statues and the odd donkey, but none was the Voice.

'My time must be up,' he thought. 'I've failed the first test. Please, Voice, where are you?' he pleaded in desperation.

It was then that the Voice he had only heard a couple of times in the past spoke to him: 'I'm here, Little Christian, living inside of you, remember? Why didn't you start asking for me sooner, instead of confusing yourself with all these gadgets?'

'I'm sorry,' said Little Christian out loud. 'But how can I be sure that it is you I am talking to in my mind, and not just my own imagination?'

'That's easy,' said the Voice. 'I will always confirm that it is me speaking, from words in the Manual. If you want more proof, I will give my Directors, like Angela for instance, the words to say to back it up. If you still need assuring, I will always fill your mind with a special peaceful feeling that only I can give.'

Little Christian was thrilled that he had found the Voice and that the Voice was so easy to hear and just as easy to contact.

Within minutes the Voice had directed Little Christian to the door and as it opened automatically for him, he walked out of the tree to the welcome sight of his two friends and the Truth Extractor. They were standing there smiling and clapping.

'Well done, Little Christian,' said the Truth Extractor. 'You have just completed and passed your first test. You now have time for a wash, meal and a short rest, then you must start the second and final test.'

Little Christian was keen to continue, and in the shortest time possible he was standing next to the Truth Extractor awaiting his next instructions. The other two Littlekids had gone to another part of the Voice's Training Module for some specialised tuition.

'Follow me,' said the Truth Extractor, and they walked together to a modern building with a see-through dome. 'This is Love Dome. Here you will learn what love is, and you have no time limit. You will be marked on how you respond to what you see.'

A sliding door opened. Little Christian entered the dome alone, and the door closed silently behind him. He was then instructed by the Voice to go and sit on a large reclining seat which was situated in the middle of the floor. 'First, I want to see if you still love me,' continued the Voice.

As Little Christian closed his eyes, he saw in his mind a rerun of the film he had seen in the Crosscountry auditorium with Hearthunter.

'What can you see, Little Christian?' asked the Voice.

'It is the most wonderful picture of all. It's about you, Voice; how you love me, how you suffered and died for me.' Little Christian opened his eyes. 'I can never thank you enough, not just for what you have done,' he cried, 'but that you are still living and talking to me now.'

'Come share a meal with me,' said the Voice, and as Little Christian looked to his right a table had appeared with some bread and wine on it. 'Eat the bread and drink the wine,' said the Voice, 'and when you do so in the future, always remember the picture that you have just seen, and be thankful.'

'Oh, I will,' said Little Christian, eagerly eating the bread and drinking the wine.

'Now I know you love me,' said the Voice. 'But let's see what you think of other people. Go over to the far side of the dome, and there you will find a laser gun.'

Little Christian did as he was told. Then, as he held the gun, the lights went out and he saw a hundred people standing right around the wall of the building. 'Now,' said the Voice, 'with the laser gun shoot all those whom you consider to be your enemies and my enemies; all those you don't like and those you think I don't like. Only spare the ones you consider to be special.'

'Great!' said Little Christian, feeling like one of the old warriors he had read about in part one of the Manual.

Laser beams were flying everywhere as he destroyed villains from the past, present and even one or two that looked like they came from the future. All the ugly ones got zapped, along with the excessively fat, the old ladies who reminded him of witches and anyone who had a lot of spots, warts or was just plain dirty. He left all the pretty girls, the oldies who reminded him of his parents and the handsome young men: in all, about fifteen out of the hundred.

As the lights came on, the bodies that had slumped to the ground under his barrage of fire disappeared, as did those who were left standing. It was all an optical illusion.

'So fifteen per cent were special enough to keep alive, were they?' said the Voice.

'Well, maybe I was a bit generous. Maybe I could have got rid of one or two more,' said Little Christian.

The lights went off again and the bodies reappeared. 'Go and have a close look at those you shot,' said the Voice.

Little Christian went up to the first, who was a person covered in sores, and he gasped as he realised that underneath the sores was his own face. Then he went to the old lady who reminded him of a witch, and again underneath the long hair was his own face.

The Voice told him to examine each one he had shot, and, yes, they were all replicas of him. The lights went up and the Voice asked Little Christian what he had learned from this lesson.

Little Christian went back to the chair, and sat deep in thought. For a long time he said nothing. Then a tear pushed its way out of his right eye. 'I see now. Just as I am special to you, so are all of these, and you want me to have the same love and concern for the ones who don't look very nice, or even act very nice, as the ones who I thought were worth saving.'

'Well done, Little Christian. You have passed the second part of your test. Just one more to go.'

Again the lights went out and cut-outs of a hundred male figures appeared around the outside of the room. They were all his well-known heroes from films he had seen and books he had read.

'Now,' said the Voice, 'you can take the legs of one, the body of another, the arms of a third, the face of a fourth and the hair of a fifth, and with these five parts make up the man you would most like to be.'

In no time Little Christian had found strong, muscular legs, a tanned, well-built body, arms that looked like they could lift the universe, the face of a catalogue model and hair that was shiny and clean and would never fall out of place.

'Right,' said the Voice. 'Stand next to your hero.' As he did so, a large mirror appeared in front of them and spotlights highlighted them.

'I look awful compared to him,' shouted Little Christian. 'Why do I look so puny and ugly?'

'Little Christian, you will always see people you wish you could look like, but what I want you to remember is that I made you like the reflection you are looking at in the mirror, and you must trust me when I say that that is how I wanted you to be. I did not want you to look like the model you made up standing next to you.

'In these tests you have shown that you love me. I have proved to you that you must love others, but can you learn to love yourself and be satisfied with the way I made you and not always wanting to be like someone else?'

Little Christian thought hard again. He promised that he would try.

The door of Love Dome opened up and as Little Christian walked out, he saw a huge crowd of Littlekids sitting on the grass facing him. Then a loud voice which he recognised to be that of the Truth Extractor shouted, 'Little Christian, come here.' As he walked through the Littlekids, he noticed that the Truth Extractor was sitting at his desk on the revolving patio. When he saw Little Christian, he jumped up smiling.

'Bring on the band,' he shouted, 'it's time to celebrate. We are going to have a Praise Party.'

In no time at all, the most up-to-date band of musicians Little Christian had ever seen had set up their electronic drums and keyboards, had tuned up their electric guitars and were leaping all over the place singing songs about how great the Voice was. All the Littlekids had joined in, and even though Little Christian felt a bit embarrassed and selfconscious to begin with, once he saw that the Truth Extractor was boogying on with the best of them, he soon lost all his inhibitions.

After what must have been hours, yet seemed like a few minutes, they finished with a song which was Little Christian's favourite. The words went:

> There is no one else around,
> In the air or on the ground,
> Who has the power (has the power) of the Voice.
> So you Enemy Superpowers,
> In your defeated final hours,
> We command you to leave, you have no choice
> (you have no choice),
> As we speak in the authority of the Voice.

After they had sung it enough times for Little Christian to learn the words, all went quiet.

'Little Christian,' shouted the Truth Extractor, 'it gives me great pleasure to inform you that the Voice believes that although you may be very young, you are mature enough to graduate. Here in my hand is your first commission.'

All the other Littlekids cheered and whistled. Then the Truth Extractor raised his arms and all went quiet as he handed a computer printout to Little Christian. 'You will no longer need a map. You have now learned how to hear the Voice and he will be guiding you direct.

'Little Christian, I commission you in the name of the Voice to plant a Power Station in Phuncity.'

The Littlekids gasped. 'Yes, I know,' continued the Truth Extractor, 'that it is heavily controlled by the Enemy

Superpowers, but you will not be on your own there. Your old friends, whom you knew before as Little Pest and Little Nuisance, are at this very moment being trained up as Flockwatchers, and once the Power Station has been established, they will come and relieve you, to allow you to move on. Remember, you are not doing this in your own strength, and there is never any need to panic because the Voice will always be with you.

'And finally,' he continued, 'on your instruction printout you will notice that this place is en route for a town you know very well. Your next mission will be the toughest assignment of all. The Voice wants to repossess Oldchurch...'

11. VICTOR

Little Christian marched out of the Voice's Training Module feeling very excited. In his pockets he had his photomap, his photo, his Manual and now his computer printout.

When he reached the bank of the lake, there were Harmony and Buddy faithfully sitting in the boat waiting to take him across. 'Do you need a lift or do you fancy another swim?' shouted Buddy, laughing.

'Oh, I think I'll come with you this time, if you don't mind,' grinned Little Christian.

As they went across the lake, Little Christian explained to them all about his mission, and as he got out of the boat on the far side and thanked them, both Buddy and Harmony promised faithfully to pray every day for his safety.

He gave them one last wave and then set off down the track towards Phuncity. Although he felt good, it was a lot colder now. He knew that he was entering the centre of Bigwideworld, and he also knew that he must be on his guard.

As he continued walking, he suddenly had the strange feeling that he was being watched, but he couldn't work out where from. He walked a bit faster now, but still he could sense that eyes were watching him. He knew he shouldn't be afraid, but he also knew that he was, and he started to run. They, whoever *they* were, started running as well.

It was then that Little Christian's foot trod on something that gave way, and he went flying through the air and landed with a thump at the bottom of a large pit. He felt bruised and a bit sick, and as he looked up towards the daylight he saw loads of little heads peering down at him. 'They can only be about eight years old,' he thought to himself.

'Give us yer Manual,' shouted one.

'Yes,' screamed another, 'or else you've had it.'

'Why do you want my Manual?' pleaded Little Christian.

'See, he is a Voice follower,' shouted another, and with this they started tipping some liquid into the hole, soaking poor Little Christian.

'Wait a minute,' he thought, sniffing. 'They're pouring petrol all over me. They're going to burn me alive.'

As he looked up, he saw one of them take a box of matches out of his pocket. 'Dear Voice, please help me,' he screamed, thumping the side of the deep pit.

It was then, as he thumped the mud at the side of the hole, that it gave way and revealed another hole. As the lighted match came hurtling down towards him, he quickly leaped through the new hole. Next second there was an explosion, but Little Christian was already falling down a black cavity to somewhere else.

After a long drop, he eventually reached the bottom and fortunately landed on something soft. Where on earth, or more to the point under the earth, was he? He rubbed the mud away from his eyes and saw that he was in an old mineshaft, but it had been done out as a small room. He had in fact landed on a bed and over on the far side, with the help of an oldfashioned oil lamp burning away, he could see a table, chair and even a cupboard.

Then he saw a slight movement from underneath a pile of rags in the corner. Little Christian got up off the bed and walked over to the rags and saw that the bundle was physically shaking.

'Come out,' said Little Christian softly. 'I won't hurt you.'

Gradually the old rags moved to one side and revealed a man.

'Who are you?' asked Little Christian. 'And what are you doing living here?'

The man got up and went over to his chair, still shaking. 'They call me Victor,' he said, 'and I am in hiding from those murdering Littlekids who live in Phuncity. Please, whoever you are, please don't take me to the Phun House.'

As Little Christian glanced around the room, he was surprised to see a well-used copy of the Manual lying on the table.

'Whose is that?' asked Little Christian.

Victor jumped up from his chair, grabbed the Manual and shouted, 'No, you can't have it. Please don't take it. You can have anything you like, even kill me if you wish, but please leave that alone.'

'Why?' asked Little Christian inquisitively.

Victor burst into tears and explained how he and his pretty sister Victoria had once lived in Oldchurch and were followers of the Voice. Then, as there was no future for Voicelovers in Oldchurch, they had left with all the other twelve-year-olds. Sadly, all their friends had deserted the Voice and now lived in Phuncity. They married people who were Voicehaters and then had children. 'My friends and their married partners didn't mind about Victoria and me believing in the Voice. They were too busy enjoying themselves in Phuncity. But when they had Littlekids, this next generation instinctively hated anything or anyone to do with the Voice. It was then that the Littlekids built their own Phun House which has a reputation of being more evil than anything that their parents could have dreamed up. Adults were not allowed in it... unless...'

'Unless what?' asked Little Christian.

Victor continued weeping, '...unless you were a follower of the Voice, like my beautiful sister Victoria. They dragged her in there two years ago, and nobody ever saw her again. And I've been in hiding ever since. If the Littlekids find me, they will take me there as well.'

'Why didn't you go to Smoke Mountain and the Voice's Training Module?' asked Little Christian.

'What are they?' asked Victor.

Little Christian explained that he too was from Oldchurch. In fact, while he was arguing with the Elder in the Real Church, an old lady shouted out about her son and daughter leaving.

'Yes, that would be my mother,' interrupted Victor.

Then Little Christian told him about Smoke Mountain

and the Voice's Training Module, and how not all Littlekids were evil. In fact, the Voice was raising up a powerful army of them to fulfil his plans. He then went on to explain his mission and how he and various others were going to plant a Power Station in Phuncity itself.

Victor was amazed and silent. He'd never heard a Littlekid speak with such authority before. He was still shaking, but he looked up at Little Christian and asked him if he would introduce him to the Voice properly. Although he did know *about* him, he wasn't sure if he really knew him.

Little Christian remembered Smoke Mountain and carefully explained what he needed to do to be a real follower, and Victor accepted all that was told him. Little Christian then saw a bucket of water in the corner of the room and, explaining the importance of being cleansed both inside and out, he threw it all over him.

Then it seemed as though the Voice breathed on Victor, in a big, loving whisper. Immediately his shaking stopped, he smiled, and together they started singing and giving thanks to the Voice.

After a bit of food and some bread and wine, Victor said that he wanted to join Little Christian, as there was still a very small chance that they might find Victoria alive.

Suddenly, Little Christian went quiet and then he jumped up shouting, 'Wow! You'll never guess what the Voice has just told me.'

'No, what?' said Victor.

'The first Power Station will be planted right in the middle of the Littlekids' Phun House. Their evil reign is about to end!'

They both cheered excitedly, then Victor told Little Christian to follow him.

Victor led him along the mineshafts until they reached a long ladder. 'Once we climb up here we will come out on Mainstreet in Phuncity,' explained Victor.

'Do you want me to lead the way?' asked Little Christian.

'No way,' said Victor with his newly-found courage. 'Follow me,' and up they both climbed.

12. PHUNCITY

Both Victor and Little Christian climbed out of what seemed like a drain cover and found themselves in broad daylight in the middle of a busy street in Phuncity. They quickly ran to the side of the road and hid behind a wall which was part of a liquor store.

As they looked around, all they could see were adults who obviously had no concern about them. They were all well and truly preoccupied with other things. Some were staggering around with half empty bottles in their hands; others were spaced out on drugs.

At the side of the road males and females were dressed in sleazy clothes and trying to encourage passers-by to join them in a room they kept pointing to upstairs, with the words, 'Come and have a phun time.' But Little Christian and Victor could see it was obvious that everyone was having anything but a fun time.

'A trick of the Enemy Superpowers,' whispered Victor. 'They have filled all these adults' minds and bodies with their cheap and nasty phun, and now they are controlled and have no ability to think for themselves.'

'Which is why we are here,' reminded Little Christian, trying his hardest to stay positive.

'Exactly,' replied Victor, though it was more out of hope than conviction.

'But where are all their Littlekids?' asked Christian.

Victor told him that some would be out on patrols, like the ones who had nearly burned him alive. 'But the vast majority would be in that building over there,' he said, pointing his finger to a very large, bright red and gold building down the far end of the street. 'That is the infamous Phun House,' he continued.

'Oh,' said Little Christian, observing this horribly tastelessly painted hall. 'So that is where our new Power Station is to be planted. We must change that colour scheme,' he mused.

'I should think that was the least of our worries,' replied Victor, looking at the mess that the Enemy Superpowers had made of what used to be intelligent human beings wandering aimlessly in front of him.

Just as they were deciding to lie low till dark because of the obvious danger they were in, they heard a noise of singing coming down the street towards them. Little Christian recognised the song—it was his favourite.

Forgetting the surrounding danger, he immediately started to join in:

> There is no one else around,
> In the air or on the ground,
> Who has the power (has the power) of the Voice.
> So you Enemy Superpowers,
> In your defeated final hours,
> We command you to leave, You have no choice
>   (you have no choice),
> As we speak in the authority of the Voice.

They could only see three singers and were quite surprised how so few could make such a noise.

As they watched the glazed, dazed adults pass by, Little Christian and Victor also noticed that they were surrounded by a small patrol of seething, swearing Littlekids who seemed powerless to harm them.

'Quick, let's join the singers,' said Little Christian, leaving the shelter of the wall and running out towards them.

'Do you think it's safe?' asked Victor. But seeing Little Christian had already left him, he was sure that it was safer to stay with him.

The trio, which consisted of two females and a male, stopped singing as they saw the two approaching them. 'Hey, you must be Little Christian,' said the male. 'What were you doing hiding behind that wall?'

Little Christian ignored the question and got straight on with the introductions. 'This is Victor,' he said, and explained a little bit about how Victor had been living since he lost his sister Victoria to the Littlekids of Phuncity.

When Little Christian had finished, the male started introducing his little band.

'We are Powerpeople. My name is Hearthunter. No, I'm not the one you met in Crosscountry,' he said, seeing that Little Christian looked confused. 'The Voice has given lots of us similar giftings so that we can spread right across Bigwideworld. These are the Wonderful Signs Sisters, Hope and Faith. The Voice said that you would need us to help you set up a Power Station in this city. So here we are, at your service.'

'Brilliant,' said Little Christian. 'Welcome to the team. The first thing we need to do is to consult the Voice as to how we are to go about this mission. We need him to give us some strategy. I suggest I find us a quiet room somewhere so we can do this.'

'What's the matter with here on the street?' asked Faith. 'Why do you want to lock yourself away? Surely you're not scared of these poor, misguided people, are you?'

Little Christian looked around him and, seeing the angry mob of Littlekids still shouting and swearing at them, he considered that there was no way he could concentrate here. But before he could answer, the matter was taken out of his hands.

Having heard all the commotion, thirty Littlekids came running out of the red and gold Phun House, and armed with ropes and primitive home-made spears, leaped on the five and proceeded to bind them up tightly. Little Christian and Victor tried to fight them off, but it was useless against so many.

They were then dragged inside the Phun House, where a trap door was opened up in the floor and then one by one they were thrown into a dirty, damp, black, dark, slimy cellar. Then the trap door was shut and a big padlock fastened.

The first one to speak was Hearthunter. 'Well, Little

Christian,' he said, 'you have got your own way. You wanted a quiet room to talk to the Voice and now you have one.'

Little Christian just mumbled that this was not the type of room he had had in mind.

It was then they heard a quiet coughing coming from what seemed to be the far end of the cellar.

'What was that?' asked Faith.

'Well, if it's a fat furry thing with whiskers and a long tail I would rather not know,' replied Victor, and all the others tended to agree. But then they heard another cough and they realised that it was no animal. It was definitely a person.

'Hello,' said Little Christian cautiously. 'Is anyone there?'

Then a tiny, quiet voice whispered between coughs, 'Please don't hurt me.'

It was the voice of a female and Victor immediately recognised it. 'Victoria, that's you, isn't it?' he shouted in excitement.

'Oh Victor,' said the little voice. 'Yes it is, but I've been in here since I last saw you, and I am in a terrible state. I think I am dying.'

Hope whispered to Victor that although it was very dark she could see with her spiritual eyes that his sister was covered from head to toe in every kind of sore and was suffering from acute pneumonia. She had only a short time left.

As Victor burst into tears, the trap door was flung open and a Littlekid screamed at them all to come up—that was, all except Victor who they had recognised. He could stay down and watch his sister die. The Littlekids all laughed. This really was phun.

When they came up out of the cellar, they could see that the very large room was packed with hundreds of the Enemy Superpower-controlled Littlekids. Behind them they noticed hundreds of evil role-playing games and machines with the most grotesque pictures imaginable on them. And these were only the things they could see in this room. Goodness knows what else was in the building. Little Christian could see that the Enemy Superpowers had been working hard to corrupt these Littlekids while they were very young, knowing that as they grew older they would be a great asset to the Enemy forces.

The four of them were tied together and then placed in what seemed like a playpen, but this was not made of wood. It was made of wire which they noticed was connected up to the electricity mains.

'Try to escape, and you will be just a smouldering black corpse,' said another voice, and again they all went into a maniacal fit of false phun laughter.

It was then that a Littlekid appeared who must have been about ten years old. He was dressed comparatively smartly and on his head he had a long blond wig. 'I am your judge,' he said, 'and this wig is in fact Victoria's hair. We had her head shaved so that I could look more like a judge.' Another bout of cruel laughter followed his words.

'You are accused of trying to infiltrate Phuncity with the false teaching of the Voice. We believe that the Enemy Superpowers are far more powerful than your Voice and that you are lying heretics. You talk about power, but take a look at poor little Victor and Victoria. They are a couple of yours and one has been locked in a cellar for two years and the other one has been hiding in fear. Your Voice has no power at all.'

Faith spoke out. 'Excuse me, your honour,' she said politely. The Littlekid judge liked that, and told her she may continue. 'Why don't you get two of your most powerful Littlekids to act on behalf of the Enemy Superpowers, and Hope and I will act on behalf of the Voice, and let's have a contest to see once and for all who is the most powerful?'

The Littlekid judge paused for thought, while all the others around them were getting quite excited at the prospect of a trial of power.

'Yes, I like that idea,' he eventually said. 'And when we win you will suffer the most excruciating pain and torture before you actually die. We'd like to see that, wouldn't we, Littlekids?'

'Yes,' they all cheered and shouted. 'That would be real phun.'

'But if the Voice wins, your honour, we want this building, and freedom in the city so that those who wish to follow the Voice may do so.'

'Yes, you have my word,' said the judge, totally convinced that he was onto a winner.

The judge decided that as males were more important than females, he would call his two champions forward first to display their supernatural powers.

Out stepped Karate and Kamikazi and, after a few minutes of calling upon the Enemy Superpowers to give them strength, they began the contest. They melted metal bars just by breathing on them, chewed bricks till they were ground into dust, then spat them out in the form of a smoke ring. They twisted their bodies until they were shaped like bulldozers, then ran at a solid brick wall and went straight through it. After many other humanly impossible feats of strength, they finished off by smashing a massive concrete pillar (which had been rolled in for the purpose) into millions of tiny pieces with their little fingers on their left hands.

The Littlekids around the room were in a frenzy of

excitement and kept giving thanks to the Enemy Superpowers for the supernatural phun they were having.

The judge stepped forward and, along with the rest of the Littlekids, gave.his champions a round of applause and a standing ovation.

'Well, ladies,' he sneered, 'you have seen just a little bit of what the Enemy Superpowers have to offer. How is the Voice able to respond to that?'

Faith and Hope were released from the pen and stood facing the enormous, now quiet crowd.

'I thought Karate and Kamikazi were very good,' said Faith, 'but I wonder if they could step forward and do one more thing for me?'

The two supernaturally-powerful Littlekids stepped forward, never missing an opportunity to show off their strength.

Faith walked up to them both and then suddenly, with a powerful voice that made everyone jump, shouted, 'In the name of the Voice I command the Enemy Superpowers in Karate and Kamikazi to leave instantly.' Then she looked at them and asked them politely to do just one of their feats of strength once more.

As they tried, they found to their horror that they couldn't even lift the metal bar and bricks, let alone melt them or smash them. They couldn't get their bodies into the shape of bulldozers, so didn't attempt to run at the wall, and when another concrete pillar was rolled in they just went back to their seats and sat down in silence.

Every Littlekid was devastated and stunned—even the judge.

'Wait, we haven't finished yet,' said Hope. 'Open up the cellar and bring out Victor and Victoria.'

The judge agreed, and everyone gasped when they saw

Victor carry his sister out. Victoria was a grey colour and, as Faith had said earlier, covered from head to toe in sores, and was coughing all the time. She was as thin as a rake and had to be held by Victor as she was not able to stand.

'Now listen, Littlekids. Not only are the Enemy Superpowers no match for the Voice, as Karate and Kamikazi have shown you, but neither are the Enemy Superpowers' plagues and diseases. You proved that the Enemy Superpowers want to break, smash and destroy. The Voice wants to restore, heal and create.'

And then with a similar voice, yet quieter than her sister's, she said, 'Enemy Superpowers that are causing all this pain and suffering in Victoria's body and are out to kill her, in the name of the Voice I tell you to leave her now, and I pray the Voice's healing power into her body.'

Instantly, it was as though a flash of lightning had hit Victoria, and all eyes nearly popped out of their heads as the coughing stopped, the sores vanished and she stood up, walked to the middle of the floor, then knelt down and thanked the Voice.

Suddenly, the whole building erupted with whistles and cheers. The Littlekids had never seen anything like this before. Even the judge was on his feet.

Hearthunter knew that this was his cue, and without even bothering to leave the pen, he started shouting out the good news of the Voice, and how they too could come to know him for themselves.

That day was a great victory for the Voice. Many of the Littlekids became followers, and immediately started smashing up all their evil phun pleasures. They then took them out onto the street and burned them. Then, under the instruction of Little Christian, they redecorated Phun House both inside and out.

The Flockwatchers had arrived right on time from the Voice's Training Module as promised, and a very lively new Power Station was in business.

Hearthunter decided to stay in Phuncity as there were enough lost adults walking the streets to keep him in work for a lifetime, a sort of Hearthunter's paradise.

Hope, Faith, Victor and Victoria also decided to stay. They felt they could be a help in training up all these new Littlekids, but Little Christian knew that now the new Power Station was successfully planted, it was time for him to move on.

Goodbyes are always sad, but Little Christian knew that he would be back to visit them all one day, so it was more a see-you-later than a farewell.

The last thing he did before leaving was to rename the city. No longer would it be known as Phuncity, because that sounded phoney. From now on it would be called Fun City. After all, now the Voice was living there he knew that people would be able to experience real fun.

13. OLDCHURCH REVISITED

As Little Christian headed back to where his journey had begun almost a lifetime ago, it seemed, he pondered over all the adventures he had been through. Although he was only slightly older than when he had left, he was now a new person with a new name. He had grown up. He wondered if his parents and the Elder would recognise him, or even still be alive. As he continued along the path towards Oldchurch, deep in concentration, he walked straight past two familiar figures.

'Gone all snooty, 'ave ya, now yer've bin given a mission?' said one voice.

'Been stuck in any tar lately?' asked the other.

Little Christian looked up and beamed. How could he not recognise the unmistakable voices of Angela and Miraclekid? He rushed over and gave them both a hug. 'Boy, am I glad to see you two,' he said with tears in his eyes.

'The Voice thought that ya might need a couple of old mates to keep ya company in what could prove to be yer toughest mission. In fact, we're waitin' for a few more reinforcements who promised to be here. Oh, 'ere they come now.'

Down the path towards him came his old friend Hearthunter from Crosscountry, and also Buddy and Harmony.

'Wow! This is like a grand reunion,' shouted Little Christian, and they all got so excited they started singing the powerful Voice song.

As they all marched along the path, they noticed that the hedges were getting more colourful with pretty flowers, and beautiful fruit suddenly appeared as if from nowhere. 'This looks familiar,' thought Little Christian. As they turned a sharp corner they all stopped. There facing them was the most repulsive sight they had ever seen.

'Yuk! What are they?' said Angela.

There blocking the whole path were six enormous Greedy Gutrots, looking more obese than ever.

'I told you I would be back to get you, Little Trouble,' said all six mouths at the same time.

Little Christian stepped forward. 'I'm afraid you're a little bit out of date, aren't you, Greedy Gutrot? My name is now Little Christian.'

'Little Christian, Little Trouble, who cares? It's all the same to me,' they snarled. 'You thought you could kill me, didn't you, Littlekid? But all you've done is made five more of me, you fool.'

'No. Correction,' said Little Christian. 'You thought that you could poison me, but all you've achieved is five more of me,' he said, pointing at his friends.

'Oh, little mister cocky, are we now? Well, you will never get past me,'said the Greedy Gutrots altogether. 'I won't let you go and spoil Oldchurch.'

'We will walk around you over the hedge,' said Little Christian.

'Well I know you've become a little angel, but I didn't know that you had learned to fly,' sneered Greedy Gutrot.

The children of the Voice looked over the hedge and saw that the Enemy Superpowers had made it a sheer cliff both sides.

'So the only way is through you,' said Little Christian.

'Impossible,' shouted Greedy Gutrot. 'Turn round and go back. You come one step nearer me and I will roll forward and flatten all the life out of you.'

'I don't believe you are really there at all,' said Little Christian. 'You are just an Enemy Superpower illusion, and I'll prove it. Take out your Manuals, everyone, and hold them up high!' This they all did. 'Right, march forward. This will scare him off.'

'You are a ****** fool,' wailed Greedy Gutrot. 'I'll kill you. I'll kill you. I'll, I'll... Aaaargh!'

As they marched up to the Greedy Gutrots with their Manuals in their hands, the Greedy Gutrots exploded into a million pieces, and the Littlekids smiled as they continued singing their power song to the Voice.

Around the next corner it appeared on the horizon: the unmistakable Oldchurch, with its grey cloud still circling high above it.

They decided at this point to stay put for the night, and while his five companions slept, Little Christian spent the night talking and listening to the Voice, to find out how the Voice wanted the mission done.

As dawn came, Little Christian woke up his friends. 'Let's go. The Voice has told me his plans,' he said, and off they set. They were still a few hours' walk from the town.

Eventually they arrived at the large gates, and as they walked through them they immediately experienced the depressing cloud overhead. It was a strange feeling for Little Christian. Understanding how he was feeling, Angela held his hand firmly.

They noticed that all the streets were deserted. There was not a sign of life anywhere, and it was only then that Little Christian realised it must be Sunday and he knew where everyone would be.

As they reached the entrance of Old Saints Church, they saw the buses just waiting there, no one around them or inside them. The whole place was as still and as quiet as a morgue. They stood silently looking at the building, and Little Christian told them to follow him. They walked through the small door, not the main entrance, and headed towards the Junior Hall. There they came face to face with a Kiddiecontroller guarding the entrance.

'How did you lot escape?' he shouted. Lifting his stick and his board to herd them back into the Junior Hall, he suddenly stopped and his mouth fell open. 'You're teenagers!' he gasped, as he collapsed in a heap on the floor.

'Who's making all that noise in the doorway?' shouted the familiar voice of Aunt Mona, and then Little Christian and his friends entered.

Everyone went silent. The Littlekids sitting on the floor looked up and stared. They had never seen a teenager before.

Eventually, Aunt Mona got her voice back. 'So it's you, Little Trouble, is it? Returned with more rebels like yourself, have you?' she said. 'Well, don't think that we are frightened of you. Lock them in the church office, Kiddiecontrollers.'

But the Kiddiecontrollers and all the other Aunties around the room didn't dare move a muscle. They were scared stiff of teenagers, especially ones who had returned from the Bigwideworld.

'Littlekids, stand up,' ordered Little Christian. 'I want you and all the Aunties and Kiddiecontrollers to follow us. We have a message that you need to hear from the Voice.'

Little Christian led them along all the winding corridors and even though he still got lost twice, he eventually reached the Real Church building door. 'We mustn't go in there,' whispered a six-year-old female Littlekid.

Little Christian bent down and picked the little girl up and put her on his shoulders. 'We must,' he said, and with that he kicked open the door and walked in with all his friends. The Littlekids and the Kiddiecontrollers followed.

'What on earth is the meaning of this intrusion?' shouted the Elder. 'You know Littlekids are banned from the Real Church.' He then stopped and looked. The whole congregation of adults lifted their heads up and looked. 'Teenagers!' they all gasped.

Little Christian walked up to the front past the Elder and climbed into the pulpit. 'We have brought you the Voice,' he said gently.

The Elder clutched his heart and slid to the floor. Buddy and Harmony rushed to help him. The Elder smiled, 'My heart is not strong enough to take such good news. At last the Voice has sent his children as my successors. Now I can be released to go and live with him for ever.'

And with that he slumped back on to his chair.

'Is he asleep?' someone cried.

'No, he's dead.'

People began to come forward, but as they did, Little Christian addressed them again.

'Now hear what the Voice has to say to you,' he shouted. 'Oldchurch is dead. Oldchurch is finished. No longer will your Littlekids be inferior to you. From now on you will be worshipping the Voice with your Littlekids, not attempting to do it by yourselves. Furthermore, no longer will there be any Little Troubles because the Voice wants them all to be Little Christians. These Littlekids are not just your children, they are the Children of the Voice and you have been given responsibility to love, honour and train them. And these are things that you have neglected to do for years.

'Finally, you have three days to leave Oldchurch before it is destroyed. Go with your Littlekids to Smoke Mountain and Crosscountry. Learn with them at the Voice's Training Module, then get into the Bigwideworld and rescue your teenagers. It is not too late.

'When you return, you will find us here waiting for you in the Newchurch Power Station, and don't expect to see any big gates or high walls, because we are going to be living in the Bigwideworld.'

'Rubbish,' shouted one adult. Angela rushed up into the pulpit next to her friend and told the people to listen as Little Christian was telling the truth.

'Why should we believe a rebellious teenager and some girl whom we have never seen before and can't even speak properly?' shouted another.

'Wait a minute,' said Miraclekid. 'You want a sign from the Voice that we are speaking the truth? OK, well here it is: as you leave Old Saints Church this morning, for the first time in living memory, the Voice is going to move that cloud of depression and allow the sun to shine down on you for one hour.'

'Oh no, not magic tricks as well,' somebody joked, and everyone started to leave the building. As the adults left the church, carrying the Elder away to bury him, the sun was shining brightly, but very few seemed to notice.

Little Christian climbed out of the pulpit and sat on the floor with his head in his hands, and Angela came and sat alongside him. 'The older you get the harder it is to face change, especially when it's brought by so-called Littlekids,' she whispered.

'Hello, son,' came a voice he recognised. He looked up and there were his mum and dad. He jumped up and gave them a hug. 'You *will* leave in the next three days, won't you?' pleaded Little Christian.

'Well, son,' they replied, 'we are getting old, and even if you are telling the truth, we don't know if we could cope with such a trip, or even if we could adjust to being part of Newchurch. But we promise we will think about it.'

For the next two days, Little Christian and his friends kept walking around telling people of the urgency to go, but very few adults were concerned about the future of their Littlekids, the whereabouts of their teenagers or, worst of all, what the Voice was saying.

With a few hours to go, Little Christian, Angela, Miraclekid, Buddy, Harmony and Hearthunter sat about a mile away from the walls of Oldchurch. They watched as quite a few were leaving Oldchurch, but they were saddened that the vast majority of these were Littlekids leaving their parents behind them because they believed, even if their parents didn't, that the Voice had a special role in life for them.

Then, with just a few minutes before the deadline, Little Christian leaped up and saw an older couple walking towards him. It was his parents.

He ran up to them, shouting, 'You decided to go!'

'Yes,' they said chuckling and looking younger than he had ever seen them look before. 'After thinking about it we decided that you are never too old to obey and follow the Voice.' And with that they ran off towards Smoke Mountain, shouting, 'See you soon, son.'

The Voice's set time had come. The grey clouds of depression turned dark blue, then black, in colour. A distant roll of thunder suddenly became as loud as an explosion. A white-hot fireball came hurtling out of the sky, smashing straight through the Old Saints Church roof. Old Saints Church was instantly blown apart. Then came an avalanche of seething fire destroying and burning up every living thing, and melting every man-made structure in its path, until all that remained of Oldchurch was a flat surface... of solid rock. Then the thunder and lightning stopped, the black and grey clouds moved away and the warm sunshine shone down.

Little Christian and his friends walked over to where Newchurch was to be built. 'The end of the old, the beginning of the new,' thought Little Christian standing on the rock. 'A Newchurch which believes that all ages are important to the Voice and have missions to complete. Thanks to the Voice, there is a fresh start for us, our adults and our future Littlekids.'

As they stood there, they heard a deep rumbling sound coming from beneath the ground surrounding the rock. The sounds were like an eerie voice which kept repeating, 'You Littlekids have no hope against us Enemy Superpowers. You think you can succeed where the adults have failed.' Then followed a horrible mocking laugh.

As the evil laughter grew louder and louder, Little Christian smiled and said, 'Who on earth do they think they are to speak to us like that? Come on, Buddy, Harmony, Hearthunter, Miraclekid, Angela... after three: one, two, three:

> There is no one else around,
> In the air or on the ground
> Who has the power (has the power) of the Voice.
> So you Enemy Superpowers,
> In your defeated final hours,
> We command you to leave, you have no choice
>   (you have no choice),
> As we speak in the authority of the Voice.

The Enemy Superpowers instantly stopped. What else could they do? But Little Christian realised they would be back, no doubt in some other deceiving disguise. But he also knew that when they did come back, they'd have to answer to all of the Children of the Voice.

Children
of the
Voice

BOOK 2

the Invasion of New Church

1. THE PARTY AT PIG HALL

The night was dark and cold. The rain fell out of the sky with the force of a water cannon, while the wind blew in every direction like it was lost and trying to find its way home.

All the paths leading to Pig Hall were just soggy, gooey, filthy, dirty, squelchy, muddy tracks. Even the moon had gone back to bed and given up trying to shine. The only illumination was the occasional lightning flash across what was presumably the sky.

However, inside Pig Hall, everything was quite different.

An enormous, gross, obese, ugly character (just to name a few of his more attractive features) was having his annual bath in his swimming pool and singing at the top of his voice one of his favourite songs which went:

All things dull and ugly
All creatures greedy and fat
All things stupid and horrible
Yes, we have seen to that.

This hideous hulk was one of the Enemy Superpowers and went by the name of Greedy Gutrot.

Gutrot was obviously very excited, and the reason for that was simple. Tonight was party night at his place, and loads of his fiendish friends had agreed to come and have a lousy time celebrating their victories over the Voice.

Once Gutrot had finished washing all the parts that he could reach, which happened to be less than one tenth of his body, he rolled out of the water and lay under a drying machine he had stolen from a car-wash. He pressed a red button and let the warm air dry him off. Once dry, he had to find something to wear. For this special occasion he decided to put on his blue and white marquee tent kaftan.

With only an hour to go before his guests would arrive, he thought he would just go and inspect the tons of cold extra-greasy chips, and gallons of stale extra-sickly clotted cream, which he felt sure all would love to eat as it was so bad for them. But having no self-control he could not help himself eating at least three-quarters of his spread before anyone else arrived.

Then the doorbell rang and in came the mud splattered, soaking wet and grumbling Enemy Superpowers, and what a terrible bunch they were. Putrid Mouthful was the first to enter, having pushed Albina Spoiltbrat out of the way and left her lying face-down in the mud by the door. Putrid was his usual self, swearing, cursing and generally making all the air around him blue with his obscene language.

Joker Dirtbox, who was his close friend, soon pushed by everyone else to join Putrid in the blue-air zone. Then came Tara Weigh, Fester Fearfinder, Connie Fusion, Funnyboy Oddfellow (plus friend), and many many more.

The last to enter was someone nobody seemed to know, except Greedy Gutrot. He was followed by a large mobile cage. As all of the Superpowers didn't like listening and only wanted to talk about themselves, it was not surprising that no one talked to this foreign-looking stranger.

As the door of Pig Hall closed, the uncontrollable riot began. Having pushed past Gutrot without even saying hello, some made their way straight to the food and ate until they were ill. Others made their way to the cellar and started opening the taps of the enormous wine vats where Gutrot's infamous homebrew had been quietly fermenting for many years, and in no time had drunk themselves unconscious. The rest started spraying the walls with graffiti, and generally smashing up Pig Hall.

It only took an hour for all the Enemy Superpowers to be either worn out, blown out or thrown out by some of their own more aggressive counterparts. Then a strange quiet came over the whole place.

Greedy Gutrot had not joined in the festivities. He was much too large to run around the mansion, and he had been content just to sit and watch everyone else enjoying themselves. But now all was quiet he saw an opportunity to try to do something a little more constructive—like organise the destruction of the Children of the Voice rather than the furniture of Pig Hall.

With the help of one or two he passed the message around to all parts of the house that he wanted everyone to be in the main banqueting hall in five minutes. Although he got the expected arguments, moans and verbal abuse, everyone made it there because they were all a little bit wary of the fat freak's size.

'Have you all had a good time so far?' growled Gutrot, who decided to chair the meeting, as he was already filling up as much of the mammoth hall as everyone else put together. A few muffled comments followed which may have been, 'Great, boss, just the job,' or, 'Get lost, you big fat slob,' but he didn't really care what they thought. He had much more important things to share.

'Now listen here, my faithful and loyal Superpowers,' began Gutrot, as though he were speaking to intelligent beings. 'Oh, get on with it!' yelled an angry Des Ruption, who was standing on his chair and gesticulating with his body to try to get people to look at him instead of the chairman.

'Will you be quiet! Some of us would love to hear what is about to be said,' whimpered Creepy Bootlicker. 'I think that wonderful very generous Mr Gutrot is doing very well.' Then two opposing factions were formed and everyone started shouting out what they thought on the subject.

'Will you all shut up!' screamed Gutrot, who had now remembered that he was not talking to intelligent beings. Then he wobbled his enormous belly which left the floor, bounced on the ceiling making a noise like an amplified bass drum, and brought three chandeliers crashing to the floor.

Everyone quietened down.

'I have had reports from various sources on how we Enemy Superpowers are doing our job. The report is in three sections, so listen carefully.

'Firstly, our Nochurch Followers: these are doing very well. In fact I think we can all be very proud of ourselves, as the vast majority of people do see sense and like ourselves think the Voice has little or nothing to do with today's generation. We must notice how much more successful we have been in times of peace than in times of war. One of the reasons for this is that war makes them think of death and their future, whereas peace keeps them happily just thinking of the lovely fun they can have in the present.

'Oh, and don't forget, we must make sure that copies of the Voice's Manual are freely available; you see, when people can't get hold of it they want it, but when they have a copy, they never seem to bother to read it.

'Any questions?'

'Yeah,' they all shouted in unison, 'what about the Children of the Voice and this Newchurch?'

'I will mention them all in good time,' replied Greedy Gutrot, trying not to appear rattled, even though he hated hearing those words. No other questions followed.

'Secondly, our Oldchurch Followers. As I'm sure we are all aware, although there are thousands of Oldchurches, they will never grow any bigger, which is the beauty of them. Any new people who choose to join will only replace those who have had a change of heart and have decided to drop out and become part of Nochurch. Again, we must congratulate ourselves that we have been able to be such an influence on what at one time was thought to be a major threat to us. It's nice when our enemies become our allies.

'I do have one suggestion, however: we need to keep making them feel that they are doing well. May I suggest that although it is breaking all our rules we do allow them to plant a few new Oldchurches. This will be such a great encouragement to the faithful, and—bless them—they deserve it, don't they? Of course the overall attendances will remain the same—it's just that they will think they are expanding, when of course we all know that all they will really be doing is weakening their resources. From our point of view, a larger number of badly run Oldchurches will make our job even easier than it is now... if that is possible.'

All the Enemy Superpowers burst out laughing. Now that was a real joke.

As the frivolity died down, again Gutrot asked if anyone had any questions.

'Yeah,' they all shouted together, 'what about the Children of the Voice and Newchurch?'

Greedy Gutrot was getting angry. 'I hate those words,' he bellowed. 'Life was so easy for all of us till they appeared.' Then he lowered his voice to the level of a whisper. 'But I have a cunning plan.'

At this a Superpower leapt up, thinking Gutrot was talking to him, and shouted, 'No I haven't!'

'Not you, stupid!' he snapped, remembering that one of his colleagues was called Cunning Plan. 'Anyway, it doesn't surprise me that you have no ideas. The last cunning plan you had was to encourage people to kill the Voice—and look how that backfired.'

'No, I have found a new friend with a cunning plan, someone you ignored when you all arrived and someone who is so intelligent that he has locked himself away all evening so he would not have to mix with you brainless rabble. He has come from another land where he has experienced a Littlekid's uprising before, and is able to give us some practical advice.'

Then with a loud voice Greedy Gutrot shouted, 'Enter Inventor!'

They all turned their eyes to the toilet door in the far left-hand corner of the hall with the 'Engaged' sign on it. They heard a rattling sound, and it was obvious the Inventor was having trouble working out how to undo the lock to make the engaged sign become vacant. But after five minutes, a short man with an almost bald head and thick spectacles appeared.

Gutrot continued, 'Ladies and Gentlemen, may I introduce you to Professor Mindwarpt. A self-made, selfconfessed genius.'

The other Superpowers responded by either shouting 'Rubbish!' or blowing raspberries, which was of course their usual way of honouring someone.

The Professor thanked them for their warm welcome and then went on to congratuate them on their job well done in both Nochurch and Oldchurch. 'Your reputations are known planetwide. You are indeed masters of your trades.' This was music to the Enemy Superpowers' ears; they loved it and started to pat themselves on their own backs and hug themselves in self-adoration.

'But,' continued Mindwarpt, 'with the Children of the Voice and Newchurch you guys are... dated, ineffectual and useless. In short, history!'

The Superpowers were furious and started cheering and shouting hooray as was their usual response to those they disagreed with, and it wasn't until Gutrot again threw his massive stomach ceilingward, this time cracking it and showering everyone with plaster, that they all quietened down.

'Hear me out,' said the agitated Mindwarpt. 'This Newchurch is young. In a few years' time you could be back in business again. But right now you are all far too obvious to them. They are too committed to the Voice to fall for your little ploys of using bad language, telling dirty jokes, having bad friendships, or being scared or greedy. You are all too blatant. But I have a plan. I am going to introduce the Children of the Voice to my own created Superpowers... the Mindwarpt Superbreed.'

Mindwarpt's large cage entered the room by remote control, as if by magic, with six coffin-type boxes in it.

Mindwarpt walked over to the cage with a half-smile and a half-sneer as he could see the other Superpowers who were so shocked their eyes were popping out.

'Inside each coffin,' he snarled, 'is a counterfeit Littlekid which looks like the real thing, will sound like the real thing, but is not the real thing. Each one is a masterpiece, skilfully crafted by me and under my personal control. They are robots that will destroy once and for all the Children of the Voice.'

The other Superpowers continued gasping until one shouted out that he wanted to see them.

'You fool!' stormed the Professor. 'You will not see, or know the identity, of any one of my magnificent six. Why do you think I've caged them in a impregnable cage? It's not so they won't get out; it is so no one will be able to get in to see them.

'Their identity will remain the most closely guarded secret since the ingredients of the Kentucky Fried Chicken.' Gutrot licked his lips at the thought. 'At the right time I will release each one of my Littlekid Superbreeds to infiltrate Newchurch, and within a year Newchurch will be back in our control.'

The Enemy Superpowers again started blowing raspberries and spitting in sheer enthusiasm, until one lonely voice shouted the words, 'What about Little Christian?'

All went deathly quiet.

Greedy Gutrot smiled. 'I have heard a rumour from a very reliable source that Little Christian is being given a job which, would you believe, will take him away from Newchurch for a year. By that time there will not only be no Newchurch, there will also be no Little Christian. I hate that Littlekid, and I am going to make it my job to see he's put out of action... for keeps.'

With this all the Enemy Superpowers went wild. In joy they started smashing up all the furniture, ripping off the roof, then pulling down the walls.

As dawn came, all was quiet, although the rain still poured down. The Enemy Superpowers had gone back to their evil deeds; the Professor and his cage had disappeared, even Greedy Gutrot had left, and all that was left of Pig Hall was a pile of wood and rubble.

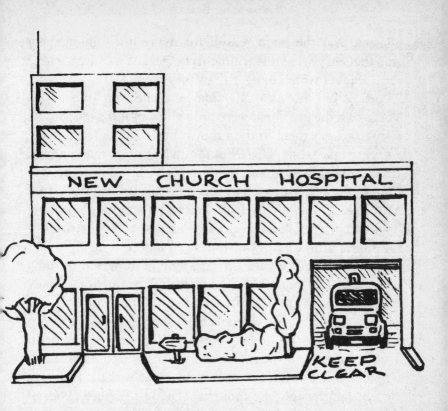

2. fIRst caLL—Last bReath

Little Christian sat in his office glancing down at the computer printout of his diary. It was hard to imagine that Newchurch had only been in action for one year; so much seemed to have happened. For him it had been quite an easy year with a few minor hiccups but no major disasters.

It was so encouraging to see that so many Littlekids had come to join them, having been rescued from the Bigwideworld, but although they had a few adults return from the Voices Training Module, still very few older adults wanted to leave Oldchurch or Nochurch to join them. He guessed that the main reason for many not joining them was that they were not willing to be part of a church where their leaders were younger than they were.

Putting his diary to one side he picked up two of his Voice-Fax sheets. These were now a few months old, but he refused to put them in the rubbish bin.

One was from Hearthunter who had returned to Crosscountry and contacted him to let him know he was busier than he ever had been. The other was from Miraclekid, who, apart from starting a school of training for other Miraclekids, also had some wonderful stories of the supernatural battles he had been involved in.

Putting the Voice-Faxes to one side he reflected on how pleased he had been with Buddy and Harmony; they really had taken over looking after the Newchurch Family.

Then (instinctively whenever he started thinking about his old friends) he looked down at a photo on his desk. Two thirteen-year-olds with their arms round each other, laughing like there was no problem in the world. 'That was eleven months ago,' he thought. 'The last picture taken of Angela and me before she was called on another Commission.'

Little Christian was missing her like mad, but he knew that being Children of the Voice, both he and Angela must put the Voice first in their lives and be obedient to him.

But why hadn't she been in touch for nearly a year?

His concentration was broken by a knock at the door, and a cheerful Littlekid entered dressed in brightly coloured shorts, kneepads, elbowpads, a helmet and worn-out train-ers with attaching olly flaps.

'Hi, you must be Little Christian,' said the smiley face. 'I'm Rhoda Skateboard. I'm learning how to be a messen-ger from the Voice, and I've come straight from the

Training Module with this sealed envelope to deliver to you personally.'

Little Christian thanked her, but couldn't help being surprised at the fact that the Voice seemed to be giving responsibilities to younger and younger Littlekids. As he looked at the envelope he saw that the Voice's seal had been broken.

'Um, Rhoda,' he said, not meaning to sound too accusing, 'you haven't by any chance opened up the envelope for any reason, have you?'

Rhoda looked stunned. 'Certainly not!' she cried. 'Who do you think I am to even consider that I would do such a thing?'

Little Christian could see that she was getting upset but still felt that he had to find out why it was open. 'I'm sorry, Rhoda,' he said. 'I didn't mean to sound like I didn't trust you, but...' Then he thought for a moment. 'You didn't by any chance stop at all between the Training Module and here, did you?'

She thought for a moment then said, 'No, I came straight here, that is, I almost came straight here. I did just stop for a few minutes when I passed a skateboard park that was full of the most wonderful ramps I have ever seen, and a kind person invited me in to have a go at some drop-ins for free. But it was only for a few minutes.'

'I see,' said Little Christian. And did you let go of the envelope?

'Oh yes,' replied Rhoda. I mean, have you ever tried to negotiate those ramps with your hands full? It's just not possible, you know.'

Just as Rhoda began to get very excited about the skateboard park, Little Christian cut in and asked her what the kind man looked like.

'Oh, he was amazing,' said Rhoda. 'He was absolutely enormous, but very kind.'

'Thank you, Rhoda. That will be all. You had better go now because I'm sure you have more work to do; but take my advice—in future don't be distracted from what the Voice tells you to do, even if it *is* a skateboard park.'

'OK,' said Rhoda, 'I'll do my best. See you around.' And off she went, closing the door behind her.

Little Christian stood up and walked around the room, quietly seething. 'So after a year of not hearing from him, Gutrot is still alive and sick, even trapping little girls now,' he thought out loud as he took the contents out of the envelope and saw that it contained a photomap and a note.

The note went as follows:

Little Christian, I have a Commission for you.

For one year now you have been leading Newchurch. It is now time for you to leave them for a while to make sure that they don't just look to you... but that they learn to look to me. They are also getting to the point where they still expect you to do things for them that by now they ought to know how to do themselves.

With this in mind, I want you to follow my photomap to a place called Deadbody. Here you will find some Voice followers who still have some life in them. They have chosen to be trapped there for various reasons. I want you to tell them all about Newchurch; then maybe they will hear what you are saying and choose to come and live, rather than stay where they are and eventually die.

Be warned, your route is not easy. The Enemy Superpowers have you on their hitlist. I will however be with you and will also be sending you a partner because, as you know, I do not commission people individually but in pairs.

Your Friend,
The Voice.

Little Christian put the photomap and letter down, then picked up a copy of the Manual to compare the handwriting and check that the letter was genuine, not a fraud. Then when he saw it was from the Voice he fell on his knees and, using a language that only the Voice understood, gave thanks to him. He also prayed that the Voice would tell him who his partner would be, but the Voice told him to be patient and to wait and see.

As Little Christian left his office he was filled with excitement and spontaneously burst into song:

> All people have a choice,
> But we are children of the Voice.
> Please help us to be faithful to the end.
> Our commission now we know
> When the Voice says 'go,' we'll go,
> For the Voice will always be
> The childrens' friend.

All the other Littlekids and adults who passed by also felt as excited as he did, and within no time at all everyone in Newchurch was singing along with Little Christian, even though very few knew why Little Christian was celebrating.

As the singing continued, the darkness of the night began to fall like a huge umbrella. The warm air soon made way for the chilling breeze; then this in turn had to give way to the authority of cold and frost.

As the singing subsided and Newchurch folk were snuggled up in their warm beds, no one was aware of a thin, badly beaten Littlekid who scarcely had the strength to drag her bruised and bleeding body over the razor sharp rocks of the Bigwideworld.

Her body was permanently shivering, and all that she had

covering her was a vest and a ripped pair of jeans. Her bare feet were red from the cuts, brown from the mud and blue from the cold.

Little Christian was so excited about his Commission that he had lost all sense of tiredness. He thought he would watch the television, but all he could pick up was depressing programmes from Nochurch and Oldchurch. Then he thought that he would go and visit someone, but then he couldn't make his mind up whom to go and see. In the end he thought he heard a voice in his mind instructing him to go for a walk, and as nothing else had come to mind this seemed like a good idea.

He had read in the Manual that the Voice had often gone onto lonely hills at night to pray, and so rather than just walk around Newchurch, he decided to put on his big warm coat, grab a torch and take a stroll over the hills of the Bigwideworld.

The little girl knew that she could go no farther. She had never stopped talking to the Voice, and her spirit was strong, but her body was giving up on her. A thought flashed through her mind that maybe the Voice was calling her home; perhaps now was the time that she was going to enter into the for ever, and to be always with him. She had no fear of death because she was one of the Children of the Voice.

Her last movement was to pull herself onto a high rock, and even though her eyes were very blurred she thought she could just make out the lights coming from Newchurch, so near yet so far. She allowed her eyes to close and pulled her thin little legs up to her chin to try and get a bit more warmth. Then with her last few lungfuls of breath she started singing in a gentle whisper:

There is no one else around
In the air or on the ground
Who has the power (has the power) of the Voice.
So you Enemy Superpowers
In your defeated final hours
We command you to leave—you have no choice
    (you have no choice)
As we speak in the authority of the...

Then her voice went quiet.

Suddenly a bright glare of a torch-beam shone straight into her face. 'Angela!' screamed Little Christian, his eyes filling with tears and staring in unbelief at the freezing little body huddled on the rock. 'Is that you?' The little girl gave a faint smile... then stopped breathing.

3.   gone but not forgotten

Very carefully, with tears running down his cheeks, Little
Christian put his coat over Angela and picked up her limp
little body. As fast as he could he rushed back to
Newchurch. Then after putting the body on his bed he ran
around waking everybody up, telling them about her.

The doctor was the first to see Angela. Having taken just
one glance at her, he shook his head, then he checked her
pulse and heartbeat, and looking up at Little Christian the
sad doctor quietly informed him he was sorry but she was
now in the hands of the Voice.

Everyone was heartbroken. They all knew that the Voice sometimes used doctors and sometimes just did the healing himself, without doctors; but here nothing could be done; it was too late and they had no suggestions or answers.

Buddy and Harmony tried to comfort the shattered Little Christian, but no words they could say seemed to help. All the excitement of the day had gone. Now was a time of mourning and sadness.

Eventually everyone went to bed, all except Little Christian who simply sat in his office sobbing and sobbing, looking at the photo on his desk. He accidentally knocked his Manual off his desk and it fell open on the floor, but he failed to notice it. In fact within a few hours he too had fallen asleep on the floor next to it. His eyes, all red, had run dry of tears.

At about seven o'clock, he could hear the birds singing as the sun began to shine through his window, but even under the warm rays that woke him he didn't want to stir. In fact he didn't want to do anything.

It was then that the door swung open and all Little Christian's burning eyes could see was the bright light glaring at him.

'Get up, Little Christian,' came a command from the doorway.

Little Christian leapt to his feet. He'd recognise that voice anywhere. 'Miraclekid, is that really you?' he stammered.

'Of course it is, Little Christian, but why are you lying on the floor when you have work to do?'

As Little Christian ran over to give Miraclekid a hug he told him to sit down as he had some sad news to tell him about Angela.

Miraclekid allowed Little Christian to tell him the whole story, and when he had finished Miraclekid stared at him.

'Did you think of asking the Voice what was going on?' he said.

'Why,' said Little Christian. 'What's the point of asking the Voice questions about a dead person? She's gone, it's over.'

'The Voice must have tried to speak to you last night. Have a look at where your Manual fell open at.'

Little Christian picked up his Manual and read how the Voice had brought a little girl back from the dead. 'Yes, but that was all very well when the Voice was walking around on the face of this earth, but that doesn't happen today... does it?'

'It's funny, you know, you remind me of someone from Oldchurch, not Newchurch,' said Miraclekid. 'Listen, get it into your mind that the Voice is as powerful today as he ever was. In fact, doesn't the Manual tell us that even greater things are going to happen in our generation?'

Little Christian just hung his head and went red with embarrassment at his unbelief.

'Obviously not everybody will be raised from the dead,' Miraclekid continued, getting into his preaching mode, 'or else the Voice would have no one living with him now, but Angela was sent here to be your partner for your Commission, so it's not very likely that she's gonna stay dead, is it?'

'But I never guessed that she was going to be my partner. The Voice never told me,' protested Little Christian.

'Well, fair enough,' said Miraclekid, rapidly running out of answers. 'Nobody understands everything the Voice does or why he does things in his way, but we do know that he has a perfect plan and that everything he does is for the best. I'm sure he had a reason for not telling you...' Then after a moment's thought he continued, 'Come to think of it, if he had told you, there would have been no reason for me being here. Anyway, come on, let's go and wake her up. She has been asleep long enough.'

They left Little Christian's office and on the way to Little Christian's house Miraclekid stopped at the cafe and asked them to prepare a nice big hot breakfast for Angela. 'She'll need that,' he said.

Little Christian didn't dare say a word as his faith was still rather low. He was still trying to work out if he was about to see a great miracle, or a great embarrassment thanks to this over-zealous nutcase of a friend.

As they entered the bedroom, Angela lay cold and still on his bed, just as she had been when Little Christian left her the night before. 'Cor, she's in a bit of a state, isn't she?' said Miraclekid.

'She's dead,' replied Little Christian sadly.

'No, she's just asleep.' Miraclekid looked at Angela and with a voice of authority that sounded like thunder commanded life back into the body, in the name of the Voice.

Immediately, Angela's eyes started to twitch. Then they opened a fraction. Then they burst open wide, and a big smile spread across her face. Miraclekid and Little Christian fell flat on the floor as they began to realise just how powerful the Voice is.

'He really has got the power over life and death!' shouted Little Christian, and after a time of giving thanks he jumped up and ran to hug Angela.

'Go gently,' said Miraclekid. 'She's very weak, and she hasn't had her breakfast yet.' Looking out of the window, he remembered that he hadn't had his, either, and he wished he had ordered one for himself as well.

Angela hadn't yet said anything. When the doctor was brought in, he explained that although he had never seen a miracle like it, Angela had still been through a terrible ordeal and needed to rest for a few days to get her strength back. Miraclekid of course didn't agree with the doctor, but Little Christian, Buddy and Harmony did; so Miraclekid reluctantly watched as Angela was taken by a praising group of Littlekids into the Newchurch hospital.

'What about her breakfast?' shouted Little Christian, but when he turned round he noticed that Miraclekid had quickly disappeared into the café and was already halfway through it. Everyone burst out laughing.

After he'd eaten, Miraclekid shouted goodbye to everyone, then turning to Little Christian gave him a hug and told him he would see him soon.

'Don't go without saying goodbye to Angela, will you?' said Little Christian.

Miraclekid didn't like the thought of that; the two things he did not relate to were hospitals and girls, but he felt he ought to see her before he went.

Gingerly he crept up to the door, then poked his head round and saw Angela lying there. 'Bye, Angela,' he whispered.

She signalled with her hand that he should come over to her bedside, which he did. Then she started opening her mouth like she was trying to say something, but he couldn't make out what she was saying, so he put his ear close to her lips. It was then that Angela cunningly moved her head to one side and gave him a great big kiss on his cheek. 'Thank you,' she whispered.

Miraclekid shot up in the air as if he had sat on a stinging nettle with short trousers on. 'Oh, think nothing of it, Angela. After all, I was only obeying the Voice. See you around.' And with that he raced out of the door.

Little Christian was waiting outside the door. 'Is she any better?' he inquired.

'Oh, I think she'll pull through,' said the red-faced Miraclekid as he raced off back towards the Bigwideworld. 'Well, her lips seem to work anyway,' he shouted. 'See ya.'

Little Christian burst out laughing again, guessing what Angela had done. 'She must be improving. It didn't take her long to get back to her usual little old cheeky self,' he thought.

Within a very short time Angela regained not just her humour but also her strength, even though she seemed a lot thinner than she used to be. Little Christian showed her the letter from the Voice and the photomap to Deadbody, and although she listened intently, she said very little. She still had her wonderful strange accent, but for most of the time she would only say words like 'yeah' and 'no' and 'maybe,' and didn't really seem to be able to enter into a conversation.

Little Christian kept asking her to tell him about how and why she was in such a bad state when he found her, but somehow either Angela couldn't or wouldn't talk about it. Sometimes she'd say that her mind had gone blank and she could not recall what had happened; then on other occasions she'd say it was too painful to think about it, and could they change the subject.

Little Christian wanted to help her. He knew that she needed it, but this could only happen when she was ready to receive his help. There would be a time when all that had happened would come out into the open and he would have to be prepared for when that time came.

Angela had been in Newchurch for fourteen days, and one day when she and Little Christian were in the office studying the Manual together there was a knock on the door. In walked Rhoda Skateboard all decked out in her usual attire.

'Hello, Rhoda,' said Little Christian. Then after introducing Rhoda to Angela he was given an envelope from the

Voice. Seeing that the seal had not been broken this time, he winked at Rhoda and she smiled back. 'Yippee!' yelled Little Christian, dancing around the table as he read the letter. 'We are off this afternoon.'

They all danced around the table together, even though Rhoda didn't have a clue what they were on about. She was a little sad when they explained to her where they were going, especially because the Voice had told her that he wanted her to come off deliveries for a bit and spend some time being trained in Newchurch. Now just as she arrived the leaders were going!

'Don't worry about that,' said Little Christian. 'Buddy and Harmony have been here with me since the beginning, and they will train you well.'

Little Christian and Angela packed a few essentials and went round saying goodbye to everyone.

Little Christian was still concerned about the lack of strong leaders in Newchurch. It was not that they had failed to train new leaders; it was just that a year is a very short time for people to come from the old and be leading in the new. Were they really ready and able to take on more responsibility? Buddy and Harmony were great, but with Angela and him away, the only other strong ones who could really take his place were Hearthunter and Miraclekid, and they too were out on Commissions and not available.

Buddy and Harmony tried to reassure him that everything would be fine. 'There are a lot of up-and-coming new leaders,' Buddy explained. 'Who knows?' he said, smiling, 'the Voice might even send in one or two mature ones after you have gone.'

After lunch everybody in Newchurch came out to wave goodbye as their dynamic duo set out for Deadbody.

Harmony had promised to look after Rhoda and had taken both her and her skateboard into her lodgings, while the other local leaders had promised to support both Harmony and Buddy in taking care of Newchurch.

The last words they heard from Newchurch came from Buddy as he shouted, 'Try not to be away too long. Remember this will always be your home.'

Unseen by anyone, from behind a rock came an evil chuckle that nobody heard. 'You mean this *was* your home,' the evil voice whispered as he unlocked the largest coffin. An imitation Littlekid stepped out.

'Welcome to my world,' said Professor Mindwarpt.

'Thank you, O Mighty Supervoice,' the Littlekid replied.

'Oh, I love that title,' said the Professor, chuckling. Then he continued, 'I have made you very wise and clever, and I've created you to be the very best leader. No other leader will ever match up to you. Everyone will be your servant... but you must do everything I say.'

'I will obey you, O Mighty Supervoice,' replied the Littlekid.

'Good,' said Mindwarpt. 'And remember, you are bugged so I will hear every word you say. I will be with you always, so watch it. If I notice any foul-ups with your obeying system you will be terminated immediately. Is that understood?'

'Loud and clear, O Mighty Supervoice,' came the reply.

'Now, what shall I call you? Yes, I know. I'll call you Shepherd, and because you are the largest and weigh more than any other of my superbreeds, your first name will be Heavy. Yes, off you go, and do your worst, young Heavy Shepherd.'

4. a BUDDY fOR BUDDY

The sun was shining down, and it was a lovely warm day to start a Commission. Both Angela and Little Christian were very excited about what they had been called to do.

'Hey, Angela, what do you know about this first place we are due to call at? It's called Treasure Iceland.'

'Do wot?' said Angela. 'Never 'erd of it, but if it's as nice as wot it is 'ere I ain't gonna grumble.'

'Well it's a few kilometres from here yet,' said Little Christian. 'So in case it's not, enjoy this while you can.'

Meanwhile, Buddy felt a bit sad with Little Christian

gone, and deep down he wondered how he would cope without him. He made his way over to Little Christian's office, which he would from now on use as his own, till Little Christian returned. There he sat down behind the desk and found himself staring at the photo of Little Christian and Angela. He thought as he began to clear the desk-top that maybe he would put it away somewhere, but then he decided he would leave it in front of him. It would be a reminder to pray for them regularly.

As he continued clearing papers away, a head came peering around the door. 'Excuse me, may I come in?' the head asked. Buddy looked up and saw a rather large Littlekid facing him, one he didn't recognise. He was a bit embarrassed as he made it his duty to know everyone's name.

'Oh, yes, please do come in and take a seat,' he said. 'I'm ever so sorry, but I seem to have forgotten your name.'

'No, it's all right, you haven't forgotten my name,' smiled the Littlekid warmly. 'You see I'm new and have just arrived this afternoon. You have never met me before.'

Buddy felt relieved, and as the Littlekid sat down he poured him out a glass of orange juice. 'Ah, I'm sorry, but I don't touch fruit or vegetables. You see I believe that the Manual speaks very strongly about cruelty, and I believe that when a fruit is picked or vegetables cut up or dug up, they feel pain. They have both life and feeling, and I would not want to deprive them of either.'

'Very interesting,' said Buddy, getting rather confused, 'So then what do you eat?'

'Well,' said the Littlekid thoughtfully, 'I live on meat. After all, meat was put on the face of the earth for us to enjoy, and the Voice has even provided us with special teeth so that we can chew it properly. I'm a very strict meatatarian.'

'Well, you have certainly made some interesting points. I must remember that,' said Buddy. 'Now tell me, what is your name and where do you come from?'

The Littlekid explained that his name was Shepherd but his nickname was Heavy due to his size. Buddy cut in and said they wouldn't call him Heavy because it was cruel to make fun of people. 'Oh no, I love it,' said the Littlekid. 'Everyone calls me Heavy, and I'd like you to as well.'

'Very well,' said Buddy, 'if you insist.'

The Littlekid went on to explain that he had come from a brand new Voice's Training Module. Although he was lying the whole time he really impressed Buddy with his wisdom, his knowledge and his qualifications.

As he got up to leave, he could see that he had already surprised Buddy, as Buddy was getting very excited about him.

'It's amazing,' said Buddy, 'and of course you wouldn't know this, but this very afternoon our leader has been sent on a Commission and won't be back for a long while. I was wondering how I would cope, but it seems that the Voice knew all about that and he has sent you along just at the right time.'

'I don't know about that,' said Heavy in mock modesty. 'I have only come to serve. I believe it's only the humble ones who will be lifted up.'

This was music to Buddy's ears. *What a great attitude*, he thought. 'You and I, Heavy, are really going to see things change around here,' he shouted excitedly.

'Well, you know me, Buddy, whatever you want me to do I'll do it.' Then just as Heavy was walking out of the door he stopped and handed Buddy a piece of paper. 'If you get time, Buddy, perhaps you could check this out. They are all the reasons why people should be meatatarians.'

'I certainly will, Heavy,' said Buddy. 'If it means that much to you, there must be truth in it for all of us.'

Heavy Shepherd left the office feeling quite pleased with himself, but even more pleased with himself was a bald-headed Professor with spectacles, who although in hiding had tuned in to the whole conversation.

5. treasure iceLand

'There it is,' said Little Christian, pointing to a snowcovered island about two kilometres out in the sea.

'Yeah, it must be, but why is it that we are standin' on this 'ot sandy beach, and that place—wot's only a little way away—is frozen solid?'

Although Little Christian had no answer to her question, he was thrilled that every hour Angela's sentences and comments were becoming more coherent and meaningful.

As they were considering how to get there, they heard a rumbling sound that seemed to be coming from the sea.

The noise grew louder and louder as whatever it was got-closer. Obviously it brought back a memory or fear into Angela's mind and she wanted to make a run for it, but Little Christian grabbed her hand firmly and reassured her that she had nothing to be afraid of as they were acting under the authority of the Voice.

Then they arrived. Driving straight out of the sea came six amphibious WarMachines with guns pointing out at every conceivable angle. On the roofs they had rockets and missiles, all with the most modern homing devices and technology imaginable.

The engines of the large vehicles stopped in unison as if someone had pulled their plugs out. Then an icy-cold voice came from the vehicle standing right in front of them. With menacing aggression the sound of the speaker echoed all over the bay. 'Who are you? What do you want, and do you realise you are trespassing by looking over at Treasure Iceland?'

Little Christian was not frightened by the WarMachine and shouted back to the vehicle, 'We have been sent by the Voice to visit you.' All went quiet for a moment, then an automatic door opened in the front of the machine from where the voice was coming. 'Enter,' it said coldly. Little Christian and Angela walked down the hot sandy beach, then as they climbed in through the small door Angela accidentally touched the side of the vehicle and let out a little cry of pain.

'What's the matter?' asked Little Christian, who had climbed in first to make sure that everything was OK.

'I've just burned me finger on the side of the WarMachine,' she whispered.

'Surely it's not that hot?' argued Little Christian in disbelief.

'No, it's that cold,' replied Angela. 'It's literally frozen.'

The door of the WarMachine closed and they found themselves alone in a small compartment. It was a bit junky, like they were sitting in the middle of an old second-hand clothes shop. There were odd garments everywhere, and there were even what looked like old-fashioned diving suits in the corner. 'Not my idea of a trendy boutique,' commented Angela, and Little Christian nodded in agreement.

Then the sound of mighty engines started like the roar of an angry lion, and the machine reversed up then went crashing back into the sea again. Angela and Little Christian didn't bother to discuss their situation as the engines were so noisy that they couldn't even hear themselves think. It seemed like only minutes, though, before the engines cut out again.

'Oh no,' said Angela. 'I 'ate the thought of breakin' down in the middle of the sea.' But before she had finished her sentence, a voice ordered them to put on as many clothes as they could and then to put on the ice-repellent thermal suits in the corner. This they did without argurnent, as they guessed that what they were putting on was for their own protection. Then, when they were all togged up, the door by which they had entered opened again.

'Get out,' a voice commanded, 'and don't touch anything.'

They found it quite hard to walk with all the gear on, but more by falling out than climbing out they soon managed to leave the WarMachine. Even with all the clothes and the thermal suits, they still felt freezing and started to shiver with cold. But as they looked around they became intrigued at what they saw. They found themselves standing in a building that was not dissimilar to what Oldchurch used to call the church building or sanctuary. There were many seats all in lines, a box like a pulpit up the front and a large table at the front with a cross on it. But what was different from Oldchurch was that it was all made of snow and ice.

'Go and sit down,' said the voice from the WarMachine. They heard bells ringing and immediately the doors of the WarMachine opened up as did many little doors all around the building.

Angela grabbed Little Christian's hand and gasped, 'I dun believe wot I'm seein',' she cried. 'Tell me it's not true.'

But it was true. In walked hundreds of adults and Littlekids, and all they were wearing were swimming costumes and sunglasses and nothing on their feet. They all sat down on the ice they were obviously all used to sitting on; then a person wearing black trunks, a sweatband and wristband walked up to the front and stood in the pulpit.

Without any warm word of welcome, he explained that he was sorry it was so hot this morning, but suggested the cause was the intrusion of these two Littlekids who claimed to come from the Voice. The man at the front used his wristband to wipe away the perspiration from his brow. 'Step up to the front,' he demanded. 'Say what you have to say, then we can get you off our island and bring the temperature back down to normal.'

Little Christian was not sure what to say, but Angela, who had been trained up as one of the Voice's directors, walked to the front, climbed into the freezing pulpit and began.

'The Voice 'as sent us to tell ya that 'e is very disappointed wiv ya. Many years ago you were warm, friendly people wot knew the warmf of the Voice's love, but now ye'r cold 'n' icy and even these subzero temperatures are too warm for yer personalities to cope wiv.

'But worst of all,' she continued, 'the Voice is sad cos this island once contained rich treasures. Years ago you were some of the first people to discover the power of the Voice. Ya learned about 'is special language before most; ya saw 'ealings and miracles reg'ler, but ya chose to keep all the treasures for yerselves on yer island and 'ated the thought of sharing 'em wiv others. That's why ye'r now the way ya are.'

Angela got down out of the pulpit and walked back to her seat. Little Christian thought she was brilliant and started to give her a round of applause but soon stopped when he saw that everyone had turned round, and he felt all those cold eyes staring at him.

The speaker with the black trunks got back into his pulpit and looked hard at the two of them. 'We don't like girls speaking,' he said, 'and that includes those girls who unlike this one can speak properly. I was expecting the boy to speak, but obviously the girl is his mouthpiece.

'What the girl said, however, was totally predictable. We have heard it all before; in fact, every misguided speaker from the Voice seems to say the same thing. Why does everyone think that we are abnormal wearing our beachwear on our very own Treasure Iceland? I think they are abnormal, not us. Can any of you imagine what it would be like if you were warm and not as cold as the ice you are sitting on? Of course not. Surely we have something very special here, and this is the way that the Voice wants us to stay. No, I believe that the reason these so-called Voice speakers come over here is because they want us to hand over our treasure to them. No way! What is ours is ours by right, and no one else will have any of it.'

Everyone nodded in agreement.

'Finally, let today be yet another lesson to us. We must keep our Island well guarded. We must be ready to use our WarMachines, our guns and rockets so that we can protect what we have for us and our own Littlekids.'

The congregation started to applaud their great orator, but noticed that putting their hands together was causing warmth, so they soon stopped.

Little Christian leaped up. 'Hold on—you don't understand,' he screamed. 'You can't last for long. A global warming is happening right across the face of the planet, and your Treasure Iceland will be the first one to melt. You haven't got a future unless you are willing to change.'

'Rubbish!' everyone shouted together. That is impossible.' Little Christian and Angela were told to get back into the WarMachine, then they were driven back to the mainland. As they walked up the beach a voice boomed out, 'If you are ever sighted even looking at Treasure Iceland again, you will be eliminated.' And with that threat the WarMachine disappeared back into the sea.

6. UNHappy familIes

Professor Mindwarpt was just finishing bragging to his friend Greedy Gutrot about how successful Heavy Shepherd had been. 'It's even surprised me how gullible they are,' he joked. 'Can you believe it? He's already got Buddy to make a statement on how vegetables and fruit are bad for the Children of the Voice.'

'Excellent,' said Gutrot with a big grin. 'But don't count your chickens yet, Professor. Newchurch may seem weak at present, but they have some very strong allies drifting all over the Bigwideworld, and we want them destroyed as well.'

Mindwarpt took his friend's advice and decided it was time to send in two more of his superbreeds. He knew they would be a great support to Heavy Shepherd.

He opened the cage and took two more of the coffin lids off. There before him was a very attractive female and a good-looking male, and these two were a little older than Heavy Shepherd.

As both got out of their coffins, Mindwarpt commented on what a nice pair they made. Then he had a brainwave. 'Hold hands!' he ordered.

'Yes, O Mighty Supervoice,' they both replied.

'I pronounce you... man and wife. You will enter Newchurch as a nice happy newly-married couple. Of course, I am not expecting you to act like you are married. I'm expecting you to wreck everyone else's idea of marriage,' he said, laughing. 'May I remind you that you are well and truly bugged and I will be listening in to all your conversations. So any hint of a malfunction, and I will terminate you both.'

'Yes, O Mighty Supervoice,' they again said together.

'Right, off you go to Newchurch and do your worst.'

Meanwhile, Little Christian and Angela were glad to be back on the mainland in the sunshine. Little Christian kept encouraging her about how dear her words had been when she was speaking from the Ice pulpit.

'Yeah,' said Angela, 'but do ya think I was right in doin' it? After all, 'e accused me of being yer mouthpiece.'

'Hey,' said Little Christian, 'I've got a big enough mouth of my own. If the Voice had given me something to say, I would have said it. But he chose to give you something to say so you were not my mouthpiece. You were the Voice's mouthpiece.'

'Well, y'er right about one fing,' said Angela thoughtfully.

'What's that?' asked Little Christian.

'Well, ya 'ave got a big mouth.' And she burst into laughter.

'You know something, I could really get to like you,' said Little Christian, half-joking.

'Then why don't ya?' replied Angela. Little Christian just grinned with embarrassment.

Heavy had been invited to move a desk in with Buddy and to share Little Christian's office so they could be more together in the work. To start with, Heavy had only had a small desk by the window. But as he needed more room to prepare, Buddy, being a very humble person, had offered him Little Christian's desk—which of course Heavy gratefully received.

The first time he was left alone in the office he tucked the photo of Little Christian and Angela into the desk drawer. Buddy did enquire about where it had gone, but Heavy convinced him that it was bad for him to keep looking at it as it would always keep him feeling inferior. Buddy tended to agree.

While Buddy was becoming close friends with Heavy, Harmony had become very close to Rhoda Skateboard, who was proving to be a wonderful little student. But Harmony still felt a bit left out when it came to more adult conversation. So you can imagine what a great thrill it was when a nice young married couple arrived on her doorstep with the hopes of becoming part of Newchurch. And they both seemed so friendly.

'And what are your names?' she asked.

'Well,' said the man, 'my name is Prophet. You see, I'm very much used by the Voice when it comes to sharing how he feels,' he lied.

'Great,' said a very excited Harmony. 'Your gift will be very welcome in Newchurch, but have you got a first name?'

'Well,' he said, 'it's a bit embarrassing, but when I was much younger I used to play a lot of ball games. The most amazing thing was that if someone ever tried to hit me, I always managed to dodge out of the way. Ever since then everyone's called me Dodgy.'

Dodgy then felt a whack on the shin. 'Don't forget me, darling,' said his wife, who had kept her mouth shut until then.

'Oh, I'm ever so sorry, Cherrylips. My wife is a very shy lady. Only just got married, and here I am forgetting her already! Harmony, this is my wife, Lucy—Lucy Morals.'

'No it's not, silly,' said Lucy. 'We are married now, darling. My name is Lucy Morals Prophet.'

'Oh yes, of course it is, sugarlumps. You see her maiden name was Morals, but now of course she's a Prophet, like me.' He was now looking very embarrassed. 'So I suppose you could say that she's now become a Prophet but still likes to be called Lucy Morals. Is that right, pigeon-pie?'

Lucy grinned furiously then gave him a massive kick on the other shin.

'Well, welcome to Newchurch, Dodgy Prophet and Lucy Morals. I'm sure we have a lot to offer you, and I'm sure you both have a lot to offer us,' said Harmony.

Dodgy, Lucy (and Professor Mindwarpt) grinned and agreed.

Within no time at all Dodgy was regularly speaking at meetings on behalf of the Voice, and although nearly everything he said was contrary to the Manual, because it got the full backing of Heavy Shepherd, nearly everyone was willing to agree with his teachings.

He also encouraged all the Littlekids to write down messages from the Voice for those they liked and those they didn't like. He explained that if they added the words 'so says the Voice' onto their message, people would take them a lot more seriously. Little notes were being passed around all the time, all claiming to be from the Voice, and within a very short time Newchurch couldn't remember what the real Voice sounded like.

Quiet, shy Lucy Morals, however, proved to be anything but quiet and shy! At the first meeting she went to she gently shook hands with both the men and women. In the second meeting she ignored the women and gave the men a warm embrace. By the third meeting she was embracing the men and kissing them on their cheeks—and so it went on. Funnily enough, she was only interested in the married men. The husbands played up to Lucy while the wives disliked her. She was beginning to accomplish her mission: she was already beginning to divide families.

Heavy Shepherd supported Lucy Morals all the way. He felt that she was a perfect example of real friendship and portrayed the love of the Voice. Many agreed with him, but many of the wives did not. He told the wives that they were being selfish and possessive and that Newchurch was one big family, not a lot of small ones. They must be willing to share everything and start being a real community. Heavy also thought she was very attractive, but he kept that to himself.

Buddy and Harmony were both in a bit of a state. Buddy could not agree with the way things were going; but he felt too weak and confused to oppose it, and his health was beginning to suffer. Harmony, on the other hand, just stayed more and more in her house feeling totally confused. Both knew that they were rapidly losing the respect and the leadership of Newchurch.

Late one night Rhoda felt like a break from her studying, so she decided she would go for a quick skateboard around the block. She knew that Harmony would not like her to be going out late, but she thought if she crept out quietly perhaps no one would notice. She crept down the stairs and saw a light in the living room, and as the door was slightly open she peeped in only to see Harmony fast asleep on the sofa.

Ever so quietly, she crept out of the door, then off she went down the road. All was quite dark and she guessed that everyone was in bed, but then she saw a light shining from the office window 'Surely Buddy or Heavy can't be working this late?' She thought. 'I bet someone's left the light on. I'd better go and check.'

She crept over to the window very quietly, because if one of the leaders was working late she didn't want to be spotted and so get into trouble with Harmony.

Standing on tiptoes and looking in, she gasped in amazement at what she saw. Immediately she turned, dropped her skateboard and ran as fast as her little legs would carry her. 'How could they?' she sobbed. 'They are wicked and evil!' Rhoda crept back to her room knowing that after what she had seen she was not going to sleep a wink that night.

The office window opened and two heads looked out into the night. 'Well now, I guess we had better find the owner of that skateboard quickly,' said one.

'Yes,' said the other. 'And we must terminate the owner, before our owner terminates us.'

7. THE ROTTER SETS IN

''Ow far is Deadbody from 'ere?' inquired Angela as she
and Little Christian sat down exhausted under a large oak
tree, with the sun still shining brightly overhead.

'Hold on—I'm just checking,' said Little Christian, carefully examining his photomap.

'Cor, we've 'arf come a long way,' she continued, looking
over his shoulder.

'Yes, we have,' he agreed, looking down at his trainers
and considering the aching feet inside them. 'Still, according to my calculations we should be reaching Deadbody

167

within a couple of hours.'

'Thank goodness fer that,' said Angela, also looking down at her feet.

Still, something seems a little fishy, thought Little Christian to himself. Why haven't we actually met anyone since Treasure Iceland, which was ages ago? Where are all the wandering Littlekids. And more to the point, where is Greedy Gutrot and his gang?

As they got up and continued their journey, they passed through a small forest then came to a clearing. In the middle of the clearing they saw a huge notice-board with some tiny writing on it and a large arrow pointing to a small footpath which left the main track and went off to the left.

'Hey, what's this?' said Little Christian, running over to the board. Squinting his eyes, he could just about read what it said.

> Before you go on... you need to look back
> If you want to progress... you'd need to back-track
> You'd need to retreat... if you want to attack
> Come learn of your history... 'cause it's knowledge
>   you lack.
> Signed: The Voice.

'Wow! It's a message from the Voice,' said Little Christian, failing to notice the spelling mistake in the signature. 'We'd better do as he says.'

'Wait a minute,' said Angela. 'This place ain't on our photomap. It may be a trap.'

'Oh don't be so suspicious,' laughed Little Christian. 'The Voice has probably just added this because there is something very strategic we need to know before we approach Deadbody. Now come on.'

Angela wasn't convinced, but she obediently followed her friend.

The path was winding and twisty and seemed to be going on for ever. Then suddenly it stopped and they saw a 'DANGER—CLIFF EDGE' sign in front of them.

Carefully they moved towards the sign and could see a sheer drop in front of them which went down to a sort of quarry. 'Be careful,' said Angela, grabbing hold of his arm. 'Ye'r gettin' too near the edge.'

'No, I'll be all right,' replied Little Christian, moving even closer towards the drop.

'Gosh,' he shouted, 'I think that I can see a...' And with that his words were cut short as the edge of the quarry that they were standing on crumbled away and both Little Christian and Angela went hurtling down the cliff-face, screaming as they fell.

Heavy Shepherd knocked loudly on the door, then as there was no answer he knocked even louder with great impatience. Eventually, the door opened and a very sleepy Harmony opened the door. 'Oh, hello, Heavy,' she said, glancing at her watch. 'This is rather late to be visiting, isn't it?'

Heavy pushed his way into the house. 'No, I'm afraid this is not a pastoral visit; this is something much more serious,' he said sternly. 'Newchurch is beginning to get out of hand due to our Littlekids severely lacking in discipline.'

'Well, I can't say that I have noticed it. Anyway, what has that got to do with me at this time of the night?' asked the perplexed Harmony.

'I'm afraid you are not bringing Rhoda Skateboard up in a way that is honouring to the Voice and our community. The girl is wild and rebellious. I have come to take her from you and put her in the hands of people I can trust.'

'But this can't be true,' said Harmony with tears welling up in her eyes. 'I've always taught her by the Manual, and she's been a wonderful Littlekid.'

'I have not come here to argue with you, Harmony. I am your leader and I know what's best. I want you to go and get her and her belongings and bring them to me now.'

Harmony started crying, 'But she's only a Littlekid. She won't understand. Who are you going to put her with?'

'Well, not that it is any of your business,' snapped Heavy, 'but if you must know she will be going to live with that highly respected couple Dodgy Prophet and Lucy Morals. They will bring her up in a way that I would be proud of.'

'No, I won't let you take her,' said Harmony, her tears turning to anger. 'Little Christian put her under my care and until he says differently, that's where she'll stay.'

'Little Christian, did I hear you say? Little Christian? Who on earth is he? Little Christian is just a bad memory; he won't be coming back here. I am your leader. No one else is, so you do what I say or face the consequences.'

'I refuse to obey you,' shouted Harmony, 'because I think you are wrong.'

Heavy roughly grabbed hold of her arm. His temper completely blown and with his eyes blazing, he stared straight into her face. With clenched teeth he whispered, 'Never, but never say that I am wrong. I am your leader, and I am never wrong.' Heavy turned to the door and gave a shout, then Dodgy and Lucy joined him in the house.

'Did you hear that wilful act of rebellion against her leader?'

Dodgy and Lucy nodded.

'Well,' he continued, 'according to my interpretation of the Manual, if there are two or three witnesses to rebellion we can take action. Dodgy, I want you to take Harmony out of

Newchurch and dump her in the middle of the Bigwideworld. From this moment, Harmony, you are banned—no, excommunicated—from Newchurch. Tomorrow I will announce your rebellion to the whole of my people and inform them that it will be a punishable offence for them in any way to communicate with you. In other words, don't even consider coming back here, because nobody will want to know you.'

Dodgy Prophet dragged Harmony out of the house and led her out into the darkness of the night.

'Well, Lucy, my dear,' said Heavy Shepherd, putting an arm around her, 'go and get your new little lodger and keep her locked up in a bedroom until we can think of a more permanent way to keep her mouth shut. And then,' he said with an evil grin, 'I will meet you back at my place in about an hour.'

8. a HISTORY LESSON

Angela opened one eye, then the other. She found herself staring into the face of a girl she had never seen before. 'Who are you?' she cried, sitting up and realising that she was on a bed.

'I'm Nurse Itbetter,' the girl replied, 'and this is my hospital. You had a nasty fall down into the quarry, you know. You're lucky that you didn't have any serious injuries. In fact your boyfriend's already up and about.'

'Me boyfriend? Oh, ya mean Little Christian,' Angela said with a smile. She felt some pain in her arm and asked the nurse what was causing it.

'Oh,' she replied, 'I had to give you both a painkilling injection.' Then, realising that she had carelessly left the vaccine bottle lying by the bed, she quickly snatched it up and put it in her pocket. Angela didn't have time to notice the words 'DECEPTION DRUG' written on the label.

She jumped up and found it strange as she looked around that the so-called hospital ward had only two beds and a nurse. The rest of the room was just windows and white walls. There was no medical equipment, no stethoscopes or trollies—in fact nothing—not even a clock or a calendar. But she didn't comment and went to the door. 'Thanks. Oh, Nurse, if yer'll excuse me, I think I'll just go and find me—ah—boyfriend.'

As she walked outside, she noticed that the sun had gone in and dusk had fallen, but what she couldn't tell was how long she had actually been there. She entered a large building that reminded her of an ancient museum and was shocked when she found out it was. The enormous hall was packed with everything from skeletons of prehistoric monsters to the first spaceship that took a man to the planet Mercury. There were spears and guns, chariots and racing cars, scrolls and computer screens, even ancient coins and credit cards. It seemed like all of history was housed here.

'Little Christian,' she yelled, and her voice echoed all around the large building.

'Over here, Angela,' came a reply. 'In between the carpenter's shop and the chocolate factory.' The building was so enormous that it took Angela another fifteen minutes to locate Little Christian.

He looked very busy. 'I thought you were never coming,' he joked. Angela stared at him. He looked so different—a pencil behind one ear, his hair grown long. He was wearing spectacles and also looked very pale and thin.

'How long 'ave we bin 'ere?' she enquired.

'I haven't got a clue,' shrugged Little Christian. 'Hours, days, weeks, months, maybe years. Who cares? This place is the place of my dreams and I am happy to stay here for ever.'

Angela's head was starting to hurt. 'Yeah,' she said, 'but I'm sure we woz goin' somewhere important before we came 'ere.'

'Rubbish,' chuckled Little Christian. 'There is nowhere as important as here.'

Angela's head was now pounding. Her mind was fighting the drug that she had been given. 'Yeah, but wot about— wot about—wot about—wot was 'is name?' Her head now screamed with pain. 'Yeah, wot about... the Voice?'

Little Christian pushed his glasses up onto the top of his head. 'Angela,' he said in a very condescending tone, 'that is what I am studying here—the history of the Manual and how we got to be where we are today. You cannot believe how helpful it's been. I feel like a new man with fascinating, fresh insights. Look, come with me and let me point out a few facts to you. Stop thinking—you're giving yourself a headache.

'Now what do you think they are?' he asked, pointing to a large, beautiful garden with two stuffed animals in it.

'They're monkeys,' Angela replied.

'Now that is where you are wrong! They are Newchurch's ancestors, Adam and Eve.'

'But they're not people, they're monkeys,' argued Angela.

'Listen, Angela, you must be open to learn. What I am discovering here is that the Voice never really created anything. For instance, did you know that billions of years ago a blob came from nowhere and everything evolved from that blob? First the blob became a jellyfish, the jellyfish became a pig, the pig became a monkey and the monkey became a human being.'

'Don't that sound a bit far-fetched?' asked Angela. 'Yer'd need a lot of faith ta believe that.'

'No, faith has got nothing to do with it,' continued Little Christian. 'It's a proven fact. An intelligent ex-monkey called Darly Charwin said so. Look, I've been studying here for ages while you have been asleep, and it seems to me that neither the Voice nor the Manual are all they are cracked up to be. Listen, let me show you two more things that actually prove that the Voice was just another human being like us. What do you think that is?' He pointed to a picture frame on the wall.

'It's a very old photo of a mum, a dad and a tiny baby.'

'Yes, that's right, an ordinary mum and dad with an ordinary baby. Read that little plaque next to it.'

Angela read it out loud. "'Ere is a picture of the Voice wiv 'is mum and dad. In the twentief century a bishop from Oldchurch proved wivout a shadow of doubt that there woz nofin' unusual or supernatural about the Voice's conception or parenthood. 'E was just a cute little baby wiv ordinary parents."

'Wow!' said Angela. 'But 'ow did 'e prove it?'

'I don't know,' said Little Christian, getting a little irritated. 'All I know is that these people are more clever than you or I will ever be, so they must be right. I mean no one threw the bishop out of Oldchurch for being a heretic, did they? So presumably all of Oldchurch must have agreed with what he taught.

'And what about this?' he went on, pulling her along to the far corner of the room. 'Look at that, a replica of the cross and the tomb. But according to scientific research the Voice never really died on the cross; he only fainted. Then when he was buried he got his strength back and then appeared to people pretending to have risen from the dead. Now read that board there,' he continued.

Angela read in big bold letters the words: 'MEDICAL RESEARCH CATEGORICALLY STATES THAT THERE IS NO SUCH THING AS RESURRECTION FROM THE DEAD.'

Little Christian stood back and started rubbing his arm.

'Wot's the trouble?' asked Angela.

'Well, Nurse Itbetter has to inject us each day to keep us healthy, and it must be due soon because I am starting to feel a bit strange.'

Sure enough, he had hardly finished his sentence when he heard the door of the building open and close and the clump of her shoes on the marble floor heading towards them.

'Little Christian, supposin' all that yer've learned is true, can ya answer me two questions? The first is wot use will it be even if ya fill all yer 'ead wiv all this knowledge if ya spend the rest of yer life in this 'ere quarry and secondly why—if ye'r learning so much vital information—are ya lookin' so thin and ill? At least the Voice seemed ta look after ya.'

Before he could answer the questions the nurse had arrived and asked them to roll up their sleeves. As he lifted his arm up he accidentally jogged the nurse and the vaccine bottle went flying through the air and smashed on the hard floor.

'I'm ever so sorry, Nurse,' said Little Christian.

'Oh, never mind,' said the nurse. 'I've plenty more where that came from. Get on with your studying and I'll just go and get another one.'

As the nurse left, Angela noticed the white wet label lying

in the vaccine. 'I wonder wot painkiller she's givin' us?' she said, picking it up. 'Oh no!' she gasped. 'Little Christian, read this!'

'DECEPTION DRUG... what does that mean?' he said.

'It means all this in 'ere is a pack of lies and a trick of the Enemy Superpowers to try and make us turn against the Voice.' She was beginning to sense the effects of the drug wearing off.

Little Christian was still under the influence of the drug. Along with the hours of lies he had been studying, it had taken its toll and numbed his once sharp mind.

Angela had to act quickly. 'Please, Voice, what do we do now?' she cried.

The Voice turned her head around and she saw a display of an altar drenched with water. By the side of it stood an old prophet who according to the Manual called down fire from heaven to prove the existence of the Voice. A table next to it contained a matchbox and a plaque which said, 'It was not possible for the Voice to send down fire from heaven, and it has been proved without any doubt that the prophet had a packet of these burnwater matches in his back pocket.'

Angela grabbed the matches, struck one and threw it on the altar. Immediately all the relics started to burn with amazing speed. She pulled Little Christian out of the door. The combination of the smell of smoke, the fresh air and the drug wearing off at last started bringing him back to his senses.

They ran as fast as they could and started to scramble up the quarry face. Although it was fairly steep there were plenty of footholds and handholds. It was like someone had gone before them and prepared it for them.

As they were nearing the top they heard a voice boom

out, 'Where do you think you are going?' Little Christian would have recognised that voice anywhere and turning around he saw the enormous body of Greedy Gutrot standing next to his evil mausoleum.

As Gutrot stood shouting and cursing, unaware that the mausoleum was on fire, he didn't notice that the fire had also started burning the bottom of his clothes. (Of course he couldn't have noticed this as his massive belly obscured his view!) It wasn't until he felt himself burning that he realised he was part of what was now an unquenchable blaze.

Little Christian and Angela reached the safety of the top just in time to see Gutrot and his evil creation melt into a gooey mess. 'That's the end of 'im,' cheered Angela.

'I'm afraid not,' said Little Christian. 'He will keep coming back until the day when the Voice finishes him off for good.'

Once back on the main path again they noticed a pretty little building called Restoration Cottage by the side of the road. It was all painted white and had the most beautiful sweetsmelling flowers growing all around it.

Little Christian opened his photomap. 'Hey, guess what?' he cheered. 'This belongs to the Voice. It's on the photomap. Let's stay here for a while as I must spend some time talking to him and also reading my Manual to get rid of all those evil lies that I have allowed to enter my brain.'

'Good idea,' said Angela, 'but first follow me.' She went into the cottage and on finding the kitchen she sat him down on a chair while she went rummaging through some kitchen drawers. 'Got 'em!' she yelled triumphantly, then seeing he was still wearing his spectacles took them off and threw them into the rubbish bin. 'Ya don't really want to keep any of Greedy Gutrot's souvenirs, do ya?' she chuckled. Then she pulled out from behind her back a shiny pair of scissors. 'And now for the hair.'

Little Christian gulped and hoped that he wouldn't end up like Samson.

Over the next few days he spent hours with the Manual. He read how he was made as a man in the Voice's image. He was pleased that he had never been a blob or a monkey. He also rediscovered about the Voice's miraculous conception to an ordinary woman—hardly more than a Littlekid herself, how his only Father was the one in heaven and finally how he was beaten up and killed, even had a spear pushed into his flesh to make sure that he was dead. And then after three days he came back to life again. 'How could I ever have believed those lies?' he thought. 'After all, if there had not been a resurrection there would be no Children of the Voice.'

9. ROBOTS RULE OK

Professor Mindwarpt couldn't help himself laughing out loud as he saw Harmony, weeping and confused, staggering over the rough rocks of the Bigwideworld but not having a clue about where she was going. 'Good,' he thought, rubbing his hands together in glee, 'another possible danger source I can cross off my list.'

Although he was reasonably happy with all the progress, he was also very angry that Heavy Shepherd and Lucy Morals had nearly blown the whole lot through some stupid lovey-doveyness—and worse still allowed a Littlekid on a skateboard to spy on them. 'When I've finished this assignment I will reprogram that pair of love-struck lilylivered lugbrains to be a couple of TV gameshow hosts. That will bring them down to earth!' He grinned.

His other worry was that none of his evil superbreeds seemed to be having any influence over the smaller Littlekids. It was as if they recognised the infiltrators, whereas the older ones didn't seem to notice.

He then opened two more of his coffins. 'Now for two nice ordinary superbreeds,' he muttered. 'We have enough at leadership level. Now it's time to hit grass roots!'

The first of his superbreeds to step out was a loudmouthed, simple character who was very theatrical and couldn't stop talking. He rarely thought—he just spoke. He was of medium build, wore a blue pinstripe suit and smart spectacles.

'Welcome, Namit Claimit,' said Mindwarpt. 'You should not only add a bit of yuppieness to Newchurch, but should also ensure that any faith in the Voice's supernatural power that may still be lurking around will soon evaporate.'

The second Littlekid was a young lady called Tiff Withallsorts—an ordinary Littlekid who would never stand out in a crowd. In fact, you would hardly notice she was there. Average size, average build, in fact the word 'average' would just about sum her up.

'Now, Tiff,' said Mindwarpt, 'I don't suppose I need to remind you that you need to be friends with all those who are discontented, and stir them up in everything. I even give you permission to stir things up against Heavy. After all, he's big enough and ugly enough to take care of himself,' he snarled.

Mindwarpt gave them the usual warning about if they were disobedient he would terminate them. Then after they had both said, 'Yes, O Mighty Supervoice,' he let them drift off to infiltrate Newchurch.

Rhoda sat prisoner, locked in a bedroom in Lucy Morals' and Dodgy Prophet's house. All she had left in the world was a skateboard and she couldn't even use that in this tiny room. It must have been a week since she had spoken to anyone, and she was really missing her friend Harmony. Although she was very frightened about what was happening in Newchurch she knew that she must escape and try to do something to help.

She'd already tried the windows and doors a number of times but there was no way she would get out through these. Then she had an idea. Once a day Lucy brought her some bread and water—opened the door, put them on a table, then walked out. This would be her only chance of escape.

While Rhoda was working out her plan, other very important plans were being discussed by all the members of Newchurch. Heavy stood up at the front, accompanied by Dodgy Prophet and Lucy Morals, and told all the people that he had some very exciting improvements and announcements to make. 'Amen,' said Dodgy, having already seen the proposals.

'First, we are changing the name of Newchurch.' The people gasped and whispered among themselves. 'Now don't look so surprised,' he continued. 'Two things I have always maintained is that we must not get stuck in a rut and we must learn to honour those in leadership over us.'

'Amen,' shouted Dodgy again.

'So we shall henceforth be known as the Newagechurch of the Heavy Shepherd.'

While the adults sat too frightened to move, a few of the Littlekids walked out in disgust.

'Secondly, we are all very sorry to hear that Buddy has had some sort of breakdown, so we feel it right to take him off the leadership for the time being for his own good. Obviously the strain of leadership was too much for him.'

The adults remembered what it was like when Little Christian, Angela and Harmony were around and sat thinking about it. The Littlekids also remembered those days and more left the meeting.

'Thirdly, first the bad news: Dodgy Prophet confided in me today that he and Lucy are, sadly, to be divorced. Of course they still have a great respect for each other, but as so often happens, they have found they are incompatible. Still, all is not lost because the good news is that Lucy has agreed to be my bride and Dodgy has agreed to be my best man.' Lucy smiled and Dodgy refrained from saying amen. The remainder of the Littlekids left the building.

'And, finally, our younger Littlekids are all getting a bit out of hand and rebellious, so I've decided that they will not be meeting with us adults any longer. "Family" is a word of the past anyway. I believe that the Voice has no time for these younger Littlekids—they just get in his way and ours. He is really only interested in us older ones. Lucy and I will take over the running of the Littlekids' meeting. We believe that there is a lot they can learn from us. We will have our first meeting tomorrow night in our ... I mean Lucy's house.' Of course, no littlekids were around to hear this statement.

As Heavy sat down, Dodgy stood up. 'Adults and Littlekids of the Newagechurch of the Heavy Shepherd: I believe you would want to join me in honouring our devoted leader and his new bride by a gift. I suggest that we build them a house, a nice brand new two-bed-roomed bungalow.'

'Rubbish,' shouted a voice in the congregation.

Heavy leaped up with a red face, ready to take some heavy authority, but Dodgy kept in firm control. 'Who said that?' he shouted.

'I did,' said a stranger walking to the front.

'Who on earth are you?' said Dodgy and Heavy together. 'We've never seen you before.'

'My name is Namit Claimit,' he shouted, standing at the front. 'And I think that it's a disgrace. If our leader is half as good as you say he is, then he and his new bride should have a *twenty*-bedroomed mansion, with an indoor swimming pool, colour televisions and a jaccuzi in every room, including the kitchen.'

Heavy looked stunned. Dodgy looked embarrassed, and Lucy looked thrilled. Everyone else looked towards the door. 'Of course it's right, what you are saying,' said Dodgy, 'but I'm not sure we've got that sort of money.'

Namit looked at the people. 'Hands up all those who believe that nothing is too hard for the Voice.' Everyone's hand went up. 'Right,' he said. 'Now hands up all those who believe that the Voice loves his children and wants to give them the best.'

Again all hands went up.

'Well, come on, Children of the Voice, let's not only believe for it, but let's name it before each other, then claim it from the Voice. After all, the Voice is no man's debtor.'

Everyone followed Namit's instructions.

'Now,' continued Dodgy, 'I believe that faith without works is dead, as the Manual says. So I suggest that on Friday night when you all get your paypackets, you bring them unopened into the office. Here we will open them for you and put nine-tenths of the money into the mansion fund and give you back a tenth.'

'Brilliant,' said Namit Claimit. 'Amazing, faithbuilding incentive. If you don't feel that you can live on the tenth, name the amount of money you need, then claim it from the Voice. Remember, his resources are unlimited and this is a surefire way to make the Children of the Voice children of mighty faith.'

The meeting closed, but everyone was asked to stay for an hour to thank the Voice for the opportunity that had been entrusted to them to provide for his work.

Unbeknown to the leaders, however, a note was being passed around the hall advertising a special meeting that had been secretly arranged for all those who were fed up with Heavy Shepherd's dictatorship. The meeting would be held in the home of a new member, Tiff Withallsorts.

While people were praying, Lucy slipped out of the side door and ran home, remembering that it was time to feed Rhoda. She was very excited at the prospect of the forthcoming marriage and even more about the forthcoming mansion; she didn't really have her mind on what she was doing. She put Rhoda's bread and water on a tray and whistled away happily to herself as she climbed the stairs.

This was Rhoda's big night, maybe her last chance to escape. The bedroom was dark as she had closed the curtains and was lying in wait behind the cupboard. She heard footsteps coming up the stairs; the lock clicked, then the bedroom door opened.

In the gloom and half-light Lucy didn't realise that she had put her right foot onto a skateboard. The minute the foot made contact, the skateboard took off, taking the screaming Lucy with it. The tray with the bread and water was thrown into the air while the skateboard stopped abruptly at the wall. Lucy, however, did not stop. The skateboard had stopped directly below the window and she continued on, flying head-first straight through it.

Rhoda leaped out from behind the cupboard, screaming as she heard the glass shatter. 'What have I done?' she yelled, not daring to look out of the window, frightened at what she might see. Rhoda grabbed her skateboard, rushed downstairs and ran for her life through the back door.

On the concrete underneath the window lay Lucy Morals. Not dead or lying in a pool of blood as Rhoda would have expected to see... but disassembled with wires hanging out and sparks flying everywhere.

The Littlekids who had left the meeting early stood gazing at the sizzling remains of the electronic Lucy and realised for the first time that their enemies were not flesh and blood. They'd seen too much. From now on life would be dangerous for them. They must go into hiding; they must take Newchurch underground.

10. DEADBODY

Professor Mindwarpt, who was usually so observant, was in his hideout overlooking Newshurch; but he failed to notice a frightened little girl carrying a skateboard run past him. He was far too busy trying to work out why one of his superbreeds had ceased to function.

Back at Newchurch a heartbroken Heavy Shepherd had found the remains of Lucy—fortunately before any of the adults had seen her. Quickly he had gathered her up in a sack and hidden her in a shed around the back of his house with the intention of taking her back to the Professor as soon as possible to see if she could be repaired. As he hid her, thinking his secret was safe, he failed to see that dozens of little eyes were watching his every move.

These same little eyes had found sanctuary in the cellar underneath the meeting hall. They spent the days reading their Manuals, spying on the invaders and praying to the Voice that Little Christian would return.

On seeing that Rhoda Skateboard had escaped and was obviously the cause of the demise of his beloved, he immediately circulated a news letter to all members explaining that Rhoda had not only gone missing, but she had also become violent and totally uncontrollable. In his opinion she had allowed an Enemy Superpower to come in and control her life.

'If anyone sees her or hears of her whereabouts, he should not approach her. She is dangerous. He must contact Heavy Shepherd immediately who, along with some experienced helpers, will give her the attention she requires. This is for her own good.'

Heavy also went on to say that no younger Littlekids had turned up to his meeting: 'Rumour has it that they have vanished. If any of these younger Littlekids are caught, they must be brought directly to me, so that I can serve them the appropriate punishment for rebellion.'

With no mention of Lucy, the letter finished.

Little Christian and Angela felt fully refreshed and restored as they entered the gates of Deadbody. It was a strange sort of place, reminiscent of Oldchurch yet with many different features. The strangest thing was that all the adults and Littlekids had smiles on their faces which were just like masks. They were obviously not happy, yet these grins tried to put over the impression that they were.

They also either wore bright red clothes or dull grey ones.

Another unusual feature was that their skin was white. In fact they really did look like walking corpses with happy faces. Angela leaned over and whispered that a few days ago she had thought that Little Christian had looked unhealthy, but she was very thankful that he had never looked like these people... though she would have loved to see Little Christian in one of the trendy red outfits.

In spite of all their strange features, the occupants of Deadbody did seem to be caring people, especially those dressed in red. One lady in red, called Mrs Ownway, beckoned them over to her house and invited them in for a cup of tea. As they entered Chalk and Cheese Cottage and sat down she pointed over to her husband who was seated with his head buried in a book and apologised that he was a grey. Her husband just grunted with a smile.

Little Christian and Angela glanced around the room and were not surprised that all its contents were either grey or red depending on whether they belonged to the husband or the wife.

Mrs Ownway explained that they had a couple of spare bedrooms and offered to put up Little Christian and Angela up for the night, apologising that the colour of the rooms might not be to their liking. But Little Christian and Angela explained that they had no preference between red and grey. Both the husband and wife looked shocked.

After a short chat both the Ownways got up and explained that it was time for their meeting. Little Christian and Angela said that they would go with them.

The church building was only a short walk away from the house. Little Christian was interested to note that the outside of the building looked absolutely awful. It was like two opposing building companies had started building from different ends and had used different plans. It was also a mixture of the grey stones from Oldchurch and the new, bright-red bricks he associated with Newchurch.

As they walked through the large doors he was again stunned by what he saw. To start with all the reds gave each other a welcoming hug, while the greys stood their distance and firmly shook each other by the hand. Little Christian and Angela, being visitors, both got a hug and a handshake each.

Then all the people in red were handed just the new half of the Manual, a songsheet and a tambourine. They all sat down on modern red plastic chairs on the left side of the building. All the people in grey, however, were handed just the old half of the Manual, an ancient hymnbook and a candle and they all sat on hard wooden benches on the right side.

Little Christian and Angela, being visitors, were handed both halves of the Manual, a songsheet and a hymnbook, plus of course the tambourine and the candle. They needed a shopping trolley to carry it all! They decided after a lot of thought to sit on the red chairs, purely because they looked more comfortable.

At the front of the building on the left side, facing them, stood a rock band dressed in red. They had a large public address system, an electronic drum kit, a stack of keyboards, lead and bass guitars, plus a whole brass section. By contrast, on the right at the front was a massive old wind organ with enormous great metal pipes stretching to the ceiling.

As things were about to start, two doors opened—one on the left and one on the right. Out walked seven leaders in red and seven leaders in grey who sat in their appropriate places facing their appropriate people. Then, from a door in the middle, a man who was obviously the chief leader entered wearing a suit that was exactly divided: fifty per cent red down one side and fifty per cent grey down the other. He even wore one red sock and shoe and one grey sock and shoe. Around his neck he had a whistle and in his hands a stop-watch and a notebook.

'Wot on earth 'ave we come to 'ere?' whispered Angela.

'That's our full-time ref.' explained a helpful red lady sitting next to her, who had to Angela's embarrassment overheard her whisper.

All went silent as a red and a grey leader rose together. The grey leader was the first to speak, 'We will begin to give thanks to the Voice by singing hymn number 301.'

'Excuse me,' said the red leader, still smiling of course, 'I do believe that it is our turn to begin this morning.' Then turning to the people in red he announced that they would begin to celebrate the Voice with song number 3 on their songsheets.

'I'm sorry,' said the leader in grey before a note had been struck, 'but you are offside.'

The whistle blew and, taking a coin from his pocket, the ref asked the grey leader to call heads or tails. The greys won. 'Greys start with hymn number 301. This will immediately be followed by the reds' song number 3.'

The mighty organ pounded out the music as the greys stood as upright and still as statues singing the words of their favourite hymn 'The Voice of old is the Voice we love'. The reds ignored them, while some even yawned.

The minute they finished and sat down, the red musicians' amplifiers were switched on. With the accompanying shriek of feedback, the chairs were pushed back and those dressed in red started to leap around bashing tambourines. Everything was at full volume as they too sang one of their favourite songs:

> Hallelujah, Voice,
> Hallelujah, Voice,
> Voice Hallelujah,
> Hallelujah, Voice.

Although the whole song was only made up of two words, they still managed to make it last twice as long as the greys' hymn. During this time the greys shook their heads and put their fingers in their ears.

As they sat down Angela and Little Christian looked at each other in disgust. 'This is terrible,' they both whispered at the same time.

The ref stood up and announced that due to the length of the reds' song, the greys now had five minutes' penalty time added on. 'It is now time for prayers,' announced the ref. looking at his notebook. 'Greys to start.'

Then the greys reopened their hymnbooks and read out some of the hymns, this time as prayers. The reds muttered 'religious' and 'contrived' under their breaths.

Then came the reds' turn. They all stood up and started speaking in what they claimed to be the Voice's special language, which of course no one understood—not even the Voice. The greys just stared at them as though they had one sandwich short in their picnic baskets.

At the end the ref stood up and holding up a yellow card told the reds that this was their first official public warning. Once again they had gone into overtime and it was his job to see that both sides prayed fairly. He also knew that later on in the meeting the reds would try and take a further unfair advantage with a healing session; they would be sure to take that into injury time.

The two preachers were about to begin. Just as the grey Littlekids who were forced to go out were preparing to go to their babysitters and the red Littlekids who were forced to stay in were climbing into their sleeping bags on the floor—Little Christian could suffer no more.

'Wait!' he yelled, walking to the front. 'I've come to bring you word from the Voice.'

The red leaders and the grey leaders stared at each other, still smiling of course, each thinking that the other was trying to gain an unfair advantage by bringing on a substitute.

'OK, Littlekid,' said the ref, 'but you will first have to tell me whose side you are on so that I can allow extra time to the others.'

'I'm on the Voice's side,' shouted Little Christian.

'Yes, and so are we,' said the reds and the greys spontaneously together.

'No, you're not. Neither of you are,' screamed back Little Christian. 'Will you please listen to me just for a few minutes? Then I will explain.'

'OK,' said the ref stopping his watch. 'I'll count this as halftime.'

Little Christian turned and looked at the ref. 'Why is he smiling all the time?' he asked. 'And why are you smiling all the time?' he said, pointing at the people.

'Because we are happy,' they all shouted back.

'No you're not,' argued Little Christian, 'you're just pretending, you're being unreal.'

'Go on. Sock it to 'em,' yelled a loyal supporter from the back, and Little Christian guessed who that was.

'That's a great idea, Angela,' he shouted back. 'Watch this, everyone,' and turning around he whacked the ref in the face. The people gasped, but then they saw the ref's face start to crack. The smiling mask fell to pieces and smashed on the floor like china. And there looking at everyone was a ref with a very sad real face.

'Now, the rest of you. I dare you to have the courage to face up to what you are really like,' shouted Little Christian. 'Go on—if you really care for the person sitting next to you, smack him or her in the face.'

Everyone hesitated for a minute, then, as the red and grey leaders walked over and started smacking each other, everyone else joined in. Masks shattered, cracked and splintered to the floor all around the building. In no time at all, a large number of sad real people sat facing the front.

Little Christian walked over to one of the grey leaders and asked him why he was there.

'We greys have been here since the beginning. This is our building. Even the walls were a revered grey to start with until the reds built on their obscene brick extensions. We enjoy worshipping the Voice in our own old-fashioned way, and we refuse to let the reds take us over with their fancy gimmicks.'

Little Christian walked over to a red leader and asked him why he was there. 'This is where the Voice has called us to be. We are here to bring change and new vision to the greys. We don't like it here and get very little from the meetings, but that's not the point. We must stay here and annoy the greys till the Voice tells us it's time to move on.'

Little Christian walked up to the ref. 'Why are you here?' he enquired.

The ref looked at him sadly. 'Many years ago I came to teach folk more about the Voice and the Manual, but that never came about. With two opposing stubborn teams both claiming to be right, it's been more than a full-time job just to keep the peace. I do wonder how much longer I can carry on in the middle though. It really takes it out of me, and my health and friendship with the Voice are suffering.'

'Good news! The Voice has an answer for all of you if you are willing to listen,' said Little Christian, turning back to face the people. 'My friend Angela is one of the Voice's directors, and I believe the Voice has already been speaking to her so that she can come and give you a solution to this terrible mess.'

Angela walked to the front with one hand covering her face. 'Are you all right,' enquired Little Christian, wondering if she was still praying.

'Of course I am, ya nitwit,' whispered Angela. 'It's just that thanks to yer hair-brained scheme of everyone slappin' each other's chops, one over-enthusiastic red slapped mine, but as ya well know I'm not wearin' a mask to protect me.' She pulled her hand down to reveal a lovely black eye. Little Christian couldn't help smiling. 'I'll sort ya out later,' she said, deliberately standing on his toe.

Fortunately, Angela's whack on the face had not stopped her from hearing what the Voice wanted to say. She explained that it was right that the greys should be allowed to continue to worship the Voice in this building in their own way. She suggested that the Voice had not told the reds to stay here and be disgruntled. In fact they were deceived and actually restricting the Voice's plans. The Voice was not interested in where people worshipped, she said, but he was concerned that they did worship and were happy and real people who honoured and loved their leaders. Angela suggested that the reds should meet in their local school hall as from next week as it would be much more appropriate for what they wanted to do.

'But that will destroy our unity,' said the ref.

Little Christian butted in, 'What unity? Sadly, at this stage there is no unity, and to keep up this pretence will never materialise. Unity will come as people live for the Voice, learn to respect those who may differ from them in certain things, but also are part of a church in which they feel secure and at home. Believe it or not,' Little Christian went on, 'to separate will actually bring you closer together. If you allow personal conflict and competition to be a thing of the past, you can then really unite in a plan that is going to help the real needy, those lost out there in the Bigwideworld.'

Angela was looking at the ref. 'Drop the name "ref." Ya don't need it any longer. The Voice tells me that there is a place waitin' for ya at the Trainin' Module if ya want it. Ye'r damaged, and ya need a few repairs.'

Immediately the ex-ref jumped up and without needing to be told twice ran out of the door. Both Little Christian and Angela guessed that he probably wouldn't stop running until he reached the Training Module.

Both the red and grey leaders could see the sense in what Little Christian and Angela had said, and would give the separate meetings and the unity a try. With that, the building emptied.

Later, Little Christian and Angela sat exhausted in the living room of Chalk and Cheese Cottage too tired even to talk. Angela had a steak over her bruised eye while Little Christian just lay back in his chair sniffing the paint fumes; their hosts were racing around the house painting everything... green!

11. the Last resort

'Psst.'

The Littlekid jumped. 'Who's there?' she cried, staring at a large thick bush in front of her.

'Are you by yourself?' the voice continued.

'Yes,' said the Littlekid, 'but who are you?'

The bush swept to one side as Harmony came out from behind it.

'Harmony!' shouted Rhoda, running up and giving her a hug. 'I thought I would never see you again.'

The two girls sat down and Rhoda related all the latest news from Newchurch. After Rhoda had finished sobbing and talking, Harmony stood up and declared that if Heavy and his evil mob wanted a war, she was prepared to give him one.

'Oh, I've never heard you speak like this before,' exclaimed Rhoda. 'I'm frightened. After all, these are very dangerous people we are going to be fighting against.'

'That's true,' said Harmony. 'But what is the difference between us and them?'

Rhoda thought for a moment then with a big beam on her face said, 'I know—we have the Voice on our side.'

'Yes, and nobody is more powerful than he is. What we are going to do now is spend some time talking to the Voice. Then we will go out and find some recruits to help us. Heavy Shepherd... your days are numbered.'

'Yeah!' shouted Rhoda excitedly as they knelt down to talk to the Voice.

As darkness was closing in, a large figure crept out of the back door of his house and undid his shed door. He put a sack over his shoulder and, making sure that no one was following him, crept through Newchurch and made his way into the Bigwideworld.

Once a safe distance away he started whispering, 'O Mighty Supervoice, O Mighty Supervoice.'

'What are you doing here?' came a gruff reply from behind a rock. Out stepped Professor Mindwarpt who stared at Heavy Shepherd. 'Did I give you permission to come and find me?' he yelled angrily. 'You are made to obey, not take your own initiative.'

'Yes, but this is different, O Mighty Supervoice,' said Heavy, grovelling at his feet. 'This is a matter of life and death.'

'Well it certainly is,' said Mindwarpt, 'and it will probably be a matter of your life and death.'

Heavy got up and pointed to the sack. 'Please, O Mighty Supervoice, can I show you what's in here?'

'Oh, for goodness sake get on with it! The sooner you do, the sooner you can get back to where you should be.'

Heavy opened the sack, tipped the contents out in front of the Professor, then jumped back in amazement.

'Very interesting,' said Mindwarpt. 'But I have seen a pile of bricks before.'

'What has happened to my Lucy?' wailed Heavy. 'I put her in this sack after she fell through a window and went out of action, and I was hoping that you would repair her, O Mighty Supervoice.' Heavy began to blub.

'Now this is serious,' said Mindwarpt, stroking his chin thoughtfully. 'Lucy's termination is of no concern to me, but I thought that like a normal person you would have buried her and no one would have known that she wasn't a normal Littlekid. But now someone has her remains and realises that an invasion has taken place.' The Professor then turned and walked away from Heavy Shepherd. 'Wait here,' he ordered.

A few minutes later he came back with what was the last of his superbreeds. Heavy looked at the Littlekid facing him and stepped back in fear. This Littlekid had a face with no emotion and eyes that were as cold as ice. His body was bulging with muscle and he looked like he had the strength of at least ten normal Littlekids. He was the meanest, nastiest Littlekid imaginable.

'Heavy Shepherd, meet Percy... Percy Cutor. From now on, Heavy, this is your right-hand man. I don't want any more democratic meetings. I don't want anyone else getting in my way, and Percy will help you achieve this. Percy, your first task is to find who has got the remains of Lucy and then you must not only eliminate that person, but see that there is no trace left of Lucy's remains, either.'

Heavy winced at the thought.

'Now move along, you two, time is running out and we have just been given a new assignment in a place called Deadbody, starting in a couple of weeks' time.'

Little Christian and Angela left Deadbody, their Commission completed. They hoped their work had been successful, but really now it was up to the people to act on what they had heard.

'It would 'ave bin so much easier if we could 'ave forced 'em ta listen to the Voice,' commented Angela.

'Yeah, you're right,' replied Little Christian. 'But you know as well as I do that the Voice does not force us to do things. He wants us to obey him because we love him.'

'Yeah,' agreed Angela. 'I know that, but it still would 'ave bin a whole lot easier.' She grabbed hold of Little Christian's hand. 'Well, wot do ya really fink of me?' she asked boldly.

'Um,' said Little Christian carefully, 'I suppose I quite like you really.'

'Is that all?' said Angela, smiling. 'Don't ya love me and fink that we make a good team and might 'ave a future togever?' she continued.

'I'll let you know when we are back in the safety of Newchurch,' laughed Little Christian.

'Promise?' said Angela.

'Yeah, I promise,' said Little Christian. 'I can't wait to get back to see all our friends in Newchurch,' he continued changing the subject. 'And according to the photomap there is a short-cut, so it shouldn't take us long to get there.'

'That's great,' said Angela. ' It's like the Voice wants us to get back quickly. Perhaps they are missing us.'

'I'm sure they are,' replied little Christian.

'I don't like it here much,' whispered Rhoda. 'It's lonely

and creepy, all dark and misty. I can't see anything that is living anywhere. It's all just like a big slag heap, and all these tombstones everywhere really give me the creeps. What are we here for, Harmony?'

'Well, Rhoda, this is the place people come to when they feel fed up with life and cannot see any point in living. This really is their last resort. If you keep walking for a few more kilometres you come to a big screen that hangs down from the sky called the final curtain. Once you go through that screen you never come back.'

'Well, that's cheered me up,' said Rhoda. 'But surely things haven't got that bad for us?'

Harmony smiled. 'No, and they never will for Children of the Voice. But I have a friend who is always hanging around here hoping to rescue people and stop them before they reach the final curtain.'

Then suddenly they heard a voice shouting out from quite a distance in front of them. 'Turn back from the final curtain. Believe in the Voice, then leave this death and darkness and experience light and life!'

'Ah, that sounds like just the person we are looking for. Is that you, Hearthunter?' shouted Harmony.

A figure seemed to come rushing out of nowhere towards them and gave both the girls a hug. 'Wow! It's great to see a friendly face,' he exclaimed. 'I've had one of those days when no one seems to listen to me. In fact they just ignore me.'

Harmony explained that she knew how he felt, but that she had some very important news to share with him regarding Newchurch. She wondered if he could spare the time to listen, then maybe to help them.

'No sweat,' he said. 'I've loads of my mates patrolling this patch twenty-four hours a day; they'll cover for me. Follow me and I'll take you out of this doom and gloom. Then you can tell me what the problem is.'

Hearthunter heard the tragic news, and tears came into his eyes. 'But we thought that Newchurch was invincible. We were convinced that we were strong and could never get into these sorts of problems. Maybe we were a bit too proud and complacent.'

'It would be good if we could find Miraclekid on the way back. We may need his gifts to sort these Littlekids out.'

'How will we find him?' asked Rhoda.

'Well, that's the problem,' said Hearthunter. 'Nobody ever finds Miraclekid. He finds you. By the way, does Little Christian know all about what's been going on?'

'I don't think he does,' replied Harmony.

'Well, when's he due back there?' asked Hearthunter.

'Again, I'm not sure,' said Harmony, 'but it must be any day now.'

'We'd better move quickly,' Hearthunter then continued. 'If Little Christian arrives back before us unaware of what has happened, he won't have a chance, He must be at the top of their hitlist!'

12. faults in the foundations

Tiff Withallsorts was achieving wonders. She had different groups meeting in her home every day and called her meetings 'The Back to the Voice Group'. It was thrilling for her to see that more and more people were becoming negative and critical.

She convinced one group that the name 'The Newagechurch of the Heavy Shepherd' was far too long and thought that they should abbreviate it to just

'Newagechurch'. After she had persuaded them all to agree, she then asked them what was the matter with the name 'Newagechurch' and in no time they were all arguing with each other again about what it should be called.

As Heavy's mansion was beginning to be built she asked an interior design group to discuss the interior. Again, within an hour, they were all at each other's throats, all of them thinking that their own ideas were the best.

She also started a men's group and began the meeting by congratulating them on their giving towards the project, but then managed to persuade them to say what they were earning. She enquired if it was fair that some were earning more than others and some were giving more than others. Yet again voices were raised as jealousy and anger reigned.

Namit Claimit had become a firm favourite with the Children of the Voice and had started his own Faithschool. So far there had been only two minor disasters. The first was when he encouraged his schoolchildren to jump off the hospital roof, claiming that the Voice would catch them before they reached the ground. Unfortunately, as the first person jumped, the Voice decided not to catch him. The rest came down and visited their friend inside the hospital, where he now lay wrapped up in bandages.

The second occasion was when he had a family faith-building session and he decided to pass around a very large snake and said that they must not be afraid to handle it. The faith level immediately shot up when he explained that the snake was not poisonous, but sank rapidly when the enormous snake decided to swallow one of the Littlekids.

Percy Cutor had been very quiet and laid-back since he arrived. He just seemed to watch and listen and take everything in. Heavy and Dodgy didn't trust him, mainly because he was so quiet and they were not. Lucy's remains and the younger Littlekids had still not been found and everyone, especially the men, were beginning to ask where Lucy was. Heavy sent out a special news letter saying that she had just gone away for a short while to see her parents and to tell them about the good news of her marriage.

Buddy meanwhile continued to lie in the hospital ward. He was getting no better. In fact, he was growing weaker all the time.

The Professor sat in the sun enjoying the feeling of success. The Children of the Voice had already started leaving Newchurch and rushing back to the security and stability of another Oldchurch, full of repentance. He could almost hear them apologising that they hadn't listened to their elders when they had warned them that Littlekids could never run a church or be of any use to the Voice.

Just as he sat there dreaming, a big cloud blotted out the sun. He opened his eyes to see it wasn't in fact a cloud but a singed, charred fat man called Greedy Gutrot.

'Well done, Gutrot!' said the Professor, laughing at his hilarious choice of phrase.

'Listen here, you, no jokes!' screamed Gutrot. 'This is no laughing matter.'

'Oh forgive me, I am sorry, sir,' continued Mindwarpt, 'but there's no need to get all fired up!' And again he went into cackles of laughter until Gutrot trod on his special cage and crushed it.

'Now will you shut up?' he said.

The Professor was hurt about having his cage wrecked; but looking at the angry mountain standing next to him, he didn't feel that now was a wise time to tell him.

As Mindwarpt explained that Newchurch was nearly all over, Gutrot calmed down and sat alongside him. He made him repeat the story again and again as he so loved to hear it. And of course each time the Professor told the story he would add extra little bits to make his plots seem even more of an achievement.

After the fifth telling, Mindwarpt asked Gutrot how he had fared against Little Christian. Gutrot immediately started to get angry again as he recollected that he had almost had him. 'Thanks to some stupid girl, he got away.'

The Professor looked up with interest. 'A girl, you say? Can you describe this girl to me?'

'Well,' said Gutrot, 'she was an ordinary looking Littlekid in her early teens, I would guess. Obviously quite experienced in the Voice's service. Skinny—oh, yeah, I know—she spoke with a funny accent.'

Mindwarpt leaped to his feet. 'Angela!' he bellowed. 'You are describing Angela.'

'So what?' said Gutrot, amazed at how the Professor had suddenly become so incensed.

'One of my top superbreeds, Percy Cutor, had given her hours of special attention and put her through the most excrutiating torture that any Littlekid has ever experienced. I heard it with my own ears. How in the name of all that's evil did she manage to live?'

Gutrot and Mindwarpt were so wrapped up in their conversation that they failed to noticed two excited Littlekids walking by them with their arms around each other. They had been on a long journey, but they were now just minutes away from Newchurch.

13. trash metal

As Harmony, Rhoda and Hearthunter jogged along the path leading to Newchurch they suddenly heard the most awful noise they had ever heard coming from behind a large hill on their left.

'What's that?' asked Rhoda as they all ground to a halt.

Hearthunter's ears pricked up and suddenly his face grew very excited. 'Wow! If that's what I think it is, we must get over there straight away,' he said enthusiastically.

'Wait a minute,' replied Harmony, looking a little bit concerned. 'You yourself said it was urgent that we find

Miraclekid then rush back to Newchurch in case Little Christian and Angela beat us there.'

'Did I?' said Hearthunter with a deliberately forgetful memory. 'Yes I probably did,' he admitted, looking at the frown that had appeared on Rhoda's face. 'Even so,' he continued, 'I'm a Hearthunter and I must get my priorities right. Over that hill there are needy people who have never heard of the Voice. I mean, at least we know that the Voice will protect Little Christian and Angela.'

Neither Harmony nor Rhoda could argue with that. They also knew that when Hearthunter got even a sniff of a lost Littlekid, nothing would distract him until he had gone and shared the good news of the Voice with him.

Hearthunter told them that they could either walk on slowly or they could come with him. Both the girls decided to follow him, as they did not know where they would find Miradekid and certainly did not want to enter Newchurch without Hearthunter.

As they climbed up the steep, grass-covered hill, the noise became louder and louder; and when they reached the top, Hearthunter cheered. The two girls could not believe their eyes.

At the bottom of the hill they saw a very large stage with enormous speakers at either side. On the stage stood four Littlekids. Two had guitars in their hands; one was playing a very large golden drum kit and the fourth was leaping around the stage twirling a microphone stand, looking like an overgrown drum majorette.

'What on earth are they?' shouted Rhoda as they descended the hill towards them and the noise reached an ear-shattering level.

'Well, they probably like to think they are musicians,' Hearthunter shouted back over the racket. 'Why I am so excited,' he continued, 'is because even though on first hearing they do not sound brilliant, I know the Voice is always on the look-out for people with some sort of musical ability that he can train up.'

'But they have no audience,' observed Harmony, also joining in the shouting.

'They don't need an audience,' laughed Hearthunter, recognising the style of music they were trying to play. 'They only play for their own ego. They think they are superior to anything else around, especially girls.'

As they approached the stage totally unnoticed by the performers, Hearthunter told them to try and listen to the words of the song they were singing. It was hard to recognise them with the accompanying din, but they did manage to pick out some of them.

> We hate chicks, yeah,
> Their brains are missing
> They're good for work, yeah,
> And for kissin'.
> But chicks they love us, yeah,
> They need us bad,
> 'Cos we're the best things, yeah,
> They ever had.
> 'Cos we're the best things, yeah,
> They ever had, Yeah, Yeah, Yeah...

'What a load of chauvinistic rubbish!' shouted Rhoda angrily. Seeing a socket at the foot of the stage, she walked straight to it and pulled out the plug.

It took a few minutes before the band realised that they had now gone into a drum solo and that no noise was coming out of their amplifiers. The one who was shouting out the words put down his microphone stand, then rushed to the drummer and told him to stop playing. 'Something's wrong!' he shrieked.

The drummer was enjoying himself far too much to stop, however, and his thrashing continued till he was pushed off his stool and was seen rolling around the stage on the floor. In no time the two guitarists joined in, and all four starting hitting and fighting each other.

Eventually everything went quiet as the arguing died down and Hearthunter, Harmony and Rhoda climbed up on the stage and walked towards them.

'Don't they look weird?' whispered Rhoda as she looked at their waist-length hair, dark sunglasses, leather jackets and skin-tight leather jeans to match. The leather was decorated with vicious-looking studs and chains. 'They need to look like that because they think it gives them a macho image,' whispered Hearthunter.

The microphone man, obviously the leader, walked over to the three Children of the Voice and pulled his hair out of his sunglasses to see who was there.

'Oi! Wot's your game?' he shouted, looking at them. 'Wos it one of you wot pulled our plug out?'

'Yes, I did,' retorted Rhoda very boldly. 'Just who do you think you are to sing such rubbish about girls?'

'Who are we?' said the singer, laughing. 'Did you hear that, boys?' he yelled to the rest of the band as they all straightened their dishevelled clothes and got off the floor.

'We only happen to be the heaviest, most famous, most wicked trash metal band in the Bigwideworld.' He then started his big introduction as though he were facing an audience of thousands.

'OK, you bozos. Right on, yeah! On drums we have *the* master of percussion... Stix Insect!' Seeing there was no audience reaction or applause, he continued, '*The* unforgettable genius on bass guitar is... uh—' temporarily forgetting his name '—Oh yeah... Tuneless Wonder!' Still no applause. 'And the fastest fingers in the West on lead guitar, may I present to you... Twang Fretfull!' Utter silence.

'And last but not least, mister wailing wall of sound himself... yours truly... Mac Throatsore!'

The band politely clapped their leader. 'Thank you, thank you, thank you, fans,' he shouted with all the panache of a mega-mega-star. 'Enough, enough,' he continued with his arms raised, long after the band had stopped applauding him anyway.

'Put all those four together and what have you got?' he said, building to a final big crescendo.

'Oh get on with it,' whispered Harmony, thinking they should be well on their way to Newchurch by now.

'Headbangers of the Bigwideworld we bring to you *the* loudest, heaviest, most digusting, scruffiest, most controversial, most wicked metal band sound of all time... '*The*... *Daisy Chains*!'

At this point all four members of the band leaped around the stage deliriously cheering, shouting and applauding themselves. After five minutes they all sat down, exhausted. (Obviously their self-admiration had worn them out, Harmony explained to Rhoda.)

'Well, it's great to meet you guys,' said Hearthunter, now taking over and ignoring the girls' comments. After introducing himself and his two friends, he started to explain that life was more than just loud music and putting girls down. He explained they could become brand new clean Littlekids if only they started loving the Voice instead of themselves.

Although Stix, Tuneless, Twang and Mac were not the

most intelligent of Littlekids he had ever met, they listened with great interest as Hearthunter was now getting into top gear and explaining all about the Voice and how he went through terrible pain and suffering because he loved Littlekids like them.

'Yeah, but does he love our music?' interrupted Stix, who was even slower than the rest at catching on.

'I'm sure the Voice loves all kinds of music, including yours,' continued Hearthunter, 'but the problem is that a lot of Littlekids who play your kind of music are very much under the influence of the Enemy Superpower. And certainly you'd need to change the words of your songs.'

'Let me put it another way,' concluded Hearthunter. 'Both your lifestyle and your music are self-indulgent. If you want to become Children of the Voice, you stop doing just what you want to do and you start living to please the Voice. He must come before your music, your image and even your personal ambitions for fame.'

As the Voice was speaking to the four musicians at the same time as Hearthunter, it didn't take the band long to realise that they were really missing out. There on that vast stage they knelt down before the presence of the Voice and asked him to make them his children.

Hearthunter then explained that they now needed to go to the Voice's Training Module to learn more about the Voice; he gave them directions on how to get there. 'I'd take your instruments with you, if I were you,' he explained. 'The Voice will always use a talent as long as it's within his control.'

As Hearthunter, Harmony and Rhoda jumped off the stage and headed back to the Newchurch path, Mac shouted after them. 'Hey, just two more heavy questions I wanna lay on you guys.'

'What are they?' replied Hearthunter.

'The first is...' he began, looking very embarrassed, 'could you tell us what a chick looks like? I don't think we'd know one if we saw one.'

'We are girls,' shouted Harmony and Rhoda, leaping up and down together, waving their arms in the air.

'Wow! Way out, baby...' gasped Mac in amazement. 'You're much better than I would have guessed. In fact, you're human, just like us. I was always under the impression that you were just sort of... very uncool, unintelligent animals.'

'Well from now on you had better start respecting girls as people and stop treating them like "uncool, unintelligent animals," said Harmony.

'Yeah, baby, right on!' said Mac. 'The other question is this: do you think the Voice will find our name "The Daisy Chains" too uncool, way out or offensive?'

Hearthunter tried to stop himself bursting into laughter. 'Ah no, I think that the Voice might just be able to cope with such a controversial name,' he said.

The band was obviously thrilled, and Hearthunter, Harmony and Rhoda set off back over the hill. 'A worthwhile intermission,' said Hearthunter, excited as always at the opportunity of introducing Littlekids to the Voice. 'Who knows? One day they may be our worship band in Newchurch.'

'Yes, if there is any Newchurch still left to be part of,' sighed Harmony, grasping hold of Rhoda's hand.

'I guess you're right,' said Hearthunter thoughtfully. 'I think we should forget about trying to find Miraclekid and make our way straight to Newchurch.'

The others agreed, and away they went, singing the Littlekids' Marching Song.

14. Locked up—in a Lock-up situation

Although the sun was shining brightly and it was the middle of the afternoon, Little Christian and Angela were surprised that the streets were deserted as they walked into Newchurch.

I wonder where everyone is? thought Little Christian. He had never known a time when there were not loads of happy, noisy younger Littlekids running around playing all over the place.

Little did they know that although they could see no one, many little eyes were well hidden but firmly focused on them.

'It's all so different from when we left... and what's that over there?' said Angela.

Little Christian looked to where she was pointing and saw a huge, half-constructed mansion. 'I've no idea,' he said. 'Perhaps there has been a flood of new people and they are having to build some new accommodation.'

'Let's go and 'ave a look at it,' suggested Angela.

As they got closer, they at last saw life and movement. 'Look, there are some of the adults,' said Angela excitedly, and they both ran over, shouting in the direction of their friends.

'We're back!' shouted Little Christian and Angela as they ran up to the workers. But the adults just ignored them.

'What's going on?' shouted Little Christian. 'We're your friends. Please stop what you're doing, and let's talk.'

Again everyone just carried on working and treated Angela and Little Christian as though they were not there.

'Let's go and see if Buddy and Harmony are in the church office. Maybe they will explain to us what is happening.'

As they approached the office door they saw a gold plaque on it which had the words 'HEAVY SHEPHERD: PRIVATE' written in large letters for all to see.

Little Christian felt his stomach churn. 'Oh Voice,' he said, 'there is something desperately wrong.' And as he prayed, he turned the handle and pushed the door open.

Angela and Little Christian could not believe their eyes. Seated there facing each other were three surprised Littlekids they had never seen before. On what used to be his desk were a pack of cards and piles of money, and the office was full of cigar smoke.

'What's the meaning of this invasion?' demanded the-largest of the Littlekids standing up and looking very important. 'Why are you not out working on the mansion with the rest of the Newagechurch of the Heavy Shepherd?'

'What in the name of all that's good are you talking about?' shouted Little Christian, looking at them angrily. 'Who are you? Where are Buddy and Harmony, and what do you think you're doing smoking and gambling in my office?'

'Now listen here,' said Dodgy Prophet, standing up next to his friend Heavy. 'No one talks to our leader like that and gets away with it. That's a punishable offence.' Namit also stood up to throw his weight into the confrontation. 'Dodgy's right, pal, you have overstepped the mark. I suggest you apologise and get back to work.'

Little Christian was furious. 'Do you realise who I am? I'm Little Christian, the founder of Newchurch. What have you done to it?' he yelled as he rushed towards them, grabbed hold of his desk, and threw it across the room sending cards and money flying in every direction. A photograph fell out of the desk drawer and dropped onto the floor right in front of them.

'It's them,' whispered Heavy. 'Look, that's their photo!'

The three Enemy superbreeds stood petrified as they realised that although there was only one of him and three of them, he seemed much more powerful than they were. Angela stood back by the door and was also a little frightened as she had never seen Little Christian this angry before.

'Name yourselves,' snapped Little Christian, 'and then I want some answers out of you.'

Just as the scared and shaking trio were about to confess all, Little Christian heard a short cry and spun round to see that a fourth Littlekid had quietly crept in and had grabbed hold of Angela. He was now painfully twisting her arm behind her back.

'So we are having a little bit of trouble are we, gentlemen? Perhaps I can be of assistance to you. Now, grab Little Christian and tie him up. If he resists I will break Angela's arm off.'

Heavy, Dodgy and Namit looked very relieved to see that Percy Cutor had arrived.

'Well done, Percy,' exclaimed Heavy. 'We were just about to tackle him ourselves, weren't we, lads? We weren't scared of these Littlekids, even if one of them is Little Christian. Now come on, lads, do as Percy says. Tie him up.'

Percy smiled an evil grin and didn't even bother wasting his breath to call Heavy a liar. Little Christian offered no resistance; he knew that if he did Angela would get hurt.

'Now then, Angela, I want you to turn around slowly and look at me,' said Percy.

She had yet to see who was painfully hurting her, but as she turned and looked at him Little Christian saw her face go a whiter shade of pale. She froze with fear and started to tremble.

'So we meet again, Angela? And isn't that nice—you do recognise your old friend—once seen never forgotten I guess. How do you like my nice new name, "Percy Cutor"? So much more subtle than the name I had when we last met—what was it? Oh yes, The Pain Inflictor.'

'I am sure you realise though, my dear, as I hold your arm, the name may have changed but my job remains the same. I must admit that seeing you here is an embarrassment to me. I thought that you would never recover from my last onslaught. Still, this time I'll make sure I do my job properly.'

'Please don't 'urt me again,' cried Angela, tears running down her cheeks.

'You touch her and you are history, pal,' screamed Little Christian from underneath the mountain of ropes.

'Brave words, Little Christian, but I'm afraid you're in no condition to dish out threats. I'll tell you what I will do though, seeing as I'm a fair Littlekid. In my pocket I have a contract. Just sign it and I will let you go and leave you both alone.'

'What will we be signing?' asked Little Christian.

'Well, not much really,' said Percy. 'It's just a simple matter of saying that you deny the existence of the Voice and swear allegiance to the Enemy Superpowers. Many greater than you have signed it in the past.'

'Never!' screamed Little Christian and Angela together. 'That would be the last thing we would ever do,' continued Little Christian.

'It very probably will be,' smiled Percy wickedly. 'Right lads, bring them over to my prison.'

'But we haven't got a prison,' remarked Heavy.

'No you haven't got a prison, Heavy,' argued Percy, 'but I have. Why do you think you have not seen much of me since I arrived? I've been preparing for this day for a long time.'

Having tied the fearful Angela up as well, Percy and Heavy dragged them up the street till they came to a side door in the hospital. There they walked along a corridor until they came to two very stout wooden doors facing each other. Percy unlocked them and pushed Angela into one and Little Christian into the other. Then he locked them both again.

'Right,' said Percy, 'I'll leave them for a few hours to reconsider my proposition. If the answer is still negative, I will get on and do what has to be done.' He grinned.

Both Angela and Little Christian sat in the dark unable to see a thing. Although they both felt very frightened, they both instinctively began to talk to the Voice.

There was no lock on the outside hospital door and as the four superbreeds walked back to the office they didn't notice a younger Littlekid dart around the corner of the hospital, creep through the outside door and run to the door where Little Christian and Angela were being held captive.

15. a Light at the Beginning of the Tunnel

The remnant of Littlekids left in Newchurch lived in fear. Having seen how Heavy Shepherd had dealt with Harmony and Rhoda was bad enough, but things had got even worse. Tiff Withallsorts' house was still packed with adults who were planning a rebellion. Some were trying to change the name of Newagechurch, and all were thinking of ways to change the leadership.

When Tiff had collected a really committed group of

rebels, she popped into the office and told Heavy all about it, making sure that she also gave him a list of all their names. In no time at all they were gathered up and banished to the Bigwideworld and warned that if they came back it would be the last thing they would ever do.

Although Tiff Withallsorts had tipped him off, Heavy didn't like or trust her because she had betrayed him by stirring everything up to start with. He arranged for his faithful followers Dodgy and Namit to see that she had a fatal accident while being escorted on a sight-seeing tour around the quickdrying concrete forming the foundations of an extension to his mansion.

Heavy held a very moving funeral service for her, explaining that she had been like a foundation stone to his work, which he was sure that she would have been proud of. But all the remaining Children of the Voice knew that she had been murdered, and their fears grew.

Every night adults would creep out under the protection of the darkness and run off into the Bigwideworld, but like sheep without a shepherd they had no idea where they were going. It was into this depleted, fearful atmosphere that Little Christian and Angela had arrived. Little wonder that everyone had been afraid to talk to them.

But although everyone seemed to be leaving through the back of the town, no one noticed three more creep in through the front. Hearthunter, Harmony and Rhoda quietly made their way into one of the many deserted houses and after speaking to the Voice opened their Manuals for a read while they waited for the right time to move.

'Oi! Little Christian, is that you?'

Little Christian stumbled through the darkness of his cell to where the voice was coming from. 'Who is it?' he whispered through the door.

'I'm a Littlekid,' the voice replied. 'My name is Ivor, Ivor Future.'

'I thought all you Littlekids had left months ago?' Little Christian said, surprised.

'No, we've just kept in hiding, waiting for you to return,' said Ivor.

Little Christian's fear went as he could see that the Voice was already answering his prayers. 'Listen, I know you can't get me out of here, but where are Buddy and Harmony?'

Ivor explained that Harmony had been thrown out of Newchurch for rebellion, while Buddy had cracked up, being full of guilt that he had allowed the evil leaders to take over. He was now in another part of the hospital suffering from a spiritual breakdown.

Little Christian was so angry at what the Enemy Superpowers had been up to that he nearly swore, but just in time he refrained and remembered that he must control himself and his language even in times like these. 'Listen, Ivor, where are you all hiding?' he asked.

'We are in the basement of the main building, right underneath the church office,' Ivor said.

'I didn't know it had a basement,' said Little Christian in amazement.

'No, and neither do those evil leaders,' chuckled Ivor.

'Well, wait there for me. I'll be out of here shortly. The Voice has told me so. One last thing, Ivor—try and get into the other part of the hospital and tell Buddy that I'm back.'

'He won't be any use. I'm afraid he's gone beyond help,' said Ivor sadly.

'Don't you believe it, Ivor. He has not gone beyond the Voice's help. So when you see him, tell those feelings of guilt and failure to leave him alone. Now, quickly, off you go and do as I say.'

Angela had not been able to hear any of the conversation Little Christian and Ivor had just had. Sitting shivering in the darkness, all she could see was the face of Percy the Pain Inflictor, and all the old hurts started to be relived in her mind. She started to cry uncontrollably, holding herself so tightly that her body started to bruise.

The hospital door opened, and the sound of Percy's boots echoed along the corridor. Hearing the sobbing coming from Angela's cell, he guessed that the memory of the pain he had already inflicted would be enough to having her screaming to sign the contract within the hour.

He opened Little Christian's door, dragged him out and pushed him into another room just a few yards away. 'This, Little Christian, is my studio,' he said with pride. 'I bet Angela never told you what she had to suffer, did she? Well, she won't have to now, because you can experience the joys of it all for yourself.' He tied Little Christian in a chair and then took hold of some headphones.

'What are you going to do to me?' asked Little Christian, still feeling brave. 'Beat me, hit me or worse?'

Percy laughed. 'Nothing as primitive as physical torture, Little Christian. It's a fact that bodily pain seems to make the Children of the Voice become even more stubborn and less likely to sign the contract. No, this is called *spiritual* torture.

'For the next few days you will not be allowed to sleep. I am going to put some headphones on you and then play you some nice cassettes. The first one will remind you of all the things you have done wrong in your life that you thought the Voice had forgiven and forgotten. We of course don't ever forgive or forget. We want to put all your past back into your mind, and by the time you have heard it a few hundred times you too will feel guilty and unforgiven.

The second tape reminds you of all those times that the Voice did not answer your prayers, or sometimes answered them in a way that you were not happy with. Again, after a few hundred hearings you will be totally convinced that the Voice is unreliable and does not really care about you at all.

'And finally the third and most important tape, from my perspective, is the one that tells you about all the advantages and all the fun that can be had when you are truly committed to the Enemy Superpowers. And now... I'll put the contract here in front of you. All you have to do is give me a wave when you want to sign it, and then I will stop the tape. Then you will be a free man.'

'I'll never sign it,' yelled Little Christian defiantly.

'Oh, I'm sure you will,' said Percy. 'Angela only got away last time because after many hours she looked so weak and thin that I thought she was going to die on me, and the last thing I needed was a Littlekid martyr. Being a fool, I thought that if I let her go she would die somewhere in the Bigwideworld from so-called natural causes. I still don't know where she found the strength from to find her way back to you.'

'Well I do,' shouted Little Christian. 'Her strength came from the Voice, where mine will come from too.'

'Very well,' sneered Percy. Then, applauding sarcastically, he put Little Christian's headphones on. 'But I fear that as true as that may be for you, you may not have noticed that Angela isn't quite as strong as she once was. In just a short while you and she will have nothing in common, because she will have signed over to become one of us. Happy listening, Little Christian!'

Ivor Future crept into the ward where Buddy was lying. 'Buddy, wake up! Little Christian is back,' he whispered.

Buddy spoke some rubbish, then turned over.

'Buddy, listen to me—Little Christian is here, and he needs your help.'

Buddy covered his face with his hands and started to sob like a baby.

'OK, so you won't listen to me, will you? Well, have it your way. Maybe you will listen to the Voice.' Ivor jumped up and stood on the bed next to the prostrate Buddy. He commanded with an authority in his voice that made the whole hospital shake: 'Buddy, I pray that by the power of the Voice you will be released from self-pity, guilt and failure and that they will no longer be part of you. Receive this. Buddy, you are one of the Children of the Voice.'

Buddy immediately went still and quiet, then slowly lifted his head and looked at Ivor. 'Thank you,' he said slowly and quietly. 'Now please pass me my Manual and my clothes. We've a war to fight!'

16. SOME YOU WIN—BUT Lots you Lose

Buddy crept through the side door of the hospital, the Voice having already given him his instructions. He put his ear next to the first door but could hear nothing. Peeping through the key-hole he saw a muscly Littlekid he did not recognise walking around the room with his fingers in his ears while his friend Little Christian was tied to a chair with some headphones on, singing at the top of his voice the Littlekids' Marching Song.

'Well, Little Christian seems to be enjoying himself, but singing was never his strong point,' he thought. Quietly he went away from the door; then, moving farther down the corridor, he heard loud sobbing. 'Thank you, Voice,' he said. 'This must be the room where she is, but the door's sure to be locked. How am I going to get in?'

The Voice told him to grab the handle and pull. To his surprise he realised the door was undone. 'That must have happened when Ivor prayed for me and the building shook,' he thought.

Opening the door, he whispered Angela's name. 'Leave me alone,' she cried, 'I'll never stop followin' the Voice, whatever ya do to me.'

'Of course you won't, Angela—and all I want to do is to pray for you.'

Angela lifted her head out of her hands and through her red tearful eyes saw Buddy. 'Buddy, is that really you?' Pulling herself out of her heap she ran towards the door and hugged him. 'Where 'ave ya bin 'idin' ?'

'Um, that's a long story,' said Buddy, looking a bit embarrassed. 'But just at this moment I've more important things to do than to talk about me... listen, Angela, you are desperately in need of some prayer for healing. You really should have talked to us, your friends, when you first went through your horrific experience with Percy Cutor. Those kinds of fears, hurts and memories do not disappear with time—they just fester away under the surface until they can raise their ugly heads again.'

'I'm sorry,' said Angela. 'I know ye'r right. I wouldn't be in the state that I am now if I 'ad bin willin' to be 'onest with ya, and 'ad allowed ya and the Voice to speak to me.'

Buddy stopped her talking by taking the Manual out of his pocket and reading some exciting words of encouragement.

Then he started to pray. He asked that she would know healing from all she had been through, and that the Voice would bring her back to full health and strength. As he prayed and she received the prayer, he could feel the power of the Voice doing exactly what Buddy had asked. Within minutes the prayers of asking turned to prayers of thanks, and together they spent some time worshipping the Voice.

Dusk fell and the cloak of darkness covered Newchurch. The coming of the night also heralded the departure of the last adults, who drifted sadly out into the nowhere land of the Bigwideworld.

Heavy Shepherd, Dodgy Prophet and Namit Claimit stood happily in the shadow of a building and watched the final exodus, while a jubilant Greedy Gutrot and Professor Mindwarpt hid behind a rock and watched the sad refugees enter their evil domain.

'Nearly there,' said Mindwarpt, rubbing his gnarled hands together. 'Newchurch is dead, and in an hour or so's time there will be no more Children of the Voice.'

'Excellent,' smiled Gutrot. 'Well done, Professor. I feel that as a final gesture—a kind of nail in the coffin sort of thing—it would be most helpful if you could programme your little superbreeds to burn down what's left of Newchurch.' He sniffed at his scorched clothes. 'After all, I know first-hand just how destructive fire can be. Let's give that Little Christian a taste of his own medicine and see how he likes it!'

'No sooner said than done,' said the obedient Mindwarpt.

Gutrot continued looking at Newchurch in the distance. Then with an even broader and uglier grin he told the Professor that as soon as the last Littlekid was in his power, he would send back the wandering adults so they could rebuild the city of Oldchurch. 'I'd much rather have them all in one place where we can keep an eye on them,' he concluded. Mindwarpt agreed. Meanwhile, Heavy, Dodgy and Namit wasted no time in obeying the Professor's commands. Soon most of Newchurch was a fiery furnace, and they laughed at the destruction they were causing.

Just as they felt that their job was completed and it was time to return to their maker, they heard a voice they recognised.

'So we meet again, do we?'

Heavy, Dodgy and Namit spun around and came face-to-face with Hearthunter, Harmony and Rhoda.

'Well, I'll be...' said Heavy. 'Not you two girls back again! But you're a bit late, aren't you? We have just destroyed Newchurch.'

'Maybe you have,' said Hearthunter. 'That can be rebuilt, but you will never destroy the Children of the Voice. And we aim to stop you trying.'

'O, come on now,' laughed Heavy. 'Do you really think you and two girls are any match for the three of us? Get them, lads.'

Immediately the Children of the Voice stepped forward and commanded in the power of the Voice that the three evil Littlekids should freeze. Although it did sound a rather strange command with the heat of all the burning buildings around them, it worked. The only part of their beings they could move was their mouths; they were imprisoned in their own bodies and just stood like statues.

'Now we just need to find out from the Voice what he wants us to do with you,' said Hearthunter, staring at them one at a time.

Inside the hospital, Buddy had finished praying with Angela and after their time of worship it was like their batteries had been fully recharged.

'Right, let's go,' said Buddy.

They walked down the corridor until they reached the studio. 'Stand back,' said Buddy with more authority in his voice than Angela had ever heard him use before. 'Let's see this wicked Littlekid jump!' And with that he lifted his foot and kicked the door down.

Percy really did jump in surprise. Then he leaped to his feet, but before he could do anything to retaliate he also heard the words, 'In the name of the Voice, freeze'—and he stood motionless with his eyes glaring and mouth wide open.

They quickly took off Little Christian's headphones and untied him. He hugged Buddy and Angela, and Buddy asked him how he felt and if he needed some prayer. Little Christian smiled, 'I always need prayer,' he said, 'but those tapes couldn't affect me as I just kept singing the Voice's song. I think my singing affected old Percy more than his tapes affected me,' he joked. 'Right now, it's time to purge Newchurch of these infiltrating Littlekids,' he said. 'All is not lost yet.'

17. THE END?

Little Christian had spoken too soon. As they dragged the stiff Percy Cutor out onto the street they all gasped as they saw the night sky lit up by blazing buildings.

'No!' screamed Little Christian. 'We are too late. They have destroyed Newchurch.'

The only buildings that were not well ablaze by now, apart from the hospital, were the church office and the adjoining meeting hall. Everything else crackled and flamed furiously.

They continued dragging Percy down the street towards

the office, weeping at the destruction of all their hard work in Newchurch. Then they suddenly saw three more people dragging three other stiff Littlekids down the street. Although it was exciting to meet their friends, the reunion was marred by the crashing timber of the town burning around them.

'Where have all the Children of the Voice gone?' Little Christian enquired, bewildered.

'They have all left to go back to the Bigwideworld and Oldchurch,' said Harmony sadly.

'Yes, I think we are the only ones left. Nobody will trust a Newchurch again,' added Rhoda.

Heavy Shepherd was lying with the other evil super-breeds in a line on the ground, and as he didn't want to be terminated he had one last plan for survival. Summoning all the emotion he could manage, he suddenly burst into a flood of tears which made the Children of the Voice turn and look at him. 'Woe is me,' he cried out. 'I've done wrong. No, we've all done wrong. Please forgive us. Let us go in peace. We really have seen the error of our ways—' he lied '—and we feel a stint at the Voice's Training Module would put us back on the straight and narrow. There I can learn to be a *good* shepherd,' he continued, 'Dodgy a good Prophet, Namit a good faith man and Percy a good... well just good.' (He stopped awkwardly, having failed to think of anything that Percy could be good at except hurting people.)

Percy, Dodgy and Namit thought he had flipped his lid until they saw Heavy wink at them through his teary eye.

'Yes, we have all been wicked,' they quickly joined in, 'but surely you must forgive four repentant Littlekids? After all, haven't we all done wrong at one time or another?'

'And let he who is without wrong chuck the first brick,'

sobbed the blubbering Namit, who was a better actor than all the rest put together.

Little Christian felt the Voice prompt him that they were lying and he must not be deceived.

Buddy felt sorry for them as did Hearthunter, Harmony and Rhoda; but Little Christian felt a righteous anger welling up inside him against them. There was something unusually evil about them, but he couldn't put his finger on what it was.

'Well, the Manual does say that we must forgive Littlekids wot are really sorry,' quoted Angela.

'So it's all agreed, then,' said Buddy, taking control. 'We shall ask the Voice to release them, and then we'll let them go to the Training Module.'

'Thanks,' said the Enemy Littlekids, their tears evaporating as quickly as they had appeared.

'We'll be eternally grateful,' grinned Dodgy.

'Not so quick,' Little Christian butted in. 'I can't forgive them. They have wrecked lives and wrecked Newchurch. They are evil and must be destroyed.'

Before anyone could move he rushed over, grabbed a burning log and threw it at the four lying on the floor. 'You seem to love fire. Well, see how you get on with this,' he yelled defiantly. Within seconds they we all ablaze, but they made no noise.

Angela, Harmony and Rhoda screamed with horror while Buddy and Hearthunter tried in vain to dowse the flames. Within minutes it was all over for Heavy, Dodgy, Namit and Percy. They just lay in a smouldering heap.

The Children of the Voice just stared. No one said a word.

Eventually Buddy walked over to Little Christian. 'What have you done?' he whispered to him. 'You have killed four

Littlekids You've tried to do the Voice's work for him. These Littlekids had repented.'

'But I felt it was right,' argued Little Christian. 'I couldn't let them just walk away.'

'Feelings ain't wot ya go on, Little Christian,' said Angela, 'Ye'r a let-down to all the Children of the Voice,' she said with angry tears. 'Just fink, I fought we might 'ave 'ad a future togever. I fought I loved ya, but I could never be married to a murderer. I never want ta talk to ya again.' She wept, turning away from him.

'Listen, they were not normal Littlekids. There was something weird about them. Surely you could all see that. I had to destroy them—I'm sure the Voice was telling me to,' explained Little Christian.

'You are as violent as they are,' said Hearthunter. 'You have their blood on your hands. I'm afraid you're no longer part of us. I suggest you leave. Newchurch is no home for you. You can no longer be known as one of the Children of the Voice,' said Hearthunter softly, putting his hand on Little Christian's shoulder. 'I'm sorry it had to end like this. Maybe in a few years' time if you really repent the Voice will give you another chance. Little Christian, go, and may the Voice have mercy on you.'

All went silent as Little Christian turned away from them. He walked down the middle of the street with houses that he had helped build just two years ago burning on either side of him. He was broken-hearted and wept uncontrollably. 'I've lost Newchurch, my friends and the girl I really did love. Why did I have to kill them, and why can't I feel sorry that I did so?' he cried. Only the Voice listened to him.

By the time Little Christian had disappeared out of sight, all the other Children of the Voice were weeping. They were sorry to lose their leader and their best friend, but they knew they had to stand by what was right.

Suddenly Rhoda's tears stopped flowing, and she screamed as she saw a face peer round from the office. Then another appeared, then another.

'Look!' shouted Buddy, wiping his eyes, '—Littlekids, come out and join us.'

'Is it safe?' said Ivor whom Buddy instantly recognised.

'Yes, it's all over,' he announced as the numerous Littlekids poured out of the cellar and wandered around looking at the charred, smouldering remains surrounding them.

'We didn't like to come out. We were waiting for Little Christian to give us the OK. Where is he, anyway?' asked Ivor.

'I'm afraid Little Christian has done a very wicked deed,' explained Buddy as gently as he could. 'Heavy Shepherd, Percy, Dodgy and Namit all confessed and were sorry for the wrong they had done, but Little Christian couldn't forgive them and killed them. Whatever anyone has done, human life is sacred and it is not for us to take it away.'

Suddenly a floppy thing was thrown at his feet.

'You fools!' yelled Ivor Future angrily. 'Is it murder to destroy an Enemy robot?' he asked, pointing to the mechanical remains of Lucy Morals. 'You've condemned your leader for destroying the Enemy Superpower's machines!'

Buddy, Harmony, Hearthunter, Rhoda and Angela could not believe their eyes.

'Robots!' exclaimed Hearthunter. 'You mean they were not normal Littlekids? Oh, no, I don't believe it.'

They all ran and looked at the charred remains of the four Littlekids, and sure enough all that was left was a pile of burned nuts, bolts and metal.

'Enemy Superpower robots sent in to invade Newchurch and destroy us and our leader—you have certainly allowed them to do that,' continued Ivor.

'So the Voice did tell Little Christian ta destroy these evil machines and we didn't believe 'im?' whispered Angela. She began to cry again. 'Oh, no. Wot 'ave I done ta the one wot I really care fer.'

'We have not only broken and condemned to exile one of the Voice's greatest Littlekids, but we have also sent him away with the guilt of a murderer,' said Hearthunter, falling to his knees in shame.

'But will he ever come back?' cried Rhoda.

'Would *you* after the way he has been treated?' Buddy asked.

'If I run, I may be able ta catch 'im,' suggested Angela, sobbing.

'That won't be any use, I'm afraid,' continued Buddy. 'You'll never find him out there in the dark, and even if you did I doubt if he will believe you or want to see any of us again. We now have to live under a cloud of guilt, and even if we try to rebuild Newchurch, it won't have—and never will have—its rightful leader.'

Angela, Buddy, Hearthunter, Harmony, Rhoda, Ivor and all the rest of the younger Littlekids knelt down in the road and prayed for the Voice's protection on Little Christian; also that one day he might forgive them and come back to them.

Greedy Gutrot and Professor Mindwarpt were dancing around, over the moon at the outcome. 'It couldn't have come out better if we had planned it ourselves,' they laughed. 'I mean we had casualties and lost Heavy Shepherd, Lucy Morals, Dodgy Prophet, Namit Claimit, Tiff Withallsorts and Percy Cutor—but look what we have achieved. You can always build more robots, but they will never be able to rebuild Newchurch, not while Little Christian is wandering depressed and alone all over the Bigwideworld. Yes... Little Christian and the Children of the Voice are gone for ever!' shrieked Gutrot with a shake of his huge belly.

Then they went quiet as they heard a voice cut through the air above them. Like a double-edged sword it threw them both to the ground.

'In the name of the Voice I call fire down from heaven. Burn them, Voice. Burn them up and all the evil they represent.'

'Oh no, not fire again,' shouted Gutrot as two firebolts shot out of the sky. Instantly he and Mindwarpt were reduced to just two pools of mess on the rocks.

'Well that will slow down their celebrations for a bit,' declared Miraclekid looking at his friend. 'By the way, I must teach you how to call down fire from heaven properly, so you'll never have to resort to using an old piece of burning wood again. Just think of the aggro that could have saved you,' he chuckled.

'Now, come on,' Miraclekid added, 'let's go back and join the others... we've got a lot of rebuilding to do.'

And he and Little Christian set off... back to Newchurch.

Children

of the
Voice

BOOK 3

DESCENT INTO NOCHURCH

1. THE RUNAWAY

It never rains but it pours, and now it really was pouring. The once-solid path had turned into a squelchy, gooey, brown, muddy stream and even the enormous giant oak trees that towered high, trying to protect Runaway Forest from such a deluge just stood looking sad, as their huge branches, like long sagging arms, allowed the torrential downpour to lash against the ground.

Though his trainers were saturated, his jeans soaked and his leather jacket unable to prevent ice-cold water from seeping down the back of his neck, Little Christian rushed on. Nothing was going to make him slow down. Yes, Miraclekid had convinced him to return to Newchurch. Yes, he had tried to forgive, forget and carry on as if nothing had happened, but he could'nt do it. It was impossible.

'I don't need them,' he mumbled to himself angrily for the hundredth time. 'Anyway, why should I forgive them after all the lousy things they said about me? It's all very well for Miraclekid, he's their hero. I mean, it wouldn't have been so bad if it was just Harmony and Rhoda Skateboard who had a crack at me. After all, they are just a couple of stupid girls, but my mates Hearthunter and Buddy, how could they even think such things about me, their leader? Well let's see how they cope with leading Newchurch without me.'

Then, as it always did, his mind went back to Angela and tears filled his eyes. 'Angela,' he continued bitterly, 'she proved to be the worst of the lot. Called me a murderer, said she never wanted to talk to me again. Well, her wishes have come true. I never want to set eyes on her again. She can go and marry Greedy Gutrot as far as I am concerned. They are two of a kind.'

'Oi!' a voice suddenly shouted.

Little Christian jumped out of his angry dreamworld and looking to his left he saw a rather well-dressed old man sheltering next to a fire under a huge rock.

'What do you want?' shouted Little Christian, rudely.

'Hey, no need to get stroppy,' said the old man. 'I just thought you might like to come under my shelter and dry off. I've got a nice hot cup of coffee over here which would warm you up a bit.'

Little Christian was not in any hurry to get anywhere. In fact he hadn't a clue where he was heading. All he wanted to do was to get as far away from Newchurch as he could.

So he wandered over and sat down next to the old chap.

'Hello,' said the old chap, smiling. 'My name's Ron, Ron Guidance. What's yours?'

'Oh, I'm Little Chris...' Then Little Christian paused. For the first time in his life he was suddenly embarrassed by his name. Then he continued, 'I'm Little Chris.'

'Well, nice to meet you, Little Chris,' said Ron, handing him a mug of coffee. As Ron stared at the fire saying nothing, Little Christian stared at Ron. He must have been in his sixties and wore a black hat partly covering short, grey hair and had a well-trimmed grey moustache. A long black coat went right down to his shoes which, although clean, had a layer of mud surrounding the soles and heels. He looked the opposite to Little Christian, which made Little Christian feel even more scruffy, dirty and angry.

Then Ron looked into Little Christian's face. 'What, may I ask, are you doing out in the middle of Runaway Forest on a day like this?'

'Mind your own business, you nosey old Buffer,' shouted Little Christian, as his uncontrollable anger began to flare up again.

'Oh, I'm ever so sorry,' said old Ron politely. 'I didn't mean to pry. You're right, it's nothing to do with me.'

Little Christian was both surprised and ashamed that he should have reacted in such a way, and he apologised. He felt desperate to talk to someone and as there was no one else around except Ron, he guessed it might as well be him who felt the bitter edge of his fury. He explained that he was once one of the Children of the Voice and the leader of Newchurch, but things had gone wrong and he had been falsely accused of all sorts of terrible things by people who were once his best friends. Now he just wanted to get as far away from them as possible.

Ron sat quietly—he didn't say a thing—and even the expression on his face didn't give away what he was feeling. Little Christian remembered his early days in Oldchurch, how he was taught that it was sensible to listen to the wisdom of older and wiser people. Although he didn't know if Ron was wiser, he was sure that he was older, so he asked Ron if he had any advice to give.

Ron Guidance stared at him. After a few moments he slowly started to speak, quietly at first, but getting louder by the sentence. 'Beware of impersonators. They may look good, they may sound good, but they are no good. The ones you have left behind are not genuine. You are right to be leaving them. You don't need them. In fact you don't need anybody except the Voice. Look at me, alone as a fish in a fruitshop—but happy, yes, there is no one happier than me.

'I too follow the Voice, only not in such a fanatical way as your ex-friends do, and it's not by chance that the Voice has put me here in your path to give you advice and direction.' Now in full swing, Ron stood up and started waving his arms around like he was conducting an orchestra of millions.

'You have no choice, Little Chris. You can't go back. You must go on. Every man is an island. Don't allow yourself to become close friends with anyone else, or you will only end up getting hurt again. Listen closely to the advice of Ron Guidance. It's as reliable as the Manual itself.' After a pause he brought his face very close to Little Christian's.

'Furthermore,' he continued in a breathy whisper, 'I suggest you make your way to a city called Nochurch—a wonderful place where many Voice followers who are fed up with being accountable go and find the freedom they need. Once you are there ask for directions to Sativision House and ask for a close friend of mine called Hugo Yourway.

He paused. 'You know, I believe the Voice wants to make you a star.'

Ron then drew away from Little Christian and sat down again mumbling, 'Here endeth the first lesson.'

This was just the advice Little Christian wanted to hear. After thanking Ron he left the shelter of the rock and the warmth of the fire and returned to the cold rain, still bucketing down, but now he didn't feel quite so angry. Now he felt like he was on a sort of commission for the Voice.

2. the secret sixty–five

'I would like to call this meeting to order,' came a polite voice from a very tall, very thin man with a black moustache which underlined his large, widely-spread nose. 'It gives me great pleasure to welcome you all to this meeting of the Grand Order Of Secretly Evil Yobs, affectionately known to us all as "GOOSEY".' His listeners smiled nervously in response. The thin man's stomach made a noisy rumbling sound as he glanced around the large, cold, sparsely-furnished Oddboys' Hall, with its old stained-glass windows and its sixty-five (including himself) all male Goosey members present.

It is worth noting that when Goosey members met together on occasions such as these they were known as a 'gaggle', and they took themselves very seriously. They would be very offended if they heard anyone giggle about the gaggle of gooseys gathering.

Of course being a secret society no non-Goosey would be allowed to gatecrash a gaggle gathering as two huge, musclebound Goosey guards, known as 'Pecks', stood to attention by both the main door and the fire exit. Now if an outsider had managed to peep around the door, they may have found it hard to take any of the Gooseys seriously. You see, the Gooseys all sat around long scruffy trestle tables looking immaculate in their black dinner jackets, white silk shirts and red bow ties, but if you peeped under the tables you would see that instead of wearing trousers they wore bright yellow shorts, with grey thermal socks and black flippers over their feet. This, believe it or not, was what distinguished the Gooseys from all other mere mortals.

'It seems like an eternity has passed since we last met,' continued the mouth below the moustache, 'and I, being your Grand Gander, bring you tidings of great joy. As you know, the perfect gaggle number for a very large city is 666. However, for a city of our size, the number should be sixty-six and for a long time we have had to function minus one goosey.' The gaggle all stared at their leader, hoping their faces were portraying an expression that he would find pleasing.

'Permission to speak!' shouted Rip Emoff, who was the owner of the Nochurch Casino.

'Yes, Rip,' said Grand Gander.

'Well, regarding our late beloved member, rumour has it that one of us around this table ran off with Amos Onmyturf's Lesserbreed, which caused Amos to go raving mad, which drove him to dumping his Littlekid in the middle of Runaway Forest and sadly to top himself.'

'Rip, please sit down and be quiet!' ordered Grand Gander, feeling embarrassed, as he tried again to forget the slight indiscretion involving himself and Amos' attractive wife. 'We have discussed this many times before and I am convinced that none of you would do such a terrible thing to a fellow Goosey as to steal his own personal Lesserbreed. And remember, it was I who heroically saved his female Littlekid and persuaded her to work for us—and where would you all be without her? (Ahem.) Now, to business!'

The Gooseys all smiled and agreed that Grand Gander was right. Arnos Onmyturf's female Littlekid kept their slave-trade thriving.

'If I may continue,' continued Grand Gander. 'Alas, Amos is no more, so we need our sixtysixth member. Well, the good news is a short while ago a new citizen moved into our community, and since then he has gained the respect of many, including myself.'

The gaggle looked nervously at each other, unsure of how to respond, as they had become very secure with just the sixty-five.

'Permission to speak?' asked Bigsby Bankbalance, a local bank manager of the Stashitaway Bank.

'Of course, Bigsby,' replied Grand Gander.

'Money is my life,' boasted Bigsby, 'and I judge a man's credentials by his credits—cashwise, if you know what I mean. Is this person of sound financial standing, because we don't want any poor people in our company? In my professional opinion they are more trouble than they are worth, hence my expression...' at which point all the gaggle joined in, having heard it so many times before, 'If not rich... ditch.'

'I assure you the person I have in mind is very wealthy, Bigsby, and unlike some he has not found the need to print his own notes.' Bigsby blushed. 'However, I'm sure he could be persuaded to use your bank if he became one of us,' added Grand Gander with a twinkle in his eye that Bigsby liked.

'Permission to speak?' asked Major Snob-Value.

'Yes, Major,' said Grand Gander.

'I say, Gander old chap, is this person of reputable employment and can he be trusted to be totally silent regarding our affairs?' He paused. 'I can't abide those working and lower classes; they have no breeding, and there is more chance of water-skiing behind the Titanic than there is of one of them keeping their mouths shut.'

Before Grand Gander could answer, or the gaggle nod in agreement, Chauvinist Pigg, a member who was born overseas somewhere but who would never reveal his nationality, interrupted by saying that he hoped they were not discussing allowing one of the Lesserbreed (the Gooseys' affectionate term for the female gender) to enlist. As Chauvinist continued, not only would they be unable to cope intellectually, but they really would have nothing to contribute once taken out of their kitchens.

The Gaggle all nodded in agreement.

Grand Gander attempted a smile, which was his first attempt for a month. 'I think we all agree with your sentiments, Major. This person has a very secure employment and has got to where he is today thanks to his utmost discretion.' Then he looked at Chauvinist condescendingly. 'You are not in some remote jungle now, my friend. You are part of our great country. You must be very careful what you say about the Lesserbreed, or people will start thinking that we Gooseys are sexist. Most of you chose to marry one, and not only do they carry out their domestic chores admirably, they also spend time with your Littlekids allowing you to forget that you've even got any. No, we are not here to put down the Lesserbreed, but we are here to say that their place is in the living quarters and not here with us.'

'Hear, hear!' shouted the Major. 'Er, that is, I mean *not* here, here,' he stammered, correcting himself.

'Permission to speak?' asked Al Kidsarbrats, a head-teacher from the exclusive Boffinswot School.

'Yes,' came the reply from the leader's chair.

'You mentioned Littlekids. I hate them. Your new member: he's not too young, is he? After all, I have these horrible Littlekid louts ruining every day of my life. I couldn't bear the thought of having to sit facing one as a member of our beloved gaggle.'

The gaggle all nodded again.

Grand Gander tried a second smile, but again failed miserably, just as his stomach made an even louder gurgling sound. 'Well actually,' he said loudly, trying to overpower what sounded like a war going on inside him, 'he is young—in fact very young—but before you all panic and think that your esteemed leader is turning our beloved gaggle into some Littlekids' playpark, take my word for it, this Littlekid is not only very mature, but in some areas is more experienced than I am.'

All the gaggle gasped at the prospect that it was possible for anyone to have more experience in anything than Grand Gander.

'Any more questions?' asked Grand Gander, hoping there weren't, as he was growing very impatient and was hating democracy more and more by the minute. He was dying to tell the gaggle the name of the one they all kept asking questions about, but he also knew it was right they had their say before he did so.

'Just a quick one,' came the almost hiss-like whisper of Arthur Theist. 'What is it, A?' enquired Grand Gander, knowing that Arthur hated the name Arthur and preferred to be called by his initial A.

'Well,' squeaked A, 'this person hasn't got any strong, dangerous beliefs, has he? We all know our beloved constitution requires us to be good religious citizens who are not allowed to believe in anything, except the Gooseys of course. This new member hasn't been contaminated by any Voice followers, has he?'

The gaggle gasped an even greater gasp than last time.

'I think I know our constitution, A,' muttered Grand Gander, now not even attempting a smile. 'After all, I did write it, didn't I?' he said angrily. 'Furthermore, seeing that you made mention of my beloved rules, may I also remind you that you have just broken one. Rule one, subsection A, clearly states that the word you have just offended us with must never be used at a Goosey meeting. Any reference to the aforementioned person must be simply V.'

The Grand Gander stood tall and put a black hat on. 'A Theist,' he bellowed, 'all rule-breakers must be punished. Pecks, do your thing.'

As one Peck grabbed hold of the hissing A and bent him over the trestle table, the other took off a flipper. 'How many, Grand Gander?' shouted the Peck.

'Oh, six of the flipper should be adequate,' snarled Grand Gander, who had now calmed down a bit.

As heavy rubber whacked the even heavier rump, A Theist wailed loudly. The gaggle enjoyed the entertainment and Grand Gander pondered the good old days when the answer to any mischief was always a good whack on the backside.

Six slaps and six screams later the Pecks were back guarding their doors, the Grand Gander was ready to continue and A Theist was back hovering over his seat as it was a bit painful to sit on it.

'Now,' said Grand Gander, 'back to where we were before we were so rudely interrupted.' Then, to everyone's utter surprise, he burst out laughing. Without more ado he spluttered, 'The person I am proposing to you was... wait for it, A... once the leader of the opposition, yes Newchurch.'

The gaggle gave vent to the loudest gasp of the day. Some even fell off their chairs and hid under the tables as they feared the name Newchurch nearly as much as the name Voice. The Pecks, whose highlight of the meeting had been to punish A, were still reliving those moments and not paying attention. They wondered what was happening and rushed around the hall thinking they were being invaded.

'However,' continued Grand Gander, still managing such a wide grin that his moustache looked horizontal, 'you will be pleased to hear that he has now seen the dark... and had his eyes well and truly closed.'

'Prove it,' whimpered all the shivering gaggle together. The tall, thin leader put his hand inside his jacket pocket and pulled out a small business card. 'Read this!' he snapped, and just as he was about to hand it to Rob Emall, a high-dass thief who sat on his right, to pass round, his stomach let out such an earth-shattering roar that anything made of glass, ranging from the beautiful stained-glass windows to Major Snob-Value's monocle, smashed into millions of tiny pieces with the vibration. The now totally confused Pecks rushed up to Grand Gander telling him to get under the table and they would soon find out who had detonated the bomb that they had just heard exploding.

All was raging chaos, so Grand Gander grabbed hold of each trestle table and, screaming, 'Shhuutt uupp!' at the top of his voice, threw them, one at a time, the whole length of the hall, breaking anything or anyone that got in their way.

Eventually everyone calmed down, and with no tables left to hide under they quietly sat back on their seats and even the Pecks returned to their doors.

'I do beg your pardon,' said Grand Gander composing himself. 'There's no bomb, Pecks. I've recently changed my eating habits and my stomach seems to be objecting. You could say it's making its feelings audibly known.

'Now, read this, Rob, then pass it on.'

As they read it they started to smile; very, very confident smiles.

'Now we've no worries here,' they laughed.

'Even old A Theist has more faith than this character,' shouted one.

'Yeah, the most influential loser I've ever heard of,' shrieked another.

'So I take it you agree that my choice has all the necessary qualifications to become one of us?' asked Grand Gander.

'He's almost over-qualified,' shouted a voice hysterically and all went into fits of totally uncontrollable laughter. Even the Pecks started to laugh, although of course they had no idea what they were laughing about.

Again the noise eventually subsided, and being a true democracy a vote was taken and all agreed that the proposed person should be approached and invited to be initiated at the next meeting, which would be at the earliest possible convenience, allowing time for the necessary repairs to be done to the Oddboys' Hall and new tables and windows to be purchased.

'Now for the final few items on our agenda,' said Grand

Gander looking at a sheet of paper that had nothing written on it. 'Pat, over to you.'

Pat Rolman, the crooked police officer, opened up a sheet of paper and started reading his report, which mentioned all the progress being made on the Gooseys' illegal money-making ventures. 'Drug-trafficking trade doing very well; extortion rackets are growing daily. Let's see...' he continued. 'Oh yes, the membership of the Muckybooks and Violent Videos lending library has multiplied at an enormous rate, especially now we have encouraged Littlekids to join.' And so his list continued. 'One other important piece of news is that Chief Officer Kleencop and the city police still have no idea that we Gooseys are responsible for all Nochurch's major unsolved crimes.' All the Gooseys laughed together at the thought of the weak and useless boys in blue.

'Thank you, Pat. I would like to mention our Littlekid slave-trade,' said Grand Gander, again taking the floor as this was a responsibility he had chosen to oversee himself.

All the gaggle listened very intently. This was of great interest to them because by exporting slaves they had all become very rich, and by holding onto a few for their own convenience it had made them all men of leisure. 'Our ally in Runaway Forest is doing a grand job in providing us with these troublesome, discontented Littlekids, and the next person to visit her will tell her so on my behalf.'

'Excuse me, Grand Gander, permission to speak.'

'Yes, Bigsby, what is it?'

'Well, whose turn is it to collect the next slave, or, I mean Littlekid?'

Grand Gander thought. 'I believe that it's the Major next, then you after him. You can collect the horse and cart from Boffinswot School, because as we all remember from our last meeting Al offered to house both of them for us.'

All seemed satisfied.

After a few very minor items were discussed, like who was giving whom a lift home, the meeting closed in the usual way, with all the gaggle holding hands and singing 'Goosey Goosey Gander' and the Pecks frogmarching everybody out of the building.

Grand Gander sat back contentedly in the deserted, almost-decimated Oddboys' Hall. It felt good having all the most influential people from Nochurch under his control, but all sixty-four around the table meant nothing to him compared to the one name written upon this business card. As he continued to stare at it he couldn't resist reading it out loud.

> *Little Chris (TV star)*
> *1 Hopelesscase Mansion*
> *Nochurch*
> *Code: WHO AMI*

Then Grand Gander looked at the small words at the bottom which looked almost insignificant, yet to him were the most important.

> *Minister of Nochurch*

Again the thin man managed a smile. 'Little Chris— or should I say Little Christian—you can call me Grand Gander when you first meet me. I doubt if you will live long enough to call me GG.' He chuckled, then he laughed until he ached, all the time waving the little card in his hand. 'But you'll never be around long enough to know who I really am.'

Tears rolled down his face. 'I'm really looking forward to meeting you,' he choked. 'My dad has told me a lot about you. I wonder if you will notice any family resemblance, like he's so fat and I'm so thin.'

Suddenly his face became serious. 'Where my fat father failed, I won't! Little Christian. I am going to destroy you... for ever.'

As Grand Gander got up to leave, a thin Oldie wearing a long coat and a hat crept into the hall, staying in the shadows.

'Oh, there you are,' said Grand Gander. 'How come you have taken so long to get here? I wondered when you were going to show up.'

Not getting a reply, he pulled out a large brown envelope that was filll of bank notes. 'Here,' he shouted, 'take this. You're doing a wonderful job.'

As the thin man caught the flying envelope and started to creep back out of the hall, Grand Gander shouted after him, 'Meet me outside here after the next Goosey meeting. I'll let you know when it is. I've got a very important assignment for you.'

The man nodded and left. Grand Gander wandered into the middle of the deserted hall and started to do a little dance by himself. 'Life is so easy,' he thought. 'Life is so good. I am so proud of myself.'

The unearthly inhuman noise that followed as Grand Gander danced around the hall is beyond description. Suffice it to say that his stomach was crying out to be filled. It was time to go and give it a treat.

3. HEADACHES AND HEARTACHE

It had been a long, long night and by the way things were going it seemed like the night would never end.

'Aw, come on now, Buddy, there's no time like the present. It's time to go for it,' shouted Hearthunter with all the enthusiasm of a powerpacked preacher prophesying over a park full of pagan people.

'Yeah, it's like time to see the blind man leap clean out of his wheelchair,' added Miraclekid getting his metaphors slightly mixed up in his excitement.

'Well, I don't really know,' replied Buddy the Flockwatcher cautiously, while scratching his head with one hand and twiddling a pen that had the words 'The Hesitator Gets There Later' inscribed on it in the other. 'Let me just read to you once more the points that I spent a lot of time meditating on last week.'

Just as Miraclekid was about to shout, 'Not again!' Hearthunter slapped a hand over his mouth and only a gurgling sound came out.

'Point number one: the Voice has been really good to us undeserving Littlekids of Newchurch, and thanks to him we have grown incredibly numerically, especially over the past year.' At this stage he walked over to his office wall where an enormous graph, which was so long it looked like a frieze on the wallpaper, displayed these facts. The graph was covered with all sorts of different coloured pen lines seemingly going in all directions. Apart from looking pretty these lines meant absolutely nothing to Hearthunter and Miraclekid, but to Buddy they held as much fascination as the Orient Express would to a Tibetan train-spotter.

'Point number two: to plant a Newchurch in Religious-city is of course part of our long-term strategy, but are we being a little premature? And finally, point number three (all good Flockwatchers have three points): our long long-term project, which is to try and restore some of the lost loners of Nochurch, well I have to say that I don't think any of us are ready for that yet.' Then, with a solemn voice he continued, 'It was not so long ago that our own future was in the balance.'

'You speak for yourself!' yelled Miraclekid. 'I never questioned my future.' His voice always grew louder when he was arguing about something that he felt passionately about. 'If we don't move out till we are ready, we shall still be here having this conversation when the Voice returns. You're sounding more like a staid boring Oldchurch pastor than a life-packed, vision-smacked child of the Voice. I've had enough of talking about strategy and projects. I say it's time to do the business.'

To Miraclekid's annoyance, Buddy always refused to get worked up—it was not in his nature—so his voice continued with the same monotone that it always had.

'I may seem staid to you, but I and many of my flock would call it stability. I may also seem boring,' he continued, 'to one as impetuous as your good self, but I believe before we "do the business" we should spend much time in planning, prayer, familiarising and fasting which are words that never seem to be in your vocabulary.'

'In other words we must do things in the Voice's timing and not ours.'

Miraclekid and Hearthunter just sat quietly. Neither attempted to argue with Buddy's theology or logic, because due to the many hours he spent in preparation, prayer and study at his desk he did seem to know more about the deeper truths in the Manual than they did.

Buddy also went quiet because deep down he wished that he had the excitement and zeal of Miraclekid and Hearthunter, and the last thing he wanted to do was to quell their enthusiasm. They all stared at each other. Eventually Buddy stared back at his graph and Miraclekid stared at his watch, so Hearthunter broke the silence.

'I think maybe we are all right and the Voice deliberately made us to think and act differently so that together we sort of balance each other out, whereas separated we would either never get round to doing anything or else we would just be racing around and doing a lot, but probably not really achieving anything.'

Buddy and Miraclekid nodded in agreement, both pleased to end the disagreement and both fed up with staring at graphs and watches. 'All right,' said Buddy, 'it looks like we need a bit of a compromise if we leaders are to move on together. How would you feel if we were to keep praying about the Nochurch loners at present and in the meantime make a hit into Religios-city?'

Miraclekid and Hearthunter leapt up and down with excitement.

'Also,' continued Buddy, 'while you are recruiting your hit squad to take with you, I will pay a visit to the leaders of any Oldchurches that may be already there. It's so important we don't just rush in, but let them know about our mission, as there may be things we can do together.'

Hearthunter again spoke up: 'Having done my home-work already on Religios-city, I'm afraid any sort of co-operation seems very unlikely. I have discovered that there are two Oldchurches in existence. One is called the Ancient Church of the Thirteenth Male Apostle and the other is called the Modern Movement of the Free Sisters' Fellowship, and both hate each other so much they have declared an all-out war with each other.'

'Oh dear,' exclaimed Buddy. 'Not so good. Still, we must do things properly, so I'll arrange a meeting with them first thing tomorrow morning.'

Miraclekid and Hearthunter were now very excited and Buddy was as near excitement as his personality would allow him to be. They decided to spend what was left of the now short, short night praising the Voice together. Leadership was important, but leaders being real friends seemed even more important. They felt very secure know-ing that their love and respect for each other went far deep-er than any disagreement that they might ever have.

While all these exciting things were happening in the Newchurch office another Littlekid was restlessly trying to sleep in one of the small Newchurch houses. This Littlekid had not had a good peaceful night's sleep for a long time. Neither had she allowed a smile or any outward show of happiness to be seen on her pretty young face for the same period. She was still part of Newchurch in as much as she lived there and attended various events that took place, but her heart was far from being the exuberant Voice director that she was once known as. Everyone who looked at her could see that she was different. No longer did she talk to the Voice or listen to him or even read the Manual. She was even rumoured to have said that sometimes she doubted if the Voice existed.

As this overtired young female Littlekid tossed and turned restlessly in her bed, she accidently bumped against her bedside cupboard and a framed photograph fell onto the carpeted floor with a gentle thud. Immediately she sat bolt upright in her bed. It had had the same effect as an alarm bell screaming in her ears. She leaned over, and by the help of the moonlit night slowly picked it up off the floor. She sat there motionless, holding it next to her heart as she had done each evening for as long as she cared to remember. She clutched it tightly, as if her life depended on it, but she didn't weep. The fact was that her eyes had cried so much and for so long there seemed to be no tears left for her to shed. The once emotional Littlekid now seemed unable to let any emotions show.

After a while, the birds outside her window heralded the soft light of a brand new day and she slowly took the photograph away from her body and directed her eyes at it. There they were, two very happy young Littlekids who seemed to have not a care in the world. They looked as though they were very close friends and maybe even loved each other.

As the dawn sun stretched up and its warm light crept through her window she glanced at her dressing-table mirror on the far side of her bedroom. Looking back at the photo she could hardly believe that the Littlekid in the photo was the same person she was staring at in the mirror.

The stress and strain of months of heartbreak and broken fellowship with the Voice had taken their toll and made the Littlekid look older and more haggard than any normal Voice follower of her age. Her face was drawn and pale and her body thin. She had no interest in food.

Guilt had become her master and she had become its slave. It had taken control of her life. As she gazed at the photo and the young male Littlekid standing beside her, she again pondered the fact that it was she who had falsely accused him of all sorts of terrible things. She wondered where he was now. She had heard nothing from him since that terrible day when he had walked out of Newchurch. She didn't know if he was dead or alive, but then she didn't really know if she was.

Over the next few days Hearthunter and Miraclekid were totally hyperactive and rushing around everywhere sharing the exciting news of the hit squad invading Religios-city-with all of Newchurch so they too would catch the excitement and start praying for it. They decided to take three of the young Littlekids with them: Ivor Future, Joy Atalltimes and Hope Itgoeswell. Buddy agreed with their choice as he too felt that these three had great potential and it would be a chance for Hearthunter and Miraclekid to train them up while on the battlefield, so to speak.

Buddy told Hearthunter and Miraclekid that he had arranged to meet both Canon Blast from the Ancient

Church of the Thirteenth Male Apostle and Pastor Kitchen from the Modern Movement of the Free Sisters' Fellowship the following day, then if all went well their hit squad could burst into action the following Monday. He felt it right that all Newchurch should pray over them on the previous Sunday.

As all seemed to be decided, Hearthunter started to say, 'What a shame...' but before he could finish his sentence he was interrupted by Buddy, 'Don't say any more,' he whispered with tears welling up in his eyes. 'I know what you are about to say. She has been loved, prayed for and given advice, but she has chosen to lock herself away so that no one, not even the Voice, has been able to get to her. I sometimes wonder if she will ever allow herself to be put right or be used by the Voice again.'

Miraclekid stayed silent for once and just looked down at his trainers. He too had unsuccessfully prayed for her, but he knew enough about miracles to know that unless she opened herself up and allowed the Voice to heal her, nothing could stop the self-destruction of this his old best friend's girlfriend. What would become of Angela?

4. BIG ON THE BOX

As the illuminated sign of Nochurch Police Station swung gently in the breeze, Chief Kleencop paced his office floor punching his right fist into the palm of his left hand in frustration. 'The crime rate of this city is rocketing, yet I can't do anything about it,' he grumbled to himself. 'I know all those bigwigs who call themselves Gooseys are behind it all, but they are the cleverest, most influential people around. How am I, a simple cop, ever going to find enough evidence to nail them?'

'Fancy a coffee, Chief?' came a voice through the door.

'Yes thanks, Pat,' said the chief 'It's good to know I've got at least one cop with me who is one hundred per cent trustworthy.'

Pat smiled to himself as he walked towards the coffee machine.

The heat was blistering as the bright spotlights shone in the small studio. 'Take one!' shouted a rather effeminate voice from behind a large doubleglazed soundproofed window that looked like it should have had fish swimming around in it. At this cue a tall young man on the far side of the window stood up from a black swivel chair and walked over to a large black microphone. The youth was immaculately dressed in a shiny bright blue suit, with a shiny pink silk shirt which had a shiny red tie hanging from beneath the collar. Red nylon socks were just noticeable between the trouser turnups and the shiny white leather shoes. His hair was immaculate, gelled down so not one strand could wander out of place, and the make-up covering the face was just enough to give a tanned rather than scorched appearance.

The mouth opened just a few inches away from the microphone to display a set of teeth that were so white and shiny that one could have thought that they had just been covered with a thick coat of high gloss white paint. Then up from the throat, over the tongue and booming out between the teeth these words broke loose: 'Now listen carefully, viewers, or should I say, my friends. I'm not just asking you. No, I'm not even just telling you. I am in fact ordering you not to stop watching me if you really want to hear what the Voice wants to say to you this very night.'

Camera 2 moved in nearer to do a close-up of his face, which due to the intense heat of the lights had started to perspire and was becoming as shiny as the clothes he was wearing. 'Yea, verily within the next hour,' the voice continued, 'I am going to explain to you not only why you need to know the Voice as your best friend, but also for a very small donation towards my ministry, how you, whoever you are or whatever you have done wrong, can also become his friend and become almost as Voice-like as myself.'

With the foundations laid, the preach then continued non-stop (except for various commercial breaks to advertise the speaker's specially-anointed videotapes and cassettes from previous programmes) for fifty-five minutes.

The face behind a million viewers' television screens would sometimes laugh, sometimes weep, but always yell into the microphone.

While the cameramen were racing around the studio like there was no tomorrow, shooting from every conceivable angle to try and keep the viewers' attention, the lighting changed after every twenty swallows from the speaker's adam's apple a bit like a sound-to-light disco.

Then came those last crucial five minutes. Success or failure would be determined in those all important 300 seconds. 'And now,' the mouth concluded so dramatically that in comparison the world's number one ranking Shakespearian actor would have sounded like an amateur, 'I've not just shared my heart with you. Nay, I have given you my all.' At this cue a technician from the other side of the double-glazing pressed a button that released the sounds of organ music followed by what could only be described as voices sounding like they'd just passed an audition to become part of an angelic choir.

'And why?' agonised the voice. 'And why?' it repeated a little louder. 'Because... I love you.' Tears came rolling down the make-up covered cheeks as they did every week at this point of the programme, and his head bowed. For the first time in an hour he whispered, which caught the sound crew off guard and sent the million viewers rushing for their remote controls to turn the volume level up. 'Good-bye. May the Voice bless you, and have a nice day.'

As tears stopped rolling in the television studio, tears continued rolling in the homes of two million bloodshot eyes. No one dared switch off their sets. It was as though they had all become hypnotised by a small electrical plastic box which communicated with them, but would not permit them to communicate with it.

The credits rolled in front of them in wonderful flowery Olde English italics, then afterwards came these words: 'Little Chris has told you everything, but it is vital that you remember what he has taught you. Send $40 immediately to the following address and receive your very own personal videotape of this programme. Remember, the first 10,000 cheques to arrive will all receive their very own handkerchiefs that Little Chris has personally wept in. So don't delay, write in today.' Then followed Little Chris's address and finally, like the Amen, the words: 'All major credit cards accepted.'

The studio crew relaxed, another programme in the can. 'Well done, lovey,' congratulated Hugo Yourway, the rather camp programme producer, as he burst in through the studio door and approached Little Chris, 'Oh my,' he continued, 'even I had a tear in my eye at one point. You really were very convincing today.'

'Wait a minute,' said Little Chris defensively picking up a towel and trying to scrape some of the make-up off his face. 'I really do believe in everything I say.'

'Oh, I am sure you do,' replied Hugo. 'You are one of the

sweetest little Children of the Voice I have ever met. You have such a nice face even I nearly believed what you were saying.' With this Hugo went into one of his giggling fits which Little Chris found most embarrassing. He decided it was time to leave.

As he reached the door Hugo contained himself long enough to shout out, 'Good-bye, Chrissy. See you soon,' and then continued his high-pitched giggling.

Little Chris span round, his make-upless face red with anger. 'I am not Chrissy! I'm Little Chris!' he yelled furiously. 'And you'd better not forget it!' With that he slammed the studio door.

Hugo immediately stopped laughing, so offended he nearly burst into tears. 'Miserable, ungrateful little hypocrite,' he whispered under his breath. 'He seems to forget he was nothing until I discovered him. Ron Guidance sent me a wreck and I made him a star. It was I who taught him good dress sense and how to speak and perform in front of the camera. I made him all he is today. He may be able to fool two million viewers with his corny rhetoric, but if they knew him like I do, they would soon see that there is more chance of me being one of the Children of the Voice than him.'

As Little Chris left Sativision House he found a crowd of female Littlekids waiting outside for him. Most wanted autographs, some wanted handkerchiefs and a few wanted a date with him that night. He was in no mood to be pleasant and just pushed them all roughly to one side and climbed into his large white chauffeur-driven limo. 'Home, driver,' he yelled rudely. Then he settled down to watch a video of his performance that afternoon.

It was exactly an hour later that his car pulled past the security guards standing next to the huge garden gates that led into his estate. He gazed at the beautiful ornate cross-shaped sign saying, 'One Hopeless Mansion' as the electronic gates glided open. The limo drove up the long driveway and the small round pebbles made a loud crunching noise as the huge wide tyres of the heavy vehicle tried to squash them flat. The sun was sinking fast behind the huge oak trees that were scattered all over the vast finely-cut lawn. Little Chris's garden may have looked unplanned to the experienced horticulturist. Nothing except the turf had been manhandled. All the rest of the garden was just like it was when he purchased it, wild and like a wilderness (which were two words Little Chris could relate to).

The large car stopped in front of the mansion, which stood like a great white castle with its ten ensuite bedrooms, three bathrooms, two lounges, a drawing room, library, offices, kitchen, plus of course the gym, swimming pool, jacuzzi and sauna. The modest sort of house every TV star who puts himself out for the Voice should have, thought Little Chris.

He stepped out of the car and, ignoring the chauffeur, climbed the twenty steps, walked between the two large mock Grecian pillars and eventually reached the large double wooden front doors. Fumbling in his pockets he eventually found his key, opened one of the huge doors and walked in, carefully shutting it behind him.

It was great to be home.

Before he was famous one of the most exciting times in the day was when the postman brought his post. Even if one morning the delivery was very early, the minute he heard the rattle of the letterbox and the gentle thud of envelopes hitting carpet, he was out of bed and downstairs like a rocket. But now it was slightly different. Once inside his hallway the first view that confronted him was three very large mail bags crammed with letters. Of course he had his own private office staff to open them, read them and answer them, but he still insisted on seeing the amount of incoming mail each day before anyone else touched it. His staff considered the reason was because he wanted to keep some sort of grassroots contact with the viewers, but Little Chris really did it to see if he was gaining or losing popularity.

Popularity brought prosperity and prosperity was what a person in his position needed to flaunt around to show everyone that he was in close touch with the Voice. Material wealth was a sign of spiritual achievement. Ninety-nine per cent of the envelopes would contain money from people who wanted to purchase his preaching products. If the number dropped dramatically, he would be in a very embarrassing position financially. All he had was rented, hired or on loan, though of course none of his admirers knew this.

Without the sackfuls of money, he would either be broke or have to do what he did a long time ago—trust the Voice to provide for him. Still, he mused, smiling to himself, three sackfuls was fine and about average. It would certainly pay offall the bills until next week.

Little Chris slipped out of his uncomfortable shoes and, walking over the luxurious deep spongelike carpet, poured himself a glass of Sacro Vino from his drinks cabinet. Nochurch really was a wonderful place to live, he thought to himself. It was the sort of place where a Voice follower could get on and do his thing for the Voice and not have to be answerable to anyone. It was great that Nochurch lived up to its name and had no churches. Who needed churches and interfering church leaders when you had the Voice? mused Little Chris in a vain attempt at theology.

It was then, as he turned around to go and sit in his favourite armchair, he noticed a very official envelope sitting on the mantelpiece above the blazing log fire. He assumed that this must have come by special delivery and that one of his staff must have put it there for his special attention. As he picked up the envelope he suddenly felt excited and his heart started beating faster. He couldn't understand why he should feel this way just by picking up a bit of paper. He hadn't felt this sort of feeling for a long time.

He sat down in his large black armchair and as he released a lever a footrest appeared. Carefully he put his drink down on the table next to him, then opened the envelope and began to read the letter.

As he gazed at it his eyes nearly popped out of his head in amazement and his heart beat so fast that it sounded like a runaway train. 'Wow!' he shouted as he leapt out of his chair and sent both table and drink flying. 'It's a miracle... thank you, Voice. Now at last I know I really have made the big time.'

5. THE WAR OF THE WORDS

Buddy knew immediately that he had entered Religios-city. It was cold and uncaring and really miserable. He had walked past a big sign on the outskirts which read: 'YOU ARE NOT ALLOWED IN RELIGIOS-CITY UNLESS YOU OBEY OUR RULES.' 'They certainly have an interesting way of making people feel welcome,' he thought.

As he walked into the shopping centre he had never seen so many noticeboards and they all started with the words, 'YOU MUST NOT...' There was 'YOU MUST NOT LAUGH OR TELL JOKES ON THE PAVEMENT.' Then there was 'YOU MUST NOT SMILE, GRIN, SMIRK OR SHOW ANY FORM OF HAPPINESS WHILE CROSSING THE ROAD.' Outside the shops were many more signs.

The butcher's shop said: 'YOU MUST NOT BRING VEGETARIANS INTO THIS SHOP.'

The greengrocer's said: 'YOU MUST NOT BRING CARNIVORES INTO THIS SHOP.'

The health food shop said: 'YOU MUST NOT BRING FAT PEOPLE INTO THIS SHOP.'

The fish and chip shop said: 'YOU MUST NOT BRING THIN PEOPLE INTO THIS SHOP.'

The fur coat shop said: 'YOU MUST NOT BRING ANIMALS INTO THIS SHOP.'

The pet shop said: 'YOU MUST NOT BRING HUMANS INTO THIS SHOP.'

The clothes shop said: 'YOU MUST NOT BRING YOUR NAKED BODY TO THE SHOP.'

The cassette shop said: 'YOU MUST NOT PLAY MUSIC IN THE SHOP.'

The supermarket said: 'YOU MUST NOT BRING TROLLIES INTO THE SHOP.'

The toyshop said: 'YOU MUST NOT BRING CHILDREN INTO THE SHOP.'

The computer shop said: 'YOU MUST NOT BRING VIRUSES INTO THE SHOP.'

The shoe shop said: 'YOU MUST NOT BRING SMELLY FEET INTO THE SHOP.'

The bookshop said: 'YOU MUST NOT BRING WORMS INTO THE SHOP.'

And that was just to name a few.

Buddy was intrigued, and as he looked more closely he realised that each sign had the words: 'BY ORDER OF BLAST AND KITCHEN.'

'Wow!' thought Buddy. 'These Oldchurch leaders really do have a major influence in this town.'

But as strange as all these posters were, the strangest thing was that he had not seen a single person walking around. He had seen a few grumpy shopkeepers' faces staring at him from out of their windows, but apart from that it was as if he had entered a ghost town.

Seeing the chemist shop with the words, 'YOU MUST NOT TRUST HERBAL MEDICINES' written outside he went towards the door deciding to ask a lady he saw through the window to tell him how he could find Canon Blast's house. As he reached the door she ran up to it, bolted it and put a sign up saying: 'YOU MUST NOT ENTER—I'M CLOSED'. He tried a few more shops and exactly the same thing happened. Buddy was shocked. He was one of the most loving and friendly people you could wish to meet and he had never been treated like this before.

It was then he heard some loud chimes from a church bell, so he ran towards the sound as fast as he could. As the last clang of the old bell rang he found himself standing looking at the great old building that it was coming from. It was typical of an Oldchurch building, beautifully built hundreds of years ago with a wonderful historic attraction about it, but it would be hard to describe it as warm, cosy and friendly, which was the environment that Buddy was used to when meeting with the Newchurch people to worship the Voice.

'Oi! What the blazes do you want?' came a ferocious voice standing outside the main wooden doors of the old building, from a man dressed in a long black robe. Buddy nearly jumped out of his skin. It was the last thing he had expected to hear as he was day-dreaming and gazing at the magnificent old building. 'Oh,' he said, 'I'm looking for the Ancient Church of the Thirteenth Male Apostle.

'Well, you've found it. Now you can clear off,' shouted the robed figure. Buddy was not scared of this rude person, whoever he was, and walked up the little cobbled path to where he was standing. No one spoke for a few minutes. They both just stood staring at each other. Buddy was rather tubby and stood dressed in his faded blue jeans, white t-shirt and white trainers. Facing him was an Oldie who was tubbier than Buddy and was wearing only a black robe and black shoes. He looked rather strange with nothing between the hem of his robe and his black shoes except two fat white hairy legs.

'I have an appointment with Canon Blast,' said Buddy quietly.

'Not dressed like that you haven't,' replied the person in the doorway. 'I am Canon Blast and you have the choice of either coming back when you're properly dressed in a robe, or not bothering to come back at all. I've got enough trouble without weirdos like you giving me more.' With that the canon turned round and walked back into the Ancient Church of the Thirteenth Male Apostle, slamming the old fourteenth-century wooden door behind him.

Buddy walked away from the old building feeling rather sad at the communication breakdown, but also realising why he was called Canon Blast. As he sat down in the warm sunshine on a grassy bank, ignoring the sign 'YOU MUST NOT SIT DOWN ON THIS GRASSY BANK', he heard a faint noise in the distance. As it slowly grew louder, he guessed that it was coming in his direction.

The first sound that he could decipher was the sound of much jingling. This was followed by loud, high-pitched shouting and a sort of chanting. He leapt to his feet and peered down the roadway in the direction of the sounds.

Then it came into view. He could just make out that it

was some kind of procession, and as it came steadily closer it reminded him of a March for the Voice which Newchurch regularly did to aggravate the Enemy Superpowers and to put them in their place. But this was very different.

It was led by a tall slim Oldie of the female variety. She was obviously in charge at the head of the procession and she was wheeling a barrow in front of her with the most enormous copy of the Voice's Manual in it that Buddy had ever seen. Her attire caught Buddy's attention as she was wearing a very smart suit, consisting of grey trousers, jacket and waistcoat, and a tie that was louder than the noise she and her followers were making. As Buddy stared, he noticed that all the marchers were female and again all dressed in smart suits with different coloured ties, and most were waving tambourines with coloured ribbons flowing in all different directions, but all very carefully synchronised.

Those who were tambourineless had banners in their hands, which they waved high as they shouted out such statements as:

> We are fighting females,
> Released, at last set free.
> It's time to lock all males up,
> Then throw away the key.

The louder they shouted, the more they waved their banners. Buddy couldn't believe his eyes as he read the wording on some of the banners. 'FIRE THE ROTTEN OLD CANON' said one. 'BLAST FROM THE PAST' read another.

Then suddenly the angry parade stopped on the road right outside the Ancient Church of the Thirteenth Male

Apostle. 'Sisters' screamed the one with the wheel barrow at the front, 'Stop!' The entourage stopped obediently, as did their shouting and tambourine bashing. Putting her barrow down she screamed in the direction of the wooden door: 'Come out, Blast, you coward. Fight if you have the guts to. We'll show you who's wearing the trousers now.'

Blast appeared through the door followed by about fifty other male Oldies all dressed in black robes, black shoes and white legs. 'Pastor Kitchen,' he yelled back, 'we are not afraid of you. In fact, as you can see we are expecting you. You should have stayed in the kitchen where you and all your rebellious army belong.'

Between the doorway of the church and the road were two tall piles of earth, and after a few further insults were thrown, both leaders shouted, 'Charge!' and the battle began. Pastor Kitchen and the Modern Movement of the Free Sisters' Fellowship leapt onto the mound on the far left, while Canon Blast and the Ancient Church of the Thirteenth Male Apostle took up their position on the mound on the far right. Then the mud began to fly. Both sides proved to be very accurate and certainly knew how to hit a person where it really hurts.

Buddy stood and watched helplessly as serious injuries were being inflicted on both sides. He gazed at the now deserted big black Manual lying face down in the barrow in the middle of the road. He could see there was going to be no let-up, as the battle became even more furious and the mudslinging seemed like it was going to last for ever.

Sadly he made his way back towards Newchurch and the blood-curdling screams of the attackers and the pain-stricken wails of the wounded slowly disappeared out of earshot.

He felt sick inside as he knew with warfare of this kind there could be no winners; ultimately all would be losers.

But the worst losers of all would be those who belonged to neither the Ancient Church of the Thirteenth Male Apostle nor the Modern Movement of the Free Sisters' Fellowship.

Now was the time to send in the Newchurch hit squad.

As all of Newchurch was excitedly awaiting Buddy's return, nobody noticed a thin female Littlekid leave her bedroom with a small bag containing all her worldly possessions. As the sun disappeared and dusk quickly fell she walked through the streets unrecognised and finally left Newchurch. She knew it would be ages before anyone even realised she was no longer around, because everyone had their minds set on far more important things than her.

6. if you go down to the woods... tonight

Dusk never seemed to want to stay around for long. It was almost as though it had an urgent prior engagement which it had to rush off to fulfil. As quickly as it moved on, darkness crept in to take its place. Runaway Forest was never a place that would scare the Littlekids of Newchurch, though of course they had been taught to be sensible and not to wander alone there after dark, as that could be asking for trouble.

Angela wasn't asking for trouble as she entered the creepy darkness of Runaway Forest. She wasn't asking for anything. When you're running away from yourself, being logical and sensible is the last thing on your mind. Fortunately, the moon had decided to shed a bit of light that night and she was able to see dimly the narrow muddy path that led into the heart of the woods. Small, inquisitive, nocturnal, furry animals ran to the edge of the path to see who was invading their territory, while the wise old owls just hooted and peered down with their large eyes wide open, wondering who would be unwise enough to be walking out alone at this late hour.

Angela shivered as she walked through the freezing night air, her thin coat no competition against the might of the weather. Ahead of her she saw an old tree stump, and feeling tired she decided to rest. Weary, she sat down.

Then she heard it.

It was louder than the owl's hooting and the other small animal noises. It was a crashing, crunching sound and was coming from a distance behind her. It sounded like horses' hooves galloping through the bracken and thick undergrowth, and as the scary sound increased in volume by the second, she knew that whatever it was, it was heading in her direction.

Now she did feel frightened. She leapt up from the tree stump and started running as fast as her tired legs could manage down the path and deeper into the forest, but with every step it sounded like the hooves, and now the snorting of the creature, were not just following her, but were almost upon her. She let out a small cry of terror, but was now out of breath, so only a faint noise escaped her tired lungs. She dare not look back. Her heart was beating like a bass drum and as she felt a painful stitch strike her right side, she realised that trying to outrun it was futile. Angela allowed herself to fall head first into the mud and lay motionless on the ground, trying to catch her breath and weeping with fear.

She didn't dare look up as the galloping became a trot then came to a standstill right behind her. A dull thud followed as someone obviously dismounted and raced over to where she was lying helpless. Rough hands grabbed her thin arms and tied them behind her back, then a smelly, dirty piece of cloth was tied tightly over her eyes. Not a word was spoken as Angela felt herself being lifted up and thrown onto the hard wooden floor of what she assumed was some sort of cart. Then came the crack of a whip and she started moving. Within seconds they were in full flight, with Angela rolling about uncontrollably as the charging horse weaved its way along the winding paths of Runaway Forest.

While all this action was taking place, Buddy had arrived back in Newchurch and, having called an emergency meeting with the excited Hearthunter and Miraclekid, was explaining to them his discoveries in Religios-city.

Many miles away Little Chris was lying in his luxury four-poster bed, dressed in his silk pyjamas, proudly watching the video of that day's programme for the fifth time.

Eventually the horse screeched to a halt. The rider dismounted again and walked over and grabbed hold of a very bruised Angela and tied something tightly around her waist. The next thing Angela knew, she was being hoisted up into the air. Now, Angela was frightened of heights, so she was pleased she was still blindfolded.

Then the upward thrust stopped and for a moment or two she felt herself dangling in mid-air. She guessed she was a long way off the ground. Again rough hands grabbed her and after carrying her a short distance threw her onto something reasonably soft, but Angela's head cracked against a wooden wall and she fainted.

'Wake up!' yelled a fierce voice. 'You heard me, wake up!' it repeated. Angela felt very dazed as she tried to open her eyes. She also felt very sick from not having eaten for a long time. She felt ice-cold water being poured over her head, which ran down the inside of her t-shirt and made her jump as though she'd received an electrical shock.

Her eyes opened. She was relieved that at least the smelly blindfold and cutting ropes that had held her arms so tightly had been taken away. By the light of a flickering candle she realised that she was in a small wooden cabin and was staring straight into the dirty face of a female Littlekid. Her captor was a bit older and taller than she was and had long black greasy hair. Her body was covered in furs and her arms were bulging with muscles.

'What are you staring at, squirt?' asked the Littlekid rudely, displaying blackened teeth that looked like they had never been introduced to a toothbrush. 'Ain't you ever seen a real body before?'

At this the Littlekid laughed as she poked Angela's skinny body with a filthy finger and even filthier fingernail. 'You were easy to find in the woods,' she continued. 'I could hear your bones rattling a mile off.'

After a few more cruel comments about Angela she picked up some raw vegetables and started to eat them.

Angela continued to look round the sparsely furnished wooden shack. Apart from the table, chair and the old mattress she was lying on, there was a bed, a small, old-fashioned wood-burning stove, and a photo of two parents and a tiny Littlekid hanging on the wall.

'Yeah, that's me,' said the fur-clad female, seeing that

Angela's eyes were gazing at the photo. 'And I think the two Oldies are my mum and dad, but I can't be sure, 'cos I haven't seen them for years. My name's Yolander and you are my prisoner.' She threw a raw potato over to Angela to eat. 'Yolander Onmyturf. Get it?' she grinned. 'Yolander Onmyturf... and you're in big trouble. And Littlekid,' she said, getting up from the table and staring at Angela, 'believe me, I ain't kidding you are in big trouble.

'Now let's have a look in your bag and see if you have any goodies that might interest me. Hello, what's this?' said Yolander, picking out the photograph of Angela and a male Littlekid that Angela treasured so much. Yolander walked closer to Angela. 'Wow, I guess this used to be you,' she commented. 'But who is this gorgeous hunk of male flesh with you?'

Angela opened her mouth, but found it painful to answer. ''Is name is Little Christian,' she whispered in her broad cockney accent.

'Well, you don't mind if I keep it, do you?' said Yolander loudly. 'I haven't got many pics on my walls as you can see, and this handsome Littlekid will make a great pin-up.' Then, smashing the glass, she took the photo out of its frame. 'Well, I don't need this bit,' she mumbled, tearing the photo in two. She screwed the picture of Angela up and threw it on the floor. 'No offence,' she laughed, 'But I don't want your picture—just his.'

Angela didn't have the strength to argue, but she winced as she saw her last reminder of the great old days destroyed before her very eyes. It was as if Yolander had pierced her heart with a sharp knife.

Angela grew frightened again. 'Are yer gonna snuff me?' she asked.

'Not unless you give me any trouble,' replied Yolander.

'Anyway, looking at the state of you it seems like you've made quite a good job of trying to kill yourself.'

Angela blushed and felt guilty.

'Now, I'm going to sleep, and if you know what's good for you, I suggest you do the same,' said Yolander after she had pinned Little Christian's photo over her bed. Then she blew out the candle and got under the bedclothes. 'You've got a busy day tomorrow, Littlekid.'

Within minutes Yolander was snoring more loudly than the fearful snoring horse that had been chasing Angela, and although she was tired, she couldn't sleep. 'I must escape,' she thought. 'This evil Littlekid obviously has somethin' awful planned for me and I'm not goin' to wait around to find out what it is.'

Although the room was very dark, the moonlight shone in around the frame of the badly-made door. Quietly, Angela put one leg out of bed. 'If I can make it to the door, I'll be able to make a run for it,' she thought. Then she put her other leg on the floor, but to her horror the potato that Yolander had thrown over to her rolled off the bed and landed with a loud thumping noise on the bare wooden floorboards. 'What's that?' shouted Yolander, but she said it in her sleep and straightaway rolled over and faced the opposite direction and started snoring again.

Angela crept across the floor, hoping that the door facing her would not be locked. Moving at what seemed like an inch a minute she eventually reached it and breathed a short sigh of relief. Then she stretched her thin right arm up to the door catch and very gently eased it upwards. 'Brilliant!' she thought, almost forgetting where she was and wanting to shout for joy. The door wasn't locked.

Slowly standing upright, she opened the door just a fraction, trying to let as little light in as possible. The snoring continued. Then she crept through it and quietly closed it behind her, realising it would be suicide to try and retrieve her bag, or the picture of Little Christian.

Her heart was now racing with excitement. 'I've made it,' she thought. 'I'm free.' Turning away from the door she was just about to make a run for it, when suddenly she halted dead in her tracks. Her face went white as all the blood seemed to drain out of it. Facing her were just branches and dark nothingness. Daring for just a moment to look down she realised it was a sheer drop of about fifty metres to the path below. She was imprisoned in a tree house.

In the past Angela had not been afraid of heights. In fact she hadn't been afraid of anything much, but since she had stopped following the Voice all sorts of fears had taken hold of her.

She glanced briefly down again and felt dizzy. Though still freezing she started to perspire. 'What can I do?' she thought. 'If I go back in the hut I know somethin' 'orrible is going to happen to me. Oh crumbs!' Deep down, even though she was panicking, she knew she had no choice. She must overcome her fear, and escape. Glancing around she saw on her left-hand side a rope-ladder tied to a strong branch. 'It's the only way,' she thought to herself, and mustering all the courage that was left in her she reached out, grabbed it, and closing her eyes started to descend.

Hand over hand, foot over foot, very slowly and all the time trying to stop the ladder from swinging, she climbed down. All of her body was now wet with sweat and her hands were finding it harder and harder to get a firm grip. 'Still, I must be at least halfway,' she thought, still not daring to look below her. Then she froze to the ladder. It was that sound again. Galloping hooves in the distance, charging through the undergrowth and trampling anything that would get in its way. Within seconds she could hear the snorting nostrils just a few metres beneath her. Still she refused to look down.

'So, you prefer my horse Nightmare's company to mine, do you?' screamed an angry voice from the top of the ladder. Angela looked up and saw Yolander staring down at her. 'Well, you have ten seconds to make your choice,' screamed Yolander even more fiendishly. 'Up to Yolander or down to Nightmare.'

As Yolander began to count up to ten, Angela just clung even more tightly to the ladder, now weeping out loud and absolutely petrified. 'Ten!' shouted Yolander and with that pulled out a sharp knife that was tucked away beneath her fur. 'Goodbye, skinny Littlekid,' she yelled as she started cutting the rope on the rope-ladder. Enjoy your time with Nightmare.' The nag below was getting highly excitable and as well as snorting even more violently, it was menacingly scraping its front right hoof in the mud and frothing at the mouth as though it had gone raving mad.

Angela didn't dare look up or down. As Yolander cut right through one of the ladder ropes, the ladder swung uncontrollably towards the tree. Screaming in desperation Angela shrieked, 'Voice, please 'elp me!' and with that her thin body swung with the ladder and thumped against the mighty tree trunk. Her fingers spontaneously released their grip of the rope, causing her to fall to the darkness below.

7.   IN NONE WE TRUST

It was very early in the morning. A white frost covered the ground of Runaway Forest like a huge white carpet. The horse and cart pulled to a halt. 'I say, have you got me someone?' came the posh voice of the driver.

'Yeah,' came the reply, 'but it ain't much of one I'm afraid; all skinny like.'

'What sort of condition is it in?' said the posh voice.

'Oh, I'm afraid it's a bit roughed up,' came the reply. 'But it's still breathing.'

'All right, throw it on the back of my cart, but if it dies

within a week you can forget about your pay. Oh, and I almost forgot Grand Gander is very appreciative of your work and sends his sincere thanks.'

Yolander felt good that her hard work was being appreciated. She lifted the thin body up and placed it in the back of the cart, and without another word being muttered the cart trundled off towards Nochurch.

That same early morning found Little Chris staring at his very expensive, highly-crystalled watch. 'Another five minutes and I must leave,' he thought. He took one last look at himself in his full-length bedroom mirror. Yes, the black shiny patterned suit with the bright yellow tie looked fine, but he put a touch more gel on his hair as he noticed one hair was trying to break free. Perfect.

He left his bedroom and excitedly ran down the stairs, picking up his briefcase as he did so. This was a meeting of a lifetime and he wanted to be sure that he hadn't forgotten anything. Once in the hallway he laid his case on a beautiful antique table and opened it. It contained a portable microcomputer, which contained his diary and would be helpful if he needed to make any notes, a portable micro-cassette recorder—that always came in handy —a pair of shades, a spare handkerchief, a chequebook, a hair brush, breath mints, a copy of the Voice's Manual and a copy of his latest show on video. 'Yes, I think that's everything,' he considered carefully, but then took out the Manual and left it on the table. 'Perhaps I won't need this today,' he thought on reflection, and with that he closed his case, picked it up and walked out of his front door to the waiting limo.

The sixty-four Gooseys fidgeted nervously as they sat facing the Grand Gander in the now-restored Oddboys' Hall.

'For goodness' sake relax,' shouted their leader, nervously pacing the floor himself. 'This is a great day, for two reasons. The first is that we have an opportunity to meet together twice in one week, and the other is that our dreams have come true. We are about to become a proper sixty-six-member gaggle.'

As Grand Gander moved away from the table, all stared at him noticing that his stomach had expanded since they had last met, but nobody dared say anything. Grand Gander could see that their eyes were aimed at a certain part of his anatomy and simply but embarrassingly explained to them that he was suffering from digestion troubles, which made him look rather larger than usual.

The limo pulled up sharply at the busiest crossroads in Nochurch in the middle of the early morning rush hour and Little Chris stared out of the window at a multicar smash up. The injured and wounded lay everywhere and the noise of exploding vehicles and the people in pain was deafening. It was a horrific scene. As he looked more closely he saw someone dressed in a traffic cop's uniform, waving his hands in all directions, seemingly ignoring the mangled mayhem. Little Chris wound down his electric window and shouted out, 'Oi! What's going on?' At this the uniformed officer stopped waving his arms and marched over towards the limo.

The closer he came, the more Little Chris thought he recognised the face, but even if he didn't, the face obviously recognised him. 'No, it can't be,' shouted the policeman excitedly, now completely ignoring the blood and chaos that continued behind him. 'Yes, it is!' he exclaimed with a huge grin spreading right across his face. It's Little Chris, isn't it?'

Little Chris still didn't have a clue who was addressing

him, then right in front of his eyes the officer started taking his uniform off, throwing his hat in the air with a yell of glee. 'Well I'll be... it's Ron Guidance,' shouted Little Chris in utter amazement, recognising the Oldie with his grey hair and his grey moustache.

'Of course it is,' replied a beaming Ron dumping the uniform on the floor. 'Who did you think it was? Robocop?' And with that he burst out laughing. 'I say, old friend,' he said amid his guffawing, 'we have done well for ourselves, haven't we?' He gazed at all the riches surrounding Little Chris. 'Now be a good chap and give me a lift away from here. You see, all this racket behind me is starting to bring on one of my migraines. I was only given this job this morning because everybody knows how brilliant I am at helping people find direction, but obviously my gifting does not include directing car drivers.'

Little Chris trusted no one, especially so-called old friends. 'But you can't just resign and walk away from this tragic mess,' he said. 'Just think of me for a moment and of my reputation as a TV star. If my fans discovered that I had not only left the scene of a disaster without giving assistance, but also gave a lift to the person who caused it, my viewing figures would be halved and I would be financially finished. Anyway, I have a very important, very private meeting that I must attend and if we don't leave right away I will be late.'

'But you owe me,' said angry Ron. The smile was now gone. 'I helped make you what you are today. It was I who advised you that you didn't need Newchurch any longer.'

'I owe you nothing,' snapped Little Chris just as angrily. 'All you scroungers want to share in my hard-earned success. Listen hard,' he continued, 'I would still be where I am today if I'd never met you. I achieved all I have today by myself and with the help of no one. Now clear off! I hope I never see you again.'

With that Little Chris closed his window and thumped his chauffeur's seat, indicating to him to drive on.

'You wait,' snarled Ron Guidance. 'I'll get even with you, Little Chris, if it's the last thing I do.' And he ran off in the opposite direction to the noise.

While Little Chris and Ron Guidance had been arguing, only one person had been doing something constructive. Sam Ariton, who hated cars and was president of the Prosecute All Polluting Vehicles Movement, had phoned for ambulances and was racing around doing all he could to help those in pain.

'Well, where is he?' grumbled Grand Gander looking at his watch impatiently for the sixth time. 'He is six seconds late and I hate being kept waiting.' This was the cue for all the other Gooseys to look at their watches and all make a tutting sound at the same time. Then outside the hall the screech of brakes silenced everyone. Grand Gander signalled to one of the Pecks to peer carefully out of the door to see who it was.

'It's a big limo,' came the reply from the peering Peck. 'And a Littlekid dressed in a smart black shiny suit has just got out and is heading towards us.' While sixty-four Gooseys looked at each other even more nervously, Grand Gander breathed a sigh of relief. 'Excellent,' he whispered to himself. 'Little Christian, you are just about to know how a fly feels when it first makes contact with a spider's web.'

8. ONWARDS INTO THE NIGHT

Neither Miraclekid nor Hearthunter had known what to say as Buddy had related the sad story of Religios-city. For the next few days they all spent a lot of time talking and listening to the Voice, as this had not been the news they had expected to receive. This was going to be no normal hit. They needed to replan their strategy.

The Voice made it very clear that now was the time to strike, which thrilled Buddy as this had been his suggestion, but both Hearthunter and Miradekid were no longer quite as enthusiastic as they were clearly about to embark upon a mission that was unlike anything they had ever experienced.

The Voice also told them that he wanted them to leave in the evening, which would mean that they would arrive in Religios-city under the cloak of darkness and be less conspicuous.

Buddy was thrilled at the turnout of Newchurch to pray over Hearthunter, Miraclekid, Ivor Future, Joy Atalltimes and Hope Itgoeswell (otherwise known as the Fearless Five) before they set off to Religios-city. Like any good Flockwatcher he also made a mental note of those who were not there. Some were obviously looking after their tiny Littlekids, others were feeling unwell, even after being prayed for, and just one or two were probably being a bit rebellious. Buddy turned to Harmony, who was also an excellent Flockwatcher, and asked if she could just pop over and ask Angela to join them. As he wasn't sure if anyone had seen her for the last few days, she might not have known that the meeting was being held.

Harmony quietly slipped out of the meeting room and ran to the small house where Angela had been staying. She went as quickly as she could because she hated missing out on the good-bye prayers. She was about to ring the door-bell, but then she noticed that there were no lights on in the house. 'She must be asleep,' Harmony thought, and look-ing up at the bedroom window she saw that the curtains were open, but again no sign of any light. This did not seem unusual though to Harmony, as she knew that Angela always slept with the curtains open.

Harmony raced back to the meeting room and discreetly pushed her way to the front. 'All her lights are off. She must be fast asleep,' she whispered to Buddy.

'Oh well,' he said, 'probably the best thing, feeling as she does.' But there was disappointment in his voice.

Although Hearthunter and Miraclekid didn't say anything, they were even more disappointed than Buddy by Angela's absence—not so much that she wasn't praying for them, more that she wasn't up to going with them. They had not been on one hit where both she and Little Christian hadn't come into their minds, but they never talked about it; it was still too painful.

The moon had decided not to bother to come out on this night, so the Fearless Five set off with small packs on their backs, containing all the essentials for a few days, a torch in one hand and their Manuals within easy reach in their pockets.

The night air was as usual bitterly cold, but they felt warm inside as they always did when they were being obedient to the Voice. Soon they reached the entrance to Runaway Forest, and Hope asked if there was any way they could walk round it and not through it, as it did look ever so creepy. The others laughed. 'It will be fine,' Hearthunter said, 'so long as we all stay together. Remember the Voice has commissioned us to do this, so he will look after us.'

Once in the wood Hope realised that she had nothing to be afraid of. In fact it was great fun all holding hands, flashing their torchlights everywhere and singing the Littlekids' marching song at the tops of their voices.

The owls peered down and the little furry animals again came inquisitively to the side of the path. It was strange for them to be disturbed twice within a few days.

As the singing continued Miraclekid suddenly shouted, 'Stop!' They all stopped instantly and went quiet.

'What is it?' asked Hearthunter, surprised.

'Wait, I think I've seen something.' He shone his torch on the path in front of them where they all saw a horse's hoofprints, followed by cartwheels.

'They are a horse's hoofprints,' said Ivor. 'I'd recognise them anywhere.'

'Yes, I realise that,' said Miraclekid rather impatiently. 'But why have they just appeared? And where have they come from?'

He shone his torch to the side of the path and saw that the bracken and bushes had been flattened. 'There's your answer,' said Hearthunter.

'What's so strange about that?'

'Something inside me says that something's not right. No, I'd go as far as to say that something is very wrong.'

With this he left the others and followed the horse and cart tracks further down the path.

'Oh, I'm getting scared,' said Hope and Joy both at the same time.

'And I don't feel so brave either,' remarked Ivor.

Hearthunter shouted after Miraclekid. 'Hey,' he said, 'go easy. You're scaring the Littlekids and we haven't even reached the battlefield yet.'

Miraclekid seemed to be ignoring all of them. He had stopped and was kneeling on the frozen muddy path. 'Look at this!' he shouted. They all ran to where he was kneeling. A large area of grass had been flattened and in the mud it was just possible to make out the imprints of clothing. Miradekid repeated, 'There's something wrong. If I'm not mistaken, not so long ago a Littlekid was lying here. Look over there to the horse and cart tracks.' They all looked to where the beam of his light was shining. The horse had obviously stopped and from then on the cart track marks were deeper. 'Something—or should I say someone has been picked up and put on the cart.'

'Come off it,' smiled Hearthunter. 'You've been watching too many mystery movies. Someone may have fallen over or been hurt and a passing cart has picked them up and taken care of them. That does happen, you know.'

Miraclekid was not convinced. 'I'm not going to move from this spot until we talk to the Voice about it. I believe the Voice is trying to show us something.'

Hearthunter knew that once Miraclekid felt something there was no changing his mind. He also knew that Miraclekid was very sensitive to what the Voice was saying, and so he agreed.

As they spoke to the Voice, he showed them all that it was no accident that they had spotted the tracks, but the Voice didn't seem to say anything else.

'I must follow the tracks,' said Miraclekid. 'I really feel that's what the Voice wants me to do.'

'Wait a minute,' said Hearthunter. 'We are on a mission. What about Religios-city? Buddy will go mad if he hears you've gone off and done your own thing. You know how impetuous he thinks you are. You must come with us.'

'I can't,' stated Miraclekid dogmatically. 'You four head towards Religios-city and I will catch you up later. It's not that I'm going against Buddy's wishes, it's just that I'm taking a detour to get there.'

Hearthunter knew he was wasting precious time trying to argue with Miraclekid. 'OK,' he said. 'We will meet you there, but do be careful.' And with that they prayed over each other again, then the four continued their singing as they headed along the path towards Religios-city, while Miraclekid left the path to follow the tracks through the undergrowth.

The further Miraclekid walked, the more quiet the singing became until soon it could be heard no more. Now he felt very alone, and he had to remind himself that he wasn't—the Voice was with him.

Although the horse and cart had made a sort of track, it was not a very good one and the brambles seemed to reach out and scratch and grab him as the stinging-nettles left painful little poisonous bumps on any piece of bare skin they could find.

Then he heard a strange sound. It was far off but certainly heading towards him. 'That's better,' he smiled, with not an ounce of fear in him. 'The horse and cart are going to find me, which will save me the effort of having to find them.' He stood boldly in the cold dark night facing towards the oncoming sound, 'Here I am! Come and get me!' he shouted.

Where he was standing, visibility was very bad, not only due to the darkness, but also due to the dense wood around him, and although the crashing noise of the horse and cart was by now extremely loud, indicating that they were very close, he couldn't quite work out how close. Then to his surprise, instead of seeing the expected sight burst out of the nearby bushes, instantly all went silent, deadly silent.

Even the owls and the furry little animals could not be heard. It was as if someone had ordered every living thing to be still or suffer the consequences. Miraclekid could just hear himself breathing rather heavily, as he now became uneasy. He felt he was being watched by evil eyes, but he couldn't work out where they were hiding.

'I know you are there,' shouted Miraclekid. 'Come out and show yourself.' Still no reply. He started to perspire and as he did so the nettle and bramble wounds seemed to hurt all the more. Then he heard a blood-curdling scream, as someone leapt out from behind him. Something hard thumped him on the back of his head, and he slumped to the ground. On this very dark night, someone had switched his lights out.

Although Hearthunter, Ivor, Joy and Hope knew nothing about all this, they did feel the Voice telling them they should wait at the edge of the forest for a while—this would give Miraclekid the chance to catch them up. But as they lay down on the grass in their thick warm clothes, even though the night was cold, their tired eyelids grew heavier and heavier until none of them could keep them open any longer, and in no time they were all fast asleep.

9. THE ADMISSION CHARGE

As Little Chris entered the Oddboys' Hall the Pecks slammed the doors behind him. Little Chris glanced around and saw sixty-five people, none of whom he recognised. He gazed at the top table, where he saw a tall man of average build with a black moustache who he assumed must be in charge.

'Welcome to the Gooseys' gaggle gathering,' said the tall man standing to his feet and making a vague attempt at a smile. 'Perhaps you would be kind enough to go over to that far corner and stand on the wooden box that we have put there especially for you.' Little Chris was escorted by the two Pecks to the box in the corner.

'I would just like to say,' said Little Chris standing on the box, 'that it is a great priv...'

'Shuddup!' snapped Grand Gander cutting him off in the middle of his sentence. 'You will say nothing until you have passed our initiation test, unless I ask you to, and even then you ask permission from me, the Grand Gander, before you utter a word.'

Little Chris went silent, while his face blushed a brilliant red.

'Listen carefully,' continued Grand Gander. 'This is a very exclusive secret society where only the elite from Nochurch ever have the opportunity to belong to the Grand Order Of Secretly Evil Yobs, and we have to check you out to see if you are made of the right material.' The other Gooseys nodded in agreement.

'There are four very simple things you must do before you can be one of us. Are you willing to attempt them? You may answer my question.'

'Yes, Grand Gander,' said Little Chris meekly.

'Well, good. First, we have to teach you to keep your mouth shut. All you have to do is to open your mouth and stick your tongue out. The Pecks will then punch a small hole in it with a sterilised instrument. This tiny hole will always be there to remind you that if you ever disclose any of the Gooseys' secrets, the Pecks will make a much bigger hole, by taking your tongue out altogether.' The Pecks liked this bit and smiled at each other.

As Little Chris opened his mouth, he saw the Pecks pull a small hole-punching instrument out of a sealed bag, 'Tongue out,' one of them growled. Little Chris hated any sort of pain and gingerly stuck his tongue out just a little way. 'Further,' grunted the other Peck. Then as one grabbed hold of it, snap, the other allowed the puncher to do it's business. Little Chris howled in pain and almost fell off the wooden box, as blood dripped down his chin.

'Oh, come on now!' exdaimed Grand Gander. 'That didn't hurt much, did it? Remember, there is no gain without pain.' All the other Gooseys nodded seriously, each relieved that they had never had to have their tongues punched.

'Secondly, you need to learn to be humble. All Gooseys, except me of course, are here to serve each other. In other words, you are here to serve us,' declared Grand Gander. 'Pecks, bring out the props.' The Pecks brought out a bucket of hot soapy water, and as they did so all the Gooseys removed their flippers. 'Well, what are you waiting for?' asked Grand Gander. 'It's feet-washing time.'

'Permission to speak please,' gurgled Little Chris, as his mouth was still bleeding. 'What do I wash and dry them with?'

Grand Gander looked hard at him and replied, 'That black suit jacket of yours would be ideal to use as a flannel, and those black trousers I'm sure would serve as a towel. Now get on with it.'

Little Chris removed his beautiful suit and started the long, horrible, arduous task, and the nearer he got to the top table, the more smelly the feet seemed to become. He wondered if any of them had ever cleaned between their toes and reckoned that if he had planted seeds there, there was enough dirt to ensure a great harvest.

Finally, feeling exhausted, he washed the Grand Gander's feet which were without doubt the worst of the lot. He was then taken back to the box in the corner.

'Do please put your suit back on,' insisted Grand Gander. 'What would people think if they walked in and saw you dressed in just your shirt and underpants?' Again all the Gooseys nodded, having put their flippers back on after admiring their clean feet. They felt very relieved that they had never been asked to perform such a humiliating task.

Little Chris put on the dirty, stinking, wet jacket and trousers and stared at Grand Gander, waiting for his next command.

'So far so good,' commented Grand Gander. 'You are now halfway through your initiation and already I feel that you are a much better person than when you first arrived.

'The third lesson you need to learn is that you are nothing compared with me. After all, there is only one leader, only one Grand Gander, and that is the one you are now facing. Within the next two hours you have to say some wonderful, nice things about me—which you shouldn't find very hard as of course there are plenty of things to choose from—but alongside those wonderful compliments, I want you to make honest comments about yourself in comparison with me. Give him an example, Bigsby Bankbalance, of what I am talking about.'

Bigsby, who had been dozing off after having a wonderful daydream about counting bank notes, sat up in surprise. 'Er, yes of course, Grand Gander,' he stammered. 'You, Grand Gander,' he continued, 'are rich in every sense of the word, whereas I, with all my worldly fortune, am like a penniless, bankrupt, broke, destitute, impecunious, needy, poverty-stricken, skint beggar in comparison.'

'Yes, that just about sums you up,' said a very condescending Grand Gander. 'Now, it's your turn, Little Chris.'

Little Chris didn't know where or indeed how to begin. 'Um, you are very good looking and I am not so good looking,' he stammered.

'Rubbish!' screamed Grand Gander, cutting him short as all the gaggle booed and hissed to give him moral support. A Peck cuffed Little Chris round the back of the head.

'I'm sorry,' came a weedy sound from Little Chris's mouth. 'What I meant to say is that you are very good looking and I am very ordinary and plain.'

'Rubbish!' screamed out Grand Gander even more loudly so his voice could be heard over the deafening boos and hisses. The other Peck cuffed him even harder.

'I'm sorry,' wailed Little Chris. 'What I meant to say is that you are the best looking, most attractive, glamorous, handsome, visually stunning, gorgeous person in the world and I am the most ugly, disgusting, revolting, nasty, objectionable piece of nothing ever to crawl out from under a stone.'

'That's much better,' exclaimed Grand Gander with the background ballyhoo now changing from boos to cheers. 'And much more truthful,' he added.

For the following one hour and fifty-five minutes Little Chris smothered Grand Gander with every compliment imaginable, while at the same time putting himself down to depths so low that he actually began to believe not only every honouring observation he made about his new leader, but also every horrible thing that he said about himself.

The two hours were up. Little Chris hardly had the strength to stand on the box. His mouth was still painful, though it had stopped bleeding, his clothes were still damp and had started to steam and smell even worse, and now he had indoctrinated himself into believing that Grand Gander was the greatest thing since the invention of the TV camera and in doing so had not just been humbled, but had allowed every bit of self-worth to be crushed out of him.

The Gooseys looked at each other in amazement, relieved that when it had been their turn they had only had to speak for ten minutes, not two hours. Grand Gander looked at him feeling well pleased with himself. 'Little Chris, so far you have learned three very important lessons. To summarise:

the first is that as a Goosey you will be sworn to silence; the second, that as a Goosey you are nobody special—you are just one of the gaggle; thirdly, you have learned that you no longer do what you want to do. You now do what I want you to do.'

Little Chris just managed a nod.

'The final part of your initiation is the most simple. It is quite painless and the only action required is that of your hand giving an autograph. Pecks, help him over here to my table.'

The Pecks almost had to carry him over to where Grand Gander was seated. Grand Gander waved a very official-looking piece of paper in the air. 'We all know that the job you do requires a certain amount of devotion to, ah, now how can I put it without upsetting the rest of the gaggle? I know, to your idea of a superior being,' whispered Grand Gander. 'The final thing you need to do to become one of us,' he continued, 'is to sign your name at the bottom of the Goosey contract of total loyalty and absolute allegiance.'

Little Chris's eyes were very bloodshot and quite bleary, but he could still read the words in front of him.

I, Little Chris, promise that no person (alive or dead) will be more important to me than Grand Gander and the Grand Order Of Secretly Evil Yobs. I am sworn to secrecy and put myself into their hands, committing the rest of my life to them. I understand that if I break this promise, my existence will be terminated.

Signed:

Witness:

Little Chris had hated the initiation ceremony and the

humiliating tasks that he had taken part in, but he also knew that if he really wanted to be somebody, he had to be part of this group.

As he read through the contract a second time, he heard a very quiet voice that he had not heard for a long time whispering into his mind the words, 'Don't do it.'

'Whose voice is that?' he thought. 'I don't recognise it.' But it kept saying the same words.

Grand Gander was now getting impatient and had started to perspire. For the first time that day his stomach gave a loud rumble, reminding him it was nearly lunchtime. 'Come on!' he snapped. 'We haven't got all day. What on earth's the matter? You do want to be one of us, don't you?'

Little Chris held the pen tightly. 'Grand Gander,' he said painfully, 'you know I want to join you, but a voice I don't recognise is telling me not to, and it's so powerful it's paralysed my right hand. Look, I can't move it.'

Grand Gander was now in a real panic. 'Listen, Little Chris,' he yelled, 'if you don't sign this you will be finished. No one turns down Grand Gander and lives to be successful.' As he said this he ran around and stood next to Little Chris and held the hand that had the pen in it. 'Now listen carefully, this is your very last chance. I am not going to ask you again,' he murmured with a murderous tone in his voice. 'Answer me. Do you want to sign it?'

Little Chris tried to speak, but now found that his lips had frozen together and he couldn't even open his mouth. But he did manage a slight nod of the head.

'That's all I need to know,' said a relieved Grand Gander, and forcing his hand painfully downwards to where the contract lay on the table he managed to manoeuvre the pen so it wrote a cross. 'Thank you,' smiled Grand Gander, snatching the contract and signing his own name next to the word 'witness'. He put it safely into his pocket. 'That is all I needed. At last,' he whispered under his breath, 'I've got you. You now belong to me. Dad, you'll be proud of me.'

He walked back to the head of the table, beaming all over his face. 'All stand!' he shouted. All the gaggle obediently rose. 'With the power invested in me as Grand Gander, I officially welcome Little Chris as our new member. Your uniform will be delivered to your dwelling place within a few days, and seeing the bad physical state you are in we will see that you receive one of the Goosey perks, which I'm sure will help you back to full health. Major, you acquired that last, ahem, servant. Can you see that he or she is delivered very quickly to our new associate.' The Major saluted obediently. 'Now, let's all raise our hands and shake our fists in the air as we sing our immortal anthem,' said Grand Gander.

As Goosey Goosey Gander was released from sixty-five pairs of lungs at full volume, the Pecks too raised their hands and Little Chris slumped to the floor feeling totally exhausted. Yet for the first time in years he finally felt accepted. This had been a morning he would never forget.

The hall emptied and as usual a very contented Grand Gander was the last to leave. As he entered the bright glare of the midday sunshine he heard a *psssst* noise coming from the shadow at the side of the building. He walked over to where the sound had come from and he could just make out the shape of a thin Oldie. 'Hello Ron,' said Grand Gander. 'It's nice to see you again.' He handed Ron a brown envelope with his agreed fee and then a small bottle with some pills in it. 'Please see that Little Chris receives these personally. I've a feeling he is going to need them.'

From the shadows, Ron's smiling white teeth stayed clenched as he replied, 'It will be my pleasure.'

Without anything else being said, the men parted company.

10. NOTHING GOES TO PLAN

'I don't believe it!' yelled a frantic Hearthunter staring at his watch. 'It's midday. We must have been asleep for hours.' The other three Littlekids were rubbing their eyes in disbelief. 'But we only put our heads down for a short doze,' said Ivor Future as the bright, warm midday sun was making it very hard to open and focus his eyes.

'What shall we do now?' asked Hope Itgoeswell. 'I remember Buddy saying that we should enter Religios-city at night.'

'I know,' frowned Hearthunter. 'You've no need to remind me.'

'I wonder where Miraclekid is,' said Joy Atalltimes, not wanting to be left out of the conversation.

'Oh, knowing him,' said Hearthunter, 'he will be in the middle of Religios-city doing all sorts of wonderful things. He will probably complete the mission before we even get there.'

'So we are going to hit it in the daylight, are we?' enquired Hope.

'We have no choice. I know Buddy will be mad at me, but what else can we do? And we still have a long walk before us,' groaned Hearthunter. 'Come on, we'd better get going.'

None of them really felt like singing any more. They just hoped they were doing the right thing.

Miraclekid ached all over and was very bored just sitting tied up in a sparsely-furnished wooden hut all morning. He had asked the Voice to burn through the rope for him so he could escape, but the Voice had told him just to wait and be patient, which were the two things he most hated doing. As he waited he gazed for the umpteenth time around his gloomy prison. 'This is very untidy,' he thought. 'Whoever lives here hasn't even bothered to make the bed.' It was as he looked at the blanket on the bed that his eyes glimpsed a torn photo above it. It was too dark to see who was in the photo so he rolled over on the floor to get a better look. Suddenly he realised who it was. 'There is only one person I know who would be carrying that photo around with them,' he said out loud. 'And I thought Angela was back in Newchurch. She must be lost—and I'm on the trail that will lead to her!'

Then he heard the faint noise of the horse and cart, and when that had stopped he heard a sort of creaking. The door burst open and he came face to face with Yolander Onmyturf.

'Hi!' said Miraclekid as cheerfully as he could manage in his painful situation. 'Wow! You must be strong for a Littlekid,' he said looking at her. 'You've certainly got the drop on me.'

'No one is stronger than me,' replied Yolander. 'You male Littlekids think you're so tough and we females are just weak little things. Well, I'm out to prove you all wrong.'

'Hold your horses,' shouted Miraclekid, suddenly realising that this was a very apt comment after the night before. 'I'm not just any ordinary Littlekid. I'm one of the Children of the Voice and I believe female Littlekids are as important and special as we males.'

'I don't believe you!' screeched Yolander. 'All you males are the same and I don't trust any of you. Mind you, I don't trust females either.'

'Well anyway, have you seen anyone around here lately?' asked Miraclekid, trying to change the subject. 'A skinny female Littlekid for instance, who is probably a bit younger than yourself?'

'Nope,' said Yolander. 'The only ones who live in this forest are me and Nightmare my horse.'

'Well, who gave you that picture of that male Littlekid stuck above your bed?' enquired Miraclekid further.

'Mind your own business,' shouted Yolander getting angry again. 'If any Littlekids like you stray into the Runaway Forest at night it is my job to capture them. I have my orders.'

'And who gives you these orders?' asked Miraclekid.

'Mind your own business,' shouted Yolander again. 'You really are a nosey Littlekid, aren't you.'

'One last question,' said Miraclekid seeing that he was getting nowhere. 'What are you going to do with me now you have captured me?'

'The same as I've done with all the rest,' replied Yolander, calming down a bit. 'I'm going to sell you to the Gooseys of Nochurch who will make you one of their slaves.'

'The Gooseys in Nochurch,' said Miraclekid looking alarmed and for the first time a little frightened. 'I've heard about them, and the Littlekid slave-trade they're mixed up in. I've also heard that once in the hands of the Gooseys the Littlekids are never seen again. Rumour has it that the strong ones are sent to faraway lands, while the weak... are killed.'

'I haven't got a clue what they do with them,' said Yolander. 'And it's none of my business. They pay me to give them Littlekids and that's all I know and that's all I want to know.'

'But you wouldn't hand me over to them, would you?' pleaded Miraclekid. 'After all, I could be your friend.'

'I don't need any friends. I didn't even need any family. They always end up leaving you,' said Yolander, now quietly.

Miraclekid could see that this was one hurt Littlekid and the Voice was encouraging her to share some of her hurts.

'Listen,' said Miraclekid gently, 'why don't you tell me your name and how you got to be working for the Gooseys.'

Yolander sat down next to Miraclekid. 'My name is Yolander Onmyturf,' said Yolander. 'I was born in Nochurch and when I was only a tiny Littlekid my mum ran off with another male Oldie. It was soon after that on one dark night that my dad, wanting to get rid of me, brought me here to Runaway Forest and left me alone to die. Although at first I was very frightened,' she continued, shivering at the memory, 'and really thought I was a gonner, it was then a miracle happened. A tall thin Oldie riding on a horse appeared, and although he never smiled he picked me up and rode into the heart of the forest until we reached this house. "This will be a nice place for you to live," said the Oldie. "And here, you can have my horse Nightmare as a gift."

'Although I never saw the Oldie again,' she proceeded, 'food would always appear and then as I grew older so did the demands. Notes were pinned to my tree saying things like, "I saved your life, now you owe me one. All you have to do is capture any Littlekids found wandering in the forest at night, then hand them over to one of my Goosey friends and I will pay you well," and the notes were signed "GG."'

'Grand Gander himself,' mumbled Miraclekid disgustedly.

'So,' ended Yolander, 'now you know it all.' Suddenly she realised that for the first time ever she had made herself vulnerable by sharing her life story. What on earth made her do it, and to an unknown male Littlekid as well? She now felt embarrassed and leapt up and walked away from Miraclekid towards her unmade bed. Then she ripped the photo of Little Christian off the wall and tore it into tiny pieces. 'See, I don't need anyone,' she growled viciously. Miracdekid was a bit worried and asked the Voice what he should do now, but the Voice just continued to say, 'Wait and be patient.'

Suddenly Miraclekid had an idea, which unfortunately was not part of the Voice's plan.

'Yolander,' said Miradekid, 'who do you think is the stronger—you or me?'

Yolander made a huffing sound and flexing her impressive muscles snarled, 'I am, of course.'

'Rubbish!' exclaimed Miraclekid. 'I have the Voice on my

side and together we could dispatch you into the middle of the next century.' Yolander didn't like this sort of talk, as she believed the only thing that she had in life of any value was her strength.

'Listen,' continued Miradekid, 'I challenge you in combat. If I win, I go free. If you win, I will go quietly with the Goosey slave-traders.'

Yolander could not refuse the chance to show off her strength, so she nodded. She then took a knife from inside her fur and walked towards Miradekid. 'Hey, no knives,' he shouted. 'Hand-to-hand combat was what I was thinking of.'

Yolander half-smiled as she cut the ropes that were binding Miraclekid. 'Follow me,' she said, 'and don't try to run away because Nightmare is even less friendly than I am.'

'Impossible,' smiled a relieved Miraclekid, rubbing his wrists, pleased that the rope had been taken off. Obediently he followed her to the wooden door. Miraclekid was surprised that they were stuck up in a tree, but seeing the rope-ladder and being very fit himself he had no trouble following Yolander down it.

As he neared the bottom of the ladder he heard those galloping hooves again, but when Yolander shouted, 'Stay,' Nightmare stopped in his tracks like an obedient, well-trained puppy.

Once on the ground they faced each other. 'I'm going to show you once and for all that female Littlekids can be stronger than male ones,' yelled Yolander.

'You haven't got a chance against me and the Voice,' shouted a triumphant Miraclekid very confidently.

As Yolander came flying towards him with her fists clenched he shouted, 'I command you to stop in the name of the Voice.'

But she didn't and the fist thumped him so hard that he lost his balance and fell over. Yolander continued to make mincemeat of him, while Miraclekid kept shouting everything from, 'Fists, be still!' to, 'Eyes, go blind!'. Eventually Yolander got off him as he lay in a moaning heap. He'd not only lost the fight, but he'd also lost his voice with all the shouting.

'If you'd stopped shouting and started fighting you may have done better,' observed the gloating and victorious Yolander.

It was then that another horse and cart arrived. 'Apologies for being a bit late, but we had a very important meeting and then I had a few things I had to attend to at the bank before I could get here,' said the voice on the cart.

'No problem,' said Yolander. 'I'll put your latest acquisition on the cart. There won't be any need to tie him up. This one's all mouth and no muscle.'

'Oh dear, he's in a bit of a mess,' said the voice on the cart as Yolander threw Miraclekid onto the wagon.

'He'll live,' said Yolander. 'And I'll be in to the bank to get my money tomorrow.' By the way, is that skinny female Littlekid I gave to the Major still alive?' she asked.

'Yes,' came the voice from the cart. 'The Major said that she is just about alive, but I wouldn't go racing to him for your wages, because it looks unlikely that she will last the week.'

With this the horse and cart and the badly beaten up and very disillusioned Miraclekid left Runaway Forest.

As Yolander dimbed back up the ladder and sat on a branch in the warm sunlight she felt a strange feeling. She didn't recognise it because she had never felt it before. She kept thinking about Miraclekid. He was different from all the others. She'd actually had a real conversation with him, and even though he did keep shouting strange things about the Voice, he had more courage than anyone else she ever captured. 'I wonder if this is the feeling you get when you make a friend,' she pondered.

As she continued thinking, she suddenly felt sick and bad inside. Something in her head was telling her that she should have let him go. Something in her mind was telling her that he was heading for great danger. And it was all her fault.

11. A DEATH AND
LIFE SITUATION

It was late afternoon when Hearthunter, Hope, Ivor and Joy approached the outskirts of Religioscity. The sun had fallen slightly, but was still providing plenty of light and warmth. They were surprised when they saw a sign saying: 'YOU ARE NOT WELCOME IN RELIGIOSCITY UNLESS YOU OBEY OUR RULES' laying on the ground— not standing upright as it obviously should have been. It looked like someone had disagreed with it, uprooted it and thrown it down in disgust. 'Well,' said Hearthunter smiling, 'it sure looks like Miraclekid has beaten us here. He always tends to leave a trail of destruction behind him. Now, quickly, follow me.'

All four hid behind a broken stone wall while Hearthunter started sharing his strategy for attack. 'We could creep in and try not to be noticed and gradually infiltrate the people by knocking on their doors this evening, but I think that would be wasting even more precious time. My suggestion is that we just walk in very confidently singing the Littlekids' Marching Song and I'm sure we will find that Miraclekid has prepared the way for us, so it should be easy.'

His three young listeners nodded in agreement.

They stepped out from behind the safety of the wall and Hearthunter positioned them in a line. 'I will go on the left, then Joy will stand next to me. Hope, you stand next to Joy and Ivor you will stand on the right.' All did as they were told. 'Now on my command of march, we will head towards the main street and not stop singing till I say so. March!'

As the eight feet started marching, so the four voices starting singing.

> There is no one else around
> In the air, or on the ground,
> Who has the power, has the power of the Voice.
> So you Enemy Superpowers,
> In your defeated final hours,
> We command you to leave, you have no choice
> (you have no choice)
> As we speak in the authority of the Voice.

So the four heroes entered Religios-city, but as they reached the main shopping centre they couldn't believe their eyes. It was as if they had just entered a riot zone. Tons of wooden signs and masses of smart clothing were burning on a large bonfire in the middle of the street, and the people were yelling and cheering every time another sign or suit was thrown into the blazing flames. Hearthunter, Joy, Hope and Ivor continued their marching and singing, although the marching was noticeably slower and the singing was considerably quieter and less tuneful.

It was then that a Littlekid who was standing by the fire turned and saw them and above the bedlam jumped up and down screaming at the crowd and pointing in their direction.

Things went quiet as angry faces turned away from the fire and stared at the four Children of the Voice. The mob looked very scruffy and untidy. All ages, from tiny Littlekids to Oldies, were present. Hearthunter told his Littlekids to stop singing and walking. Only the crackling of the blazing fire could be heard.

Nobody said anything for several moments. Both sides just stared at each other, wondering who was going to say or do something first. It was a tall Oldie who broke the silence. 'Who are you and what do you want with us?' he yelled.

'We are from Newchurch,' shouted back Hearthunter boldly, 'and we have come to tell you about the Voice.'

The crowd looked round at each other and started whispering.

'Do you have the same beliefs as Canon Blast and Pastor Kitchen?' shouted a young female voice this time.

'Well,' replied Hearthunter truthfully, 'having met neither of these people I am not sure, because I've never talked to the Canon or the Pastor to find out what they really do believe.'

'Well I think you should meet them,' shouted the Oldie who had spoken to them first. 'Get 'em, lads, and let's give them a formal introduction.'

The next thing that Hearthunter, Joy, Hope and Ivor knew was that they were roughly grabbed and their arms painfully forced up their backs. 'Have no fear,' Hearthunter shouted, 'the Voice is with us.' But his voice was by now very shaken and it did not instil a whole heap of confidence in his three junior friends.

The large crowd walked a short distance then stopped opposite what Hearthunter presumed must be the Ancient Church of the Thirteenth Male Apostle.

All went quiet again. Hearthunter was dragged through the church gate by the gang spokesman and stopped a short distance from the large doors. 'Let me introduce you to Canon Blast and Pastor Kitchen,' said the Oldie who still had a tight grip on his arm.

Hearthunter stared at the doors, expecting them to appear. 'I think you're looking for them in the wrong direction. Try looking to your right and down a bit.'

Hearthunter couldn't believe his eyes as he found himself staring at a very large new gravestone. His captor allowed him to go free as he walked over to read the inscription upon it.

Here lie Canon Blast and Pastor Kitchen,
Otherwise known as the 'you must nots'.
They made everyone's lives miserable when
they were alive.
May they continue to make each other's lives
miserable now they are dead.
They won't R.I.P.

Hearthunter was lost for words, but just managed to ask what had happened.

'They tried to make all us ordinary non-religious people live under their religious laws,' shouted a voice from the crowd. 'They told us what we could and couldn't do—even what clothes we must wear. They made living unbearable.'

'Yeah, and they never stopped warring between themselves,' shouted another, 'and finally the inevitable happened: they destroyed each other and also their poor confused followers.'

'So we won't allow Newchurch to bring in another set of rules,' said the Oldie, who had grabbed hold of Hearthunter's arm again. 'From now on there will be no religious laws and no religiosity. We will all believe what we choose to believe.' All the crowd cheered in agreement.

'Wait, you're right,' shouted Hearthunter, pulling himself free and leaping up onto a wall. At this point Ivor, Joy and Hope all knew he was now getting very excited and was about to launch into a full-scale attack.

'We are not here to bring you religious laws which end up like chains and imprison you. We are here to tell you that the Voice came to earth and gave his life to set captives free. Look at us: no suits, and Littlekids who are full of fun. Can you see any similarity between us and Blast and Kitchen?'

He heard the crowd whispering 'no' to each other, which fired him up all the more.

'We will never force you to do anything, I promise. All we want is the chance to tell you about the love the Voice has for you, then leave you to make up your own minds whether you want to be Voice followers or not. It will be your choice, not our laws.'

The crowd looked at each other, not sure what to think.

'Listen,' pleaded Hearthunter, 'to prove that we are genuine we will help you break down and burn all the "YOU MUST NOT" signs. We hate them as much as you do.'

This was just the proof the crowd needed. Although some were still uneasy about the Voice followers, others invited them into their homes to discuss things further.

12. WHAT a way to go

Rhoda Skateboard had been feeling a bit fed up. It seemed that while all her best friends had been invited to take part in different adventures for the Voice, she had been left back at Newchurch where the only action taking place was Buddy updating his graph each day.

She had been to have a chat with Buddy, but the most audacious thing that he had offered to break her boredom was to deliver some of his letters on her skateboard. She reluctantly agreed and set off with her pile of letters. 'Oh well,' she thought, 'my first responsibility was to be a postwoman, and here I am back in the same job.' As she rode her skateboard to the first house, she allowed her mind to drift back to that first letter she had delivered. It had been a commission sent from the Voice's Training Module to Little Christian, who was at that time the leader of Newchurch. She missed Little Christian. He had been quite a tough leader, but she still had great respect for him.

She pushed the first envelope through the appropriate letter box and then looked at the following one to see where her next destination was. It was for Angela. Back on her skateboard, her memory started working overtime and she remembered arriving in Little Christian's office and seeing a photo of Little Christian and Angela. They both looked so happy, and if she hadn't known better she would have thought that they were in love.

Rhoda knew that Angela was in a bad way—well, everyone did—and realising that she hadn't seen her for a long time she decided not just to push the letter through the letter box, but to ring the bell and give it to her in person. She might like to have a female chat, even though Rhoda knew Angela was a lot older and would probably not want to talk much to her. The bell rang, but there was no answer. She rang it again and looked up at the window. The curtains were open.

'She must be in. Everyone knows Angela never goes out.' Rhoda plucked up courage and tried the door handle. The door opened. She shouted up the stairs: 'Angela!' but there was no reply. Quietly she crept up the stairs, and as the bedroom door was open she peered in. 'Wow!' thought Rhoda in surprise as she rushed into the room. 'She's gone!'

Rhoda knew that Angela didn't possess a lot, but she could see that her clothes' drawers were empty and her coat was missing. She almost fell down the stairs. There wasn't a minute to lose. It was full speed on her skateboard back to Buddy's office where she literally fell in through his door.

'Angela's gone!' she gasped breathlessly.

Buddy leapt up. 'Gone where?' he asked.

'How should I know?' said Rhoda. 'All I know is that all her things have gone from her house.'

'There's no time to lose. Follow me,' said Buddy, looking worried. They made their way as quickly as they could back to the house to see if she had left any clues. There was nothing except a stale smell which indicated that the windows hadn't been opened for quite a time.

'Pack some warm clothes, Rhoda. We're going to find her. I am a Flockwatcher and if any Littlekid wanders off, it is my responsibility to search for them until I find them.'

Buddy told Harmony to get Newchurch praying and left her in charge. 'We will head for Religioscity first to see if she joined the Miraclekid and Hearthunter hit squad. I'm hoping that is where she will be.'

Within a very short time Buddy and Rhoda were walking briskly through Runaway Forest. 'It shouldn't take us too long at this pace,' said Buddy striding out, but already Rhoda had a stitch. She was not used to walking. It was always easier to skateboard everywhere—except maybe on a grass path through a forest.

'Well, Junior, I'm glad you managed to drop in for a few days,' said Greedy Gutrot smiling all over his obese face. 'It's always nice to see you, but it's even nicer when you bring me such good news about the biggest pain of my career, Little Christian.' That last name was more spat than spoken by the old arch enemy of the Children of the Voice. Junior was pleased that he had done something to please his father. His upbringing had not been a very happy one, as the whole family had argued and fought every minute of the day.

'Well, Father, the minute I found I'd achieved something that you never managed to achieve I just had to come and see you. You may be a big fat failure, but it must please you to know that your son is a success.'

'Don't push it, Junior,' snapped Gutrot. 'I've had Little Christian in the palm of my hands before. I suggest you don't count your chickens yet. He's a slippery, slimy, cool customer.'

'Correction, Father, he was, but that was in your day. Now he's a blubbering mess who has given himself over to my control—and I have the contract to prove it. I can destroy him anytime I like.'

'Well do it straightaway, fool. Don't play games with him—he's dangerous.'

'Don't you tell me what to do, fatso. I'll destroy him when I choose and not when you tell me to...'

And so the arguing continued. Happy days were here again.

'By the way,' said Greedy Gutrot in a pause between fights, 'I'm glad to see you've managed to put on some weight. You're looking more and more like your old dad every time I see you.'

'Pig off,' snarled Junior, and the arguments continued.

Back in Nochurch, life had taken a turn for the worse for Little Chris. His health had gone steadily downhill since becoming a Goosey. Every television appearance he made became more pathetic—not helped by the fact that the hole in his tongue meant he couldn't even speak properly. Each failure became a more successful failure than the last.

'What on earth has happened to you, lovey?' wailed Hugo Yourway. 'Your charisma has left you, your viewing audience has deserted you, and now Sativision have told me I have to fire you. I thought we had a future together, but the way you're looking and sounding, Chrissy darling, I don't think you have a future - certainly not in television.'

Little Chris left the studios for the last time, without saying a word. It seemed like he'd managed to become a Goosey, but lost everything else. He had never known such depression as he was experiencing now.

'Wait a minute, Little Chris,' came a familiar voice just as he was about to crawl into his car. He turned and saw Ron Guidance smiling at him. 'Hey, no hard feelings,' he said. 'I'm sorry about the little argument we had last time we met at the pile-up in town. I was a bit upset and didn't mean what I said.'

Little Chris didn't say a word. He just nodded sadly as he sat in the back seat staring blankly downwards. 'Listen,' said Ron in a comforting tone, 'you look bad and Ron is always good at directing people to an exciting future, however bad they may look. Have you ever seriously thought,' he continued, 'that perhaps your future good times are not here on earth? Perhaps you would be happier if you ended it all.'

Little Chris had never contemplated suicide before, but then he had never ever felt this low. He continued to look at the floor of the car and nodded. Ron pushed a bottle of pills into Little Chris's hand. 'Take these when you get home. All the best in your future life.' Ron shut the door and walked off, rubbing his hands together and smiling. 'Good-bye and good riddance,' he whispered under his breath.

On reaching his home Little Chris almost fell out of his car and staggered up his steps. In his hallway were still plenty of letters, but these were no longer pay cheques and fan mail. They were bills and letters from numerous debt collectors.

He slouched in his chair with an uncorked whole bottle of Sacro Vino in one hand and Ron's pills in the other. He took a swig out of the bottle, then putting it down on the floor he slowly started to unscrew the lid on the pill bottle.

'The Gooseys have destroyed me!' he whispered. 'They have ruined my life.' Then he thought, 'Perhaps I have destroyed myself. I left Newchurch. I could not forgive those who wronged me. Yet I guess they were the only ones who really loved me. I told the Voice what I was going to do for him instead of listening to what he wanted to do with me. A Little Christian living in Nochurch is a contradiction in terms. I've fallen too far to be rescued. Voice, please forgive me. I really am sorry.'

He tipped a handful of pills into his hand and opened his mouth.

Suddenly the door-bell rang and a voice shouted, 'Two gifts for Little Chris special delivery.'

'Leave them inside the front door,' Little Chris whimpered pathetically, but just loud enough for the delivery Oldie to hear. The door opened and he heard something soft, then something heavier, fall onto the floor before the door slammed shut.

Holding the pills in his hand he slowly made his way into the hall. 'What the...' he exclaimed as the pills fell from his hand and bounced all over the wooden floor. There in front of him were two packages. The small one was obviously his new Goosey gear (he could make out the shape of the flippers), but the larger one was a body wrapped in brown paper. He ran over to the body and read the label which said: 'Your very own personal slave, with love from the Gooseys.'

He could see that the body was breathing, but with the

brown paper covering the face he was scared stiff that it was about to suffocate. He carefully tore the paper covering the mouth and nose, then ripped it a bit higher to reveal two eyes wide open and staring at him. Suddenly his whole body went numb. 'Angela!' he whispered.

'Little Christian, is that really you?' she replied.

13. GOING NOWHERE... fast

'I can't believe this,' groaned Miraclekid. 'For the first time
in my life I am surrounded by more money than I ever
dreamed existed, yet I can't get out to spend it.' At that
point he heard a few buttons being pressed and the huge
bomb and bullet-proof door opened. Bigsby Bankbalance
brought in a tray with a plateful of burgers and fries on it,
plus a large diet cola. 'Well, thanks very much,' said
Miraclekid with genuine appreciation, and started eating.

'Perhaps you could tell me, Mr Bank Manager, how
long I have been locked away in your vault and how

long you are planning to keep me in it?'

Bigsby glared at him and was surprised that he was in such high spirits after all these days. 'The answer is simple, Littlekid. You have been entertained by me for just a couple of days, and in a very short time you will be leaving us and be taken to another country far away.'

'Well,' said Miraclekid smiling, 'I hope it's somewhere hot and you have packed me some swimming gear, because I'm about due for a vacation.'

Bigsby sat on some money bags and had to admit he was fascinated by Miraclekid. 'Why are you so relaxed?' enquired Bigsy.

'Well, no point in getting stressed out, is there?' chuckled Miraclekid. 'I mean, stress is a major cause of many illnesses and I don't want any of them if I'm about to travel to somewhere nice, do I: And anyway,' he added, as an afterthought, 'the Voice is looking after me.'

Bigsby squirmed at that name. 'Well the... one you are talking about hasn't done too well so far, has he?' sneered Bigsby. 'I would say you are now in my hands, not his hands, wouldn't you?'

'Well now, that's interesting,' argued Miraclekid, 'cause I thought just for a few seconds when I was losing that fight with Yolander that he had let me down, but then I realised I was trying to tell him what to do, which of course was right out of order, because he wanted me to be here with you.'

Bigsby didn't like that answer and it made him feel very uneasy in the presence of this strange Littlekid. 'Why do you think he wants you here?' asked Bigsby nervously.

'Well,' replied Miraclekid, 'I'm not one hundred per cent sure, because he hasn't told me yet, but I've got a feeling he is about to destroy the Gooseys. What do you think, Mr Bank Manager?'

Bigsby didn't answer. He got up and walked straight out, locking the vault behind him. He was now very scared of his prisoner.

As Buddy and Rhoda walked past the Religioscity sign lying on the ground, Buddy smiled to himself thinking that Miraclekid had passed this way before.

He was even more surprised when they reached the main shopping area to see that there were no signs or suits, but friendly people. 'I can't believe it,' he whispered to Rhoda. 'The hit squad must have been a devastating success. Everything is the opposite to how it was last time I was here.'

'Hey, Buddy, Rhoda! It's great to see you! What are you doing here?' They looked over by the chemist shop and saw Ivor shouting and waving to them. After hugging each other Buddy asked where the other Littlekids were. 'Well,' said Ivor, 'Hope and Joy are teaching some tiny Littlekids about the Voice in school, and Hearthunter is in the Town Hall, as the people here have allowed us to use one of their rooms to hold our Newchurch meetings.'

'Brilliant!' said Buddy and Rhoda together.

'And where is Miraclekid?' asked Rhoda.

'Oh, he hasn't been here. He left us in Runaway Forest to try and find a horse and cart, and we assumed that he had returned to Newchurch.'

'What?' stormed Buddy. 'He left Hearthunter and you three Littlekids in the middle of Runaway Forest in the middle of the night to go and do his own thing? He will be in trouble next time I see him!

Not only has he been disobedient, but he's also been totally irresponsible.'

'Hey, calm down,' said Ivor. 'All the shoppers are looking at you. I suggest you'd better come and talk it over with Hearthunter.'

They walked a short distance to a modern building which had an attractive sign outside saying 'Town Hall.'

'We meet just in here, through the door on the right,' said Ivor, leading the way into a nice warm bright room with plenty of windows.

'Well, well, Buddy and Rhoda—how great to see you,' came a voice behind the door that happened to belong to Hearthunter.

After a hug Buddy and Rhoda sat down and listened while Ivor made them all a cup of tea and Hearthunter told them the whole story. He explained about the horse and cart in the forest, and how Miraclekid was convinced that the Voice told him that he must go and investigate it, to which Buddy just made an obviously disapproving huffing sound.

He then went on to explain that they hadn't taken the signs down, it was the locals who had done that after the fight to the bitter end between Canon Blast and Pastor Kitchen. Finally he told them of how well they had been received and that many Oldies and Littlekids through their own choice had become Voice followers.

Buddy now forgot about his anger against Miraclekid; he and Rhoda were impressed and very excited at what the Voice was doing in this town. What have they done to the Ancient Church of the Thirteenth Male Apostle and the Modern Movement of the Free Sisters' Fellowship buildings?' asked Buddy inquisitively.

'Well, one of the conditions that we were allowed to stay was that we must not use any buildings that would remind them of the bad old days, which of course suited us,' continued Hearthunter. 'But I believe the Sisters' building has now become a community cinema and the Males' building, which of course has the advantage of a high ceiling is now being used as a badminton hall.'

'But what are they going to call the town if they don't want to be known as Religios-city?'

'That's an interesting one,' butted in Ivor. 'They are still discussing that, but they haven't told us anything.'

At this point Hope and Joy walked in, having finished their lesson, and again it was hugs all round. As they all gave thanks to the Voice, Buddy was aware that the Voice was speaking to them. 'We must find Angela and Miraclekid,' Buddy said. 'Being the cautious type of person I am,' he continued, 'I wouldn't usually do this, but Ivor, I want you to continue to oversee the work here as you have a little more experience than Hope and Joy, but I want them to stay here and support you.' All three looked pleased at being given such major responsibilities at such young ages. 'Well, the Voice seems to be using younger and younger Littlekids nowadays, so I'm certainly not going to put a cork on what he's doing. Hearthunter, Rhoda and I will go and try to find the other two, as I feel they are both in great danger.'

After more prayer and a few practical instructions Buddy, Hearthunter and Rhoda left the three Littlekids and set off. 'Where are we heading for?' asked Rhoda.

'Well, Runaway Forest seems as good a place to start as any,' said Buddy. But he really had no idea how they were going to find their two friends.

14. foes 'N' friends

After Little Chris had unwrapped Angela, he carefully lifted her up and helped her onto the sofa. He made a couple of hot drinks and a plate of cheese sandwiches (he remembered they were Angela's favourites). Then they started to say sorry to each other. Tears were flowing freely down both their faces as Angela began apologising for the terrible things she had thought about Little Christian back in Newchurch all that time ago. Little Chris butted in to say sorry for running away. Miraclekid had told him that Angela was really sorry, but he wanted her to suffer as he had done.

Angela picked up the story at that point and explained how from that time onwards she had lived under a cloud of guilt and had not been able to be part of Newchurch or be in contact with the Voice.

'It was all my fault,' wailed Little Chris. 'I'm sorry. The suffering I must have put you through.' Little Chris knelt down and held Angela's hand gently. 'Do you know I've been part of Nochurch since I left you? I even made everyone call me Little Chris because I knew deep down I wasn't right with the Voice, but from now on I want to be called Little Christian again.'

'Can you forgive me?' they both said to each other at the same time.

'Of course,' they both replied, still at the same time.

'I think now it's time we said sorry to the Voice,' said Little Christian. 'Hopefully it's not too late to put right all the things we have done wrong.'

Angela and Little Christian spent a long time confessing to the Voice, and the Voice assured both of them that not only were they forgiven, but he had a very important task for them to do, which he would tell them about as they read the Manual together over the next few days.

For hours they shared stories. Angela shared how she had been captured by a horrible muscular female Littlekid called Yolander in Runaway Forest, who had stolen her prize photograph from her. She then told of how she had been a slave of the horrible Major Snob-Value. She wept as she told it, still feeling the deep pain he had inflicted on her.

Little Christian explained how he had become rich by ripping off weak Nochurch Voice followers who watched his television show.

'I always thought ya were a star,' smiled Angela, wiping away her tears.

Little Christian smiled.

'Oh dear, what 'ave ya done to yer tongue?' she asked. There's an 'ole in it.'

Little Christian went bright red with guilt and embarrassment. He walked over and picked up the other package that had arrived with Angela. Tearing it open he allowed the Goosey uniform to fall onto the carpet.

'Yer a Goosey!' said Angela in disbelief.

'Yes, I'm afraid so,' confessed Little Christian. 'You see, in Nochurch all the top people are. It was the only way for me to be among the elite, which was where my stupid pride wanted me to be.'

'Ya must resign straightaway,' said Angela. 'They're evil. They're the lot what captured me, and I dare say many uvver Littlekids, and made us their slaves.'

'It's not that easy, Angela,' whispered Little Christian. 'If I do resign they will kill me—and probably you as well.'

As they both sat quietly thinking, Angela noticed the half-empty pill bottle. What are these for?' she asked.

Again Little Christian blushed. 'What I haven't told you is that I am no longer a star. I am now a nothing. Since I joined the Gooseys everything has gone wrong. I've been sacked from my TV programme, I've been ill, I have no money and will very shortly be thrown out of this wonderful house. A friend called Ron Guidance gave me those pills so that I could get away from all these problems by ending it all. If you'd arrived five minutes later I would have been dead.'

Again both went silent, but this time Angela leaned over and squeezed his hand reassuringly. Angela and Little Christian had no answers to the dangerous situation they were in, but as time passed and as they continued to talk to the Voice together and read his Manual, he started giving them some. But they were answers that were going to require a lot of bravery and trust.

'Well, here we are in the middle of Runaway Forest, but what do we do now? Please, Voice, tell us,' prayed Buddy desperately.

'I think we should spread out and try to find some horse and cart tracks,' suggested Hearthunter, 'and then follow them. After all, that was the last thing we saw Miraclekid doing.' All agreed that this was a good idea and they spread out to search for tracks.

It wasn't long before Rhoda was heard shouting out excitedly, 'Look over here! It hasn't been long since the horse passed this way.'

'How can you be sure of that?' asked Buddy, as he and Hearthunter ran over to where she was.

'Well,' she said pointing, 'that mound of brown stuff over there is still steaming, so the horse must have dropped it fairly recently.'

As they all stared at the fresh horse dung Buddy said, 'Thank you, Rhoda,' and quickly changed the subject. 'Let's get moving then.'

They walked along, their eyes glued to the grass in front of them, frightened that they may take the wrong track, when again Rhoda made them both jump by shouting, 'Look—over there!'

They both looked up and saw a horse happily grazing at the edge of the path, while a rather muscular female Littlekid was sitting on the cart looking very miserable with her head in her hands.

'We will ask her if she has seen Angela or Miraclekid,' said Buddy, walking briskly up to the cart and taking control of the situation.

'Excuse me,' he said politely as he stood facing the Littlekid.

'What?' came the rude reply.

'I say,' Buddy continued, 'have you seen a couple of friends of ours?'

'I haven' t seen anyone for ages,' she said glumly.

'Well, it would have been quite some time ago actually,' said Hearthunter taking over. Then he started to describe Miraclekid. 'A male Littlekid, would have been about my height, totally fearless and always asking the Voice to do things to other people.'

Suddenly she looked up. 'Yes,' she said. 'What did you say his name was?'

'Oh, I don't think we did,' continued Buddy, happy that they were getting a response. 'His name is Miraclekid.'

'That must have been him,' said the Littlekid jumping down off the cart. 'I captured him, beat him up a bit, then gave him over to Bigsby Bankbalance of the Gooseys to take back to Nochurch.'

'You did what?' shouted Rhoda. 'You beat up our friend? How could you?' Then staring at her muscles she could see how easily she could.

Both Hearthunter and Buddy knew about the Gooseys and the evil deeds they were involved in. Buddy stared at the Littlekid, looking very stern. 'You realise that it's very likely that Miraclekid has been sold to become a Littlekid slave and sent far away. The Gooseys have contacts all round the world.'

The female Littlekid burst into tears. 'I really am sorry,' she said. 'I've captured a lot of Littlekids for the Gooseys, but your friend seemed different from anyone else I've ever met. You see, I've never had any friends, and I think that he could have been my first one. I've not been able to capture anyone else since him. I feel so rotten.'

The Newchurch Littlekids looked at her, not knowing what to say. 'What's your name?' said Buddy eventually, feeling both guilty himself at the way he had spoken to her and compassionate for the situation she was in. He gently put his hand on her shoulder, which scared her as she had never been shown affection before.

'I'm Yolander Onmyturf,' she replied.

'Well, Yolander,' said Hearthunter, getting everyone out of the pastoral care mode, 'I suggest that you and we climb up on your cart and you get your horse moving at full throttle, I mean full gallop, and take us straight to Bigsby's bank. Who knows, we might still get there in time to rescue Miraclekid before the Gooseys export him.'

Yolander agreed, and in no time they were racing at breakneck speed through the forest towards Nochurch.

15. WHEELS WITHIN WHEELS

'Everything OK, Ron?'

'Yes, fine thanks, Bigsby. Have you got my package? My car is waiting outside the bank.'

Bigsby walked towards the open door of the vault and saw a wriggling large brown parcel on the floor.

'He's a lively one,' commented Ron.

'Yes, he certainly is,' agreed Bigsby, 'and a powerful one. I will be relieved to get him out of my bank. He should fetch a good price from our overseas agents.'

Bigsby grabbed one end of the parcel while Ron grabbed

the other, and with great difficulty they dragged it out into the street and put it onto the back seat of Ron's car, slamming the door behind it. 'Well, I must dash—I've got a meeting to attend,' said Bigsby, carrying a plastic bag with his Goosey gear under his arm.

'I understand,' said Ron, winking. 'I'll just take my parcel to the docks and wish it bon voyage.' They shook hands then went their separate ways.

It was rush hour again in Nochurch. In fact, with far too many cars for far too few roads, every hour was rush hour in Nochurch. Chief Kleencop took his cap off and scratched his head. 'This is all I need,' he shouted, looking at the cart with three wheels on it while the fourth had broken free from its axle and was racing down a hill chasing a large grey fluffy cat. The four Littlekids stood next to him, staring hopelessly at the place where the wheel once was. Nightmare the horse just stood still, waiting for Yolander to give it its next instructions.

'These contraptions should be banned in cities!' yelled the Chief. 'I've got enough trouble with motor vehicles.'

With that, the quickly-growing jam of motor vehicles started hooting their horns even more loudly. 'Why did you have to lose your wheel in the middle of the busiest crossroads in town? Ah well,' he mumbled, 'we ain't going to move you quicky, so I'd better move the rest of these cars then put a road block up and divert the traffic.'

They watched as Kleencop wandered down the queue of traffic and they could hear all the drivers moaning and swearing at him. Then he stopped alongside a large red car and was looking in the back window and shouting something to the driver. The driver got out while the Chief opened the back door and was leaning in the car.

'Oh oh, this looks like trouble,' observed Hearthunter, and all of them ran over to see what was happening.

'Look!' shouted Rhoda as the driver pulled a large heavy jack handle out of the front of the car and raised it above the cop's head. Suddenly, before he could bring it down and crack the skull of the officer, strong muscular arms had grabbed his arm and the heavy handle fell harmlessly into the road. Yolander twisted his arm high up his back as the cop leapt back out, realising that he had nearly been a gonner.

'Thanks, Littlekid,' Kleencop said, snapping his cuffs on the smartly-dressed Oldie with grey hair and a thin grey moustache, 'Now, before I throw you in the slammer, perhaps you would like to tell me who you are and why you have a Littlekid wrapped up in the back of your car?'

'It's me!' shouted a wriggling Miraclekid, who had managed to bite through the paper, roll off the back seat and get jammed on the floor between the front and back seats.

Buddy was both surprised and relieved, and along with Hearthunter and Rhoda gave thanks to the Voice there and then in the middle of the road for leading them to Miraclekid and for his safety. Yolander didn't know the Voice, but she did know Miraclekid, so she leapt enthusiastically onto the back seat and started unwrapping him.

The hooting was getting louder, but Chief Kleencop ignored it as Miraclekid managed to pull himself free from the wrapping paper and Yolander's clutches, and explained to him that he was on his way to the docks to be sold as a slave, and all under the instruction and for the benefit of the Gooseys.

'This could be just the break I need to bust the lot of them,' thought an excited Police Chief. Grabbing the driver, he asked him what his name was.

'Ron,' said the driver, now very frightened. 'Ron Guidance.'

'So you're a Goosey, are you?' shouted Chief Kleencop.

'Oh no,' said Ron, almost in tears. 'I'm just their delivery man.'

'Well, tell me where I can find the Gooseys,' he continued.

'I can't,' said Ron, now blubbing like a baby. 'They will kill me.'

'Well it's your choice. Either you take their blame and I throw the book at you, or you let them take their own blame and I will be much more lenient with you.'

'All right,' wailed Ron. 'It's a fair cop. You'll find them in the Oddboys' Hall. Just don't hurt me and don't let them hurt me. I can't stand pain.'

'Excellent,' said the Chief, as more officers arrived to take away the quivering Ron Guidance and to try and get the traffic moving again.

'OK, you Littlekids, jump into my squad car. We have a visit to make.'

'But what about my horse and cart?' asked Yolander.

'Yes, good point. It's probably better if you stay as the horse knows you. I'm sure my boys will help you take them both safely back to the station,' said the Chief, smiling.

16. THE BIG ENDING

'All quiet!' shouted Grand Gander as he stood up and tried to squeeze in behind his table. All the gaggle stared at him and gasped. Realising what they were looking at he explained to them that he had a bit of a weight problem, which now accounted for him being the size of a barrage balloon. 'To continue,' he said, trying to change the subject, 'you may have noticed that we are back to our good old number of sixty-five.'

'Where's our new member?' shouted A Theist, forgetting to get permission to speak as usual.

'I'm afraid he wasn't really up to being one of us and he never really recovered after the initiation ceremony.'

'Permission to speak?' asked Al Kidsarbrats.

'What is it, Al?' said Grand Gander.

'Well, you were a bit rough on him at the initiation. I mean, none of us had to go through what he went through, did we?'

All the gaggle nodded in agreement.

'Oh dear,' said Grand Gander, 'I have gathered here the finest brains in all of Nochurch, but not one person has any idea of how my mind works. Listen, you fools, did you really think I wanted him here with us? As you know, I am not human like you. I am one of the Enemy Superpowers and Little Chris, or Little Christian as he was once known, in his heyday gave us more problems than anyone on the face of the earth. He humiliated my dear father, he blew up Oldchurch, he founded and led Newchurch, and every plan we made to destroy the Children of the you-know-who, he always discovered it and foiled us, making us look like a bunch of halfwits.

'But then his best friends did something to bring him down that we could never do. They really hurt him. Our job was then simple. All we had to do was to make sure that he would not forgive them. Our good friend Ron Guidance directed him away from the security of Newchurch to become a lone-ranger in Nochurch. Without a church he became weak and vulnerable.

'Hugo Yourway then came into the picture, and although we would all agree that he is a little strange, we would also agree that he does his job well. Little Chris became a TV star with all the trimmings. He had such a big ego, he didn't even miss his friends.

'But I knew all along that his ego would not be satisfied

until he joined us, the aristocracy of Nochurch. Then it was my turn. I broke him till he felt more useless than a worm. I took away his fame, his fans, his fortune and finally his future.'

Grand Gander took out the contract signed by Little Chris and as he tore it into little pieces he whispered, 'Little Chris will bother us no more. Little Chris has committed suicide.'

At that very moment the door burst open, knocking one of the Pecks flying, and a male and a female Littlekid ran into the middle of the room. 'Gooseys, I destroy you in the name of the Voice!' shouted Little Christian and immediately all the gaggle fell to the floor in fear, screaming and holding their ears.

'I destroy yer evil slave-trade and every uvver evil that yer've instigated, in the name of the Voice!' screamed Angela above the rising din.

The Pecks tried to approach and silence Little Christian and his Lesserbreed accomplice, but the Voice had paralysed them. Little Christian leapt onto the nearest table and ran down them till he came face to face with a very fat, very scared, very sweaty Grand Gander, who was so big he couldn't move anywhere.

'So we meet again, Grand Gander—or, judging by the size of you, and your generally ugly appearance, should I say a young Greedy Gutrot?'

'How did you manage to live?' stammered Gutrot.

'Easy. The Voice sent me a little present in my time of need,' he said, his face now radiant and glancing over at Angela. 'She gave me the will to live.'

'Now it's time for you to leave Nochurch for ever. I think they have had enough of your evil influence, don't you? In the name of the Voice I call down fire from heaven. Burn him, Voice, and make him and all the evil he represents disappear.'

A thunderbolt shot straight through the ceiling of the Oddboys' Hall and all that was left of the devilish dictator was a pile of burned ash on his chair. All went instantly quiet.

'Bravo, Bravo!' came a lone voice from the back of the hall. 'I couldn't have done better myself.'

Little Christian spun around and saw his old friend Miraclekid looking up at him.

'Yea, not bad for a Littlekid!' shouted Buddy Hearthunter and Rhoda all together.

While Chief Kleencop arrested all the gaggle and the Pecks and put them into waiting vans outside the building, he told them to take their last look at daylight, because where they were going they were not likely to see it again for a very long time.

Little Christian hugged each one of his friends in turn and, weeping with joy, apologised to them, explaining how everyone needed real friends, and how they were the best friends anyone could wish to have.

'You'd better believe it,' they all replied with wet eyes as well.

Then while the Police Chief personally cuffed and escorted his one-time friend Pat Rolman to the last van, all the Children of the Voice gave thanks both for his protection and for bringing them all back together again. As the Chief returned to the hall to make sure that he had not left any behind, he mentioned that he only had sixty-four. Would the fat one be returning? Everyone smiled and shouted that they hoped not. He then asked if they'd like a reward.

As Buddy started to explain that their reward was serving the Voice, Hearthunter and Miraclekid, never wanting to miss an opportunity, took the policeman to one side, out of everyone's earshot, and asked if as a reward they could return later in the year to tell the Nochurch people how they were missing out by not having a Newchurch in their city. The Chief shook their hands and said, 'It's a deal. I'll even help you arrange it.'

When they rejoined the others Buddy was suspicious and asked Miraclekid, 'What was all that about?'

'Oh, I'll tell you later,' he said, smiling and winking at Hearthunter.

The Chief gave them a lift to the Police Station where a smiling Yolander was waiting for them with Nightmare and a repaired cart. 'Anyone want a lift home?' she shouted. As Angela was about to ask what she was doing there they all shouted, 'Yes please!' and jumped up on the cart.

'Don't worry, I'll explain,' said Rhoda as the cart moved off, with a very grateful Chief Kleencop and many other honest policemen waving to them.

17. THE BURNING QUESTION

'Never mind, Junior,' said the old fat Gutrot to the young fat Gutrot.

'But, Dad, I so nearly had him,' wailed Junior.

'Yes, I know the feeling,' said Senior.

'Perhaps if you hadn't been such a bigheaded arrogant young twit and listened to the wisdom of your old dad you may have succeeded.'

'Wisdom!' screamed Junior. 'I've got more wisdom lodged under my big toenail than you have in your enormous body.'

'Now, Junior, there's no need to get personal. By the time you get to my age you will be twice my size. Anyway, let's not argue, because in the end we Enemy Superpowers will get him, Remember, there is always another day...'

Greedy Gutrot Senior's face suddenly lit up. 'I've got it!' he shouted. 'Divided we failed, but what about if we teamed up, combined evil forces?'

Junior reached out, grabbed his father's hand and shook it in agreement, then smiled, 'It's a deal!'

Then Junior spoke very slowly. 'Father,' he growled, 'now we are partners, I would like to share with you a long-term plan that won't only destroy Little Christian, it could even knock Newchurch right back into Oldchurch in just a few years.'

Gutrot Senior stared at him in disbelief 'How do you propose to do that?' he asked cynically.

'Simple,' said Junior. 'We wait patiently until Little Christian gets married and has Littlekids of his own. Then we will turn him into a nice normal family man.'

'It's a great thought, son,' he smiled. 'Once someone in Little Christian's position marries and settles down with his own Littlekids, it really does knock the heart out of the Voice's plans. There is, however, one slight flaw to your plan.'

'What's that?' enquired Junior.

'There's no chance of Little Christian getting married, blockhead.'

The Littlekids' Marching Song was sung so loudly it would have deafened anyone within a ten-mile radius. But that's not surprising, because Newchurch had so much to celebrate and to thank the Voice for. To start with, the Newchurch planted in Nonreligios-city (at last they had decided upon a name, even if it was a very long one) was growing every day. Ivor Future, Hope Itgoeswell and Joy Atalltimes had so impressed Buddy with their leadership ability that they now lived there and had been asked to take responsibility for it indefinitely.

Hearthunter and Miraclekid had been given the all-clear from the Voice and Buddy to take a hit squad to Nochurch later in the year and had kept in close contact with Chief Kleencop, who was very close to becoming a really clean cop and a Voice follower himself.

Then there was Yolander Onmyturf, who had become a committed Voice follower and now lived in Newchurch, not her tree house. Of course she had to change Nightmare's name. She wanted to call it Gee Gee, but Buddy thought that Peaceful may be more appropriate. Yolander still had a slight problem in that she really fancied Miraclekid, who as yet had not returned the feelings. In fact, although he was known as the fearless one, some thought that the only person he was frightened of was Yolander.

But what made Newchurch most thankful to the Voice was the return of their founder leader Little Christian, along with Angela. Both were much closer to the Voice than they ever had been. Yes, there was a lot of praising and singing to be done by the Children of the Voice.

It was a burning hot Sunday afternoon. Little Christian and Angela were having a lazy afternoon walk through Runaway Forest. There was no fear in the forest now with Ron Guidance securely locked away and Yolander and Peaceful now happily living in Newchurch.

Little Christian slipped his hand into Angela's and she giggled and blushed. She was not used to Little Christian showing any physical affection. He seemed to think it was a bad example for a leader to do that sort of thing when so many Littlekids were looking up to him. He stopped in the middle of the path and stood looking at her. 'I did miss you so much,' he said, his cheeks now stariing to go red. 'I am so thankful to the Voice that he has given us another chance.'

Although Angela agreed, she kept quiet. She was enjoying listening to her friend's voice again and it was nice for her to hear him share his feelings, because she was never quite sure how he felt about her.

Eventually she did speak. 'What d'ya think the future 'olds for yer?' asked Angela.

'I don't know. The Voice hasn't told me yet. What about you?'

'I dunno,' Angela replied. 'The Voice 'asn't told me yet either.'

'Maybe we're not asking the Voice the right question,' continued Little Christian thoughtfully.

'What d'ya mean?' said Angela.

'Maybe we should be asking the Voice what the future holds for us.' And with that he kissed her on the lips. It was the first real kiss he'd ever given her—or anyone, for that matter—and although Angela was surprised that he would do such a thing, she felt warm and excited.

They stared at each other, then suddenly Angela shouted, 'Little Christian! Open yer mouth!'

Little Christian obediently opened wide, but was somewhat surprised by the request.

'Yep!' she beamed. 'It's gone! The 'ole in yer tongue 'as healed over.'

Little Christian was so thrilled and relieved that a great big smile spread all over his face. 'Thank you, Voice. That was just the sort of sign I needed.'

'What d'ya mean, sign?' asked Angela looking at him suspiciously.

Little Christian kissed her again. 'It was as I kissed you that the Voice healed me. I believe that the Voice wants us to be together... permanently.'

'Angela, I love you... will you marry me?'

Before Angela could open her mouth to answer they were disturbed by two noisy Littlekids running towards them shouting.

'Slow down, Miraclekid,' yelled a puffed out Yolander trailing a few metres behind him. 'I only wanted to go for a short romantic walk—not a crosscountry run.'

'Personally,' replied Miraclekid, keeping up the pace, 'I believe a good fast jog is much healthier for both of us, so stop moaning and save your breath for running.'

'Hi, Little Christian, Hi, Angela,' they both shouted as they ran past them. 'Hope we haven't interrupted anything.' Miraclekid and Yolander giggled as they disappeared into the distance.

Little Christian was now feeling a bit embarrassed. Proposing once was one thing, but proposing twice?

He glanced at Angela. She looked stunning, and that was all the encouragement he needed. Plucking up his courage for the second time he whispered, Angela, will you... ?'

Before he could finish his sentence he jumped with surprise as he heard a familiar voice behind him. 'Angela! Little Christian! There you both are. We've been trying to find you for ages.'

Hearthunter and Buddy were walking briskly towards them. 'I hope we're not disturbing you,' continued Buddy. 'But we have a female Littlekid who needs a bit of encouragement. Normally I'd ask Harmony but she seems to have gone for a ride on Peaceful. If you're not involved in anything too important, Angela, I wondered if you could come and have a word with her.'

Angela glanced at Little Christian, her eyes sparkling in the sunlight, and then she smiled a warm smile. 'Of course I will, Buddy,' she answered. 'Nothing is more important than working for the Voice, is it?' and with that she squeezed Little Christian's hand and walked off with Buddy.

Hearthunter stood next to his friend and slapped him playfully on the shoulder, 'We didn't come at an inappropriate moment, did we?' he asked. 'I mean, you weren't discussing something important, were you?'

Little Christian stood quietly for a moment watching Angela disappearing in the distance. He shrugged his shoulders. 'Nothing is more important than working for the Voice, is it?'

'Spoken like a true leader,' grinned Hearthunter. 'Come on, wake up, loverboy.' With that he gave the thoughtful Little Christian a hefty thump. Little Christian lost his balance and toppled into a muddy ditch by the side of the path.

Laughing at his rude awakening from cloud nine, Little Christian tried to pick himself up, but could only slide about in the slippery mud. 'You wait till I get my hands on you!' he shouted.

'Again, spoken like a true leader,' repeated Hearthunter, chuckling and retreating down the path. 'But you will have to catch me first.'

The two friends chased each other back to Newchurch, laughing all the way.

The Littlekids Marching Song

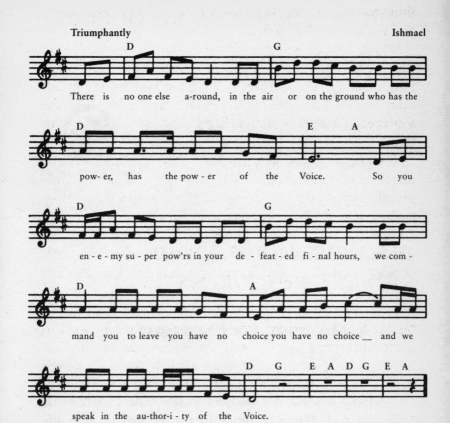

There is no one else a-round, in the air or on the ground who has the pow-er, has the pow-er of the Voice. So you en-e-my su-per pow'rs in your de-feat-ed fi-nal hours, we com-mand you to leave you have no choice you have no choice __ and we speak in the au-thor-i-ty of the Voice.

ISHMAEL/RADICAL RESOURCES

Ishmael/Radical Resources can be contacted at Revelation Church Centre, PO Box 58, Chichester, West Sussex, PO19 2UD, UK.

For further information on any other products that Ishmael has available, please enclose an S.A.E.

radical resources

also available from radical resources

A HISTORY OF CHILDREN
By Irene Smale

An easy to read study book on children and religion from ancient civilisations to the time of Christ. It gives a practical and informative insight into the way children were brought up and trained in spiritual matters in the Old and New Testament periods.

This book is a valuable study for all those working with children and who are interested in learning lessons from history.

Send S.A.E. for further information to the address above.